JOHN DAVID ANDERSON

WALDEN POND PRESS

An Imprint of HarperCollins*Publishers*

Walden Pond Press is an imprint of HarperCollins Publishers.
Walden Pond Press and the skipping stone logo are trademarks and
registered trademarks of Walden Media, LLC.

Minion
Copyright © 2014 by John David Anderson

Library of Congress Cataloging-in-Publication Data
Anderson, John David, date
  Minion / John David Anderson. — First Edition.
    pages   cm
  Summary: "Michael Morn is a supervillain-in-training and the adoptive
son of the brilliant criminal mastermind whose sense of right and wrong is
thrown into question when a new superhero arrives in town." — Provided
by publisher.
  ISBN 978-0-06-213312-0
  [1. Criminals—Fiction. 2. Supervillains—Fiction. 3. Superheroes—
Fiction. 4. Good and evil—Fiction. 5. Adoption—Fiction.] I. Title.
PZ7.A53678Mi 2014   2013043188
[Fic]—dc23   CIP
                                                                   AC

Typography by Erin Fitzsimmons
15 16 17 18 19   OPM   10 9 8 7 6 5 4 3 2 1
❖
First paperback edition, 2015

For Nick and Isabella, my own little minions.
May you someday rule the world.

"Whatever is done for love always occurs beyond good and evil."
—*Friedrich Nietzsche*

Minion: A servile dependent, follower, or underling. From the Middle French word mignon, *meaning "darling."*
—*From Merriam-Webster's 11th Collegiate Dictionary*

I want you to know, right from the start, that I'm not evil. I'm not saying I'm Captain Fantastic, either. I just don't want you to misinterpret everything that I'm about to tell you. Because being the bad guy is really all about intent, and I never intended to hurt anyone. If anything, it was the opposite. It's just sometimes it's hard to know what's right and what's best and why there even has to be a difference.

There are those moments in your life, you know, when the last screw is tightened and the green light flashes and you realize that your whole worldview is a loose thread dangling from the blanket you've wrapped so tight around you. And somebody's gotten ahold of that one thread and is starting to pull. And most of you wants to tug back. To stay warm. To stay safe. To keep things as they are.

And then part of you wants to watch it unravel. Just to see how far it will go.

My name is Michael Marion Magdalene Morn. And this is my side of the story.

MY HERO

When I was twelve years old, give or take, my father strapped a bomb to my chest and drove me to the First National Bank and Trust so we could steal $27,500. I know what you're thinking: if you're going to go through all the trouble of rigging your son with explosives and send him to rob a bank, you should set loftier goals, but my father has a policy that he only steals what he needs at the time, and at the time he needed $27,500 to finish one of his projects and to buy groceries. We were out of frozen waffles.

Dad parked outside the BP across the street to distract himself by playing Angry Birds and eating cashews while I walked through the bulletproof doors of the gray-bricked building. Me, a pale, wispy-banged preteen, green eyed and skinny, wearing a dark-brown overcoat and an impertinent expression, walking into a bank all by myself. There was no guard at the door, but there were plenty of little black globes hanging from the ceiling. Security cameras. My heart caught in my throat, but I forced it down—Dad had told me not to worry about the cameras. They were taken care of. He had my back.

I approached the first teller—a young woman in a navy blazer with her hair pulled into a stern bun and too much makeup masking a potentially pretty face—and opened my jacket, showing her the bomb. I could tell she was impressed by her platter-sized eyes and the choked-down, quietly-pee-your-pants scream, which came out all muffled, like a dog's squeak toy under a couch cushion. I gave her the speech. The one I had recited at least a dozen times the night before and three more on the way over while finishing off a bag of Skittles for breakfast.

"There's a horrible man outside," I said, nodding back toward the glass. "You can't see him, but he can see you, and he says if you don't fill this"—produce Transformers backpack, old-school cartoon, not those overstuffed Michael Bay movies—"with twenty-seven thousand five hundred dollars, he will hit the detonator and you and me will both be carried out of here in Ziploc bags." It was a speech prepared by my father, at least most of it. I added the Ziploc bags part myself.

And it probably would have worked. The bomb. The speech. The Ziploc line. It *would* have, if I had even tried, if I had bothered to get into character. Someone in my position, a kid picked up off the street, three pounds of explosives taped under his chin, a juvenile IED about to commit his first

4

felony—you'd expect I'd be snot faced and crying, shaking uncontrollably, begging the woman to hurry or to call the police. But I just couldn't make myself do it. I came off flat, I'm sure, as if I couldn't care less.

As if I wasn't worried at all.

Don't get me wrong. I was. A little. I just knew more than I was letting on.

I glanced at the teller standing next to her. A man, mid-forties. Receding hair. Pencil lips. Probably his second job. Or third. Formerly an accountant, or a used-car salesman. I felt sorry for him. Maybe he liked the girl with the bun. Maybe he would try to impress her by leaping over his teller station and tackling me. Maybe he'd always wanted to be a hero when he grew up.

Understandable. But there aren't any heroes left in New Liberty, and I'm pretty sure if Captain Bald Spot had super-powers, he wouldn't be here cashing checks and wearing that stupid-looking paisley tie.

I watched him twitch, his wrinkle-wreathed eyes darting back and forth from me to another man—the bank manager, I figured, a much younger guy, skinny like me and better dressed, cluelessly staring at his computer across the room.

This wasn't going as well as I had hoped.

I turned back to the young woman and whispered, "The bad man outside told me that I only have three minutes."

Actually the last thing my father had *really* said to me was to watch for traffic. "Look both ways." Because *that's* what you worry about when you are going to rob a bank. Still, it's nice that he worries.

The teller blinked at me. Maybe she was in shock. Or maybe somehow she realized that the explosives sitting above my heart were just Lincoln Logs rolled in Reynolds Wrap, with wires and a pulsing LED light attached with electrical tape. Either way, she wasn't moving. The bag sat empty on the counter between us. The accountant/car salesman/bank teller next to her made a little move, a twitch of the arm, no doubt reaching under the counter and triggering the silent alarm.

Now I really did only have three minutes.

"Listen, lady," I said, pushing the bag a little closer to her. "It's okay. No one is going to blame you. You aren't going to get fired over this. Insurance will cover it. And even if not, this job isn't worth it, am I right? You don't really even want to be a bank teller for the rest of your life anyway, and you certainly don't want to explode. So just toss the money in the sack, and I'll go."

I said it in the same even tone I said everything else, except this time I looked square into her eyes, tractor-beam style. Locked on. Sucked in. She looked back into mine, and I saw the little black dots of her pupils blow up big and glassy like a stuffed bear's.

This time I had her. It was a last resort, but I knew when I walked in there that I might have to use the gift God gave me. The bank teller nodded and then knelt down to access the safe under her cash drawer, taking the bag with her.

"You're not going to say anything, are you?" I asked Captain Chrome Dome, giving him the same penetrating stare. It took a moment longer, but eventually he went all glassy-eyed too, and shook his head.

"Come to think of it, you won't really even remember what I look like," I added coolly.

The man put his finger to his lips. Mum's the word. The woman in the blue blazer handed me my bag and smiled too. I zipped it up and slung it over my shoulder.

"You shouldn't wear so much mascara," I said. "Your eyes are pretty enough."

Fifteen seconds later I left the bank with my backpack full of cash and crossed the street to the gas station where our little white Civic was parked, taking care to look both ways. Dad was hunched over his tablet.

"We should go," I said, buckling in.

"Almost finished," he said. His tongue stuck out of his mouth like a curious turtle, and his big orange caterpillar eyebrows were crowding the bridge of his nose. There were cashew crumbles down the front of his Hawaiian shirt. My dad had never been to Hawaii, but he found the shirts cheap at the Goodwill and had a closet full of them. Wore one each day. His green eyes dashed across the screen.

"Seriously, I think it's time to go," I said a little more sternly.

"I've almost got it," he mumbled. I could hear the sirens now. Several blocks away still, but it's not as if we were driving a Lamborghini. The Civic was eight years old and ran

7

mostly on good intentions. It was our only getaway car. I drummed my fingers impatiently on the dash. I could have tried to make eye contact, insisted. Insisted that we go. But I had a rule against using my power on my own father. Instead I hummed.

"*There* it is!" he said triumphantly. "Take that, you lousy pigs! Hah!" He thrust a fist in the air and then turned the screen so I could see he had three-starred another level.

"I'm proud of you," I said. "Now can we please get a move on?"

"Sure," he said. He started the car and pulled slowly out into the street, headed away from the bank. Away from the sirens. Away from at least thirty years in prison for him and several years of juvie for me, and that was being generous given the things we'd done.

He also pressed a button on a little black box about five inches square that had been sitting in one of the drink holders between us. I instinctively held my breath.

Like all my father's little black boxes, this one had three buttons. Green, white, and red. Green to activate, white to deactivate, and red . . . you never press the red one—I learned that the hard way. Also like all his little black boxes, it had a sticky label telling you what it did. This one was called the Scrambler, and if it worked, it meant Dad had just fried every security camera in a three-block radius. There would be no footage of me entering or leaving the bank. No trace of our white Honda sitting in the gas station. Only the bank employees would be able to offer the cops a lead, and I was confident they wouldn't remember much. The box vibrated a little and then went dead. Exhale.

As we pulled away, I glanced out my window and up at the sky. I'm not sure what I expected to see. A helicopter maybe. Some schmuck in cape and tights. But the sky was crystal blue and beautiful and as empty as the pretty bank teller's safe.

"How'd it go?" Dad asked as we merged onto the interstate.

"Exactly as planned," I said, finally removing the fake explosives from my chest and tossing them in the backseat next to the backpack full of cash. He could have made a real bomb, of course, but we both knew it was only a prop. The hope was for me not to have to use my powers, but if I did, the wires and blinking lights would add to my natural charm, make me even more persuasive. "You should have seen the look on her face when I opened the jacket. She was seriously freaked."

Dad reached over and ruffled my hair. It was a habit, and I didn't have the heart to tell him that it was kind of annoying.

"See?" he said. "People will believe just about anything."

Yes, I thought to myself. They certainly will.

It was the first serious crime I ever committed, robbing that bank. Unless you count aiding and abetting, which I had probably been doing for two years before that. I'm not exactly sure what *abetting* means, but I would microwave my father hot dogs while he was downstairs fidgeting with his inventions, and I once told him that a high-powered laser he had constructed was "freakin' awesome" as it burned a pancake-sized hole in our ceiling. So if *encouraging* is the same thing as *abetting*, then I was an avid abettor.

That was before I started going down there myself. Before he let me help with the boxes. Then I became an aider. And then an accomplice. I'm only thirteen years old, and I've already accompliced a lot with my life.

No doubt you are thinking that any father who would duct tape a toy bomb to his son and make him rob a bank isn't exactly Hallmark-card material. I guess you're right. The professor isn't your typical dad. He doesn't do backyard barbecues and baseball games. He never coached soccer or took me camping. He doesn't ask me to fetch him beers, and he doesn't pretend to suck at sports sometimes so I will win. He sucks at sports for real, so I always win. But make no mistake: he *is* a hero.

He saved me, after all.

I grew up in the St. Mary of the Woods School for Wayward Boys. When I say *school* I really mean *detention facility*, and when I say *wayward* I pretty much mean *abandoned*, though I also mean *delinquent*, *deranged*, and sometimes *downright criminal*. St. Mary's was a tossed salad of juvenile dysfunction. There were boys who were there because they liked to light things on fire. Boys who liked to steal from their parents. Boys who stole things from their parents so they could light them on fire. There was even a boy, Charlie "Chuck It All" Chamberlain, who once took a twelve-pack of glass Coke bottles to the top of the I-80 overpass and started catapulting them at the cars below, causing an eight-car pileup and an instant invitation into St. Mary's open arms.

And then there were boys like me who didn't have a mother or father to steal from. Who were a little afraid of fire. Who never really had a home outside St. Mary's. We were the "perms." Permanent residents. Mary's Kids. We didn't have a home to go back to, but at least we were destined to inherit the earth. Or so we were told.

That's right. I was an orphan, just like every little freckled-girl and every farmer-boy hero in a fantasy book. Just picture it: swaddled infant, abandoned on the church doorstep in the pouring rain, poor overwrought mother stealing away into the night, shedding a solitary tear that you can tell isn't a rain-drop by the way she wipes it with the sleeve of her torn coat, looking back, just once, her face half illuminated by the pale moon before she turns into a shadow and disappears around the corner.

Except that's not me. I wasn't left on the church doorstep. I was actually dumped at a White Castle. The counter jockey working the night shift found me in a corner booth with an envelope full of twenties and a mangled onion ring. I was a quiet baby: it was a half hour before he even noticed I was there, apparently.

That's it. The whole origin story. Child of the White Castle. Home for belly bombers and abandoned babes. The cops made inquiries. Tracked down customers through credit cards. The teenager working the register was a half zombie and not much help. The state set out to reunite me with my family, but in the meantime, St. Mary's came for me. They took me and the four hundred in cash as a donation. A nameless kid with a polka-dot onesie and a wet diaper and a deep-rooted aversion to onions that wouldn't surface until years later.

Not that I ever ate onion rings. I was served three meals a day in the main hall of St. Mary's dormitory, all the normal food groups with a side of bless us, O Lords, and an extra helping of trespass-forgive-us-ness. The teachers at St. Mary's were incredibly sweet, providing comfort in a whisper or a hug . . . until you turned six or seven. Then, for some reason, they assumed you had been possessed by the evil spirit and did everything they could to drive it out of you.

Luckily for me, I had discovered my power by that point. In fact, by the time *I* was seven, I had learned how to get most anything I wanted.

Except the thing I wanted most.

Right. That's the other thing you should know about me. I'm not exactly normal. I mean, nobody's *normal*. But I'm, like, *extra*-not-normal. I've got this little thing I can do. Kind of a mental magic trick. A little abracadabra.

I can make you do my bidding.

Dad calls it "suggestive hypnosis" or a "mild form of tele-pathic manipulation," but I think "do my bidding" sounds more dark lord of the Sith. It's not easy. It requires intense concentration, a kind of hypermental focus where I guess I unlock some part of my brain that everyone else keeps shut tight. Tapping my chi or whatnot. And eye contact—that's a must. The key, really. Without that, I'm just another whiny kid pouting to get my way. There are other tricks, subtle nuances, all learned over time. Don't blink. Use a polite but firm tone. No questions—never give them the chance to say no. Insist, but don't be overly bossy. And always keep your cool. If your attention slips, the spell is broken and you've lost them.

It's okay if you don't believe me. Just look into my eyes and I'll convince you.

My power just came to me, gradual, like how fingernails grow. It wasn't a radioactive blast or a nuclear bug bite. I wasn't sucked into a black hole. Didn't fall into a toilet transporting me to an alternate dimension where I learned I was actually a demigod sent to the planet earth or any load of bull like that. I know those things happen sometimes—I'm not an idiot. I watch the news. I read the headlines. But they didn't happen to me. In fact, I had probably been using my power for years without even knowing it. It just took a while to recognize what was really going on, to understand why, every now and then, people seemed to do *exactly* what I wanted them to.

I know what you are thinking. Lame, right? It's no laser beams from the eyes. I can't fly, or turn my body to fire, or flip a tank. I don't have a cybernetic arm or a rocket pack, though I know where I could have one built. But a little bit of mind control is nothing to sniff at. It came in especially handy at St. Mary's.

"I think I should get a *double* portion of pudding today, Sister Margaret."

"You don't really *need* me to make my bed this morning, Father Matthew."

"We aren't the boys you're looking for."

Once I learned how to control it, I could get away with almost anything. And no one ever suspected. At least, almost no one. Once Father Gabe, who oversaw most of the home's academics, told me I had a silver tongue. I said thank you, and that I really admired his Friar Tuck haircut. He said it wasn't a compliment, adding that the Devil used the same gift when he tempted Eve and that I should be careful. He tossed some proverbs at me. I reached into my pocket and pulled out a pack of Juicy Fruit that I had convinced Charlie Madison to give me. I looked into Father Gabe's eyes and told him he should have a piece and stop worrying so much. He left, chewing happily.

That was about as close as I ever got to being caught.

But I still had to be careful. With great power comes a great need to hide it from other people so they don't turn you into their tool. I learned that one the hard way.

"Hey, Mikey, see if you can make Sister Katheryn get us out of math today."

"Hey, Mike, tell Sister Grace to take us out to the field this afternoon."

14

"Mike, make Sister Beatrice dance again. That was freakin' *hilarious*."

Granted, if you've never seen a nun break-dance before, you are missing something. But it became necessary to keep things under wraps, not to end up as everybody's lackey. As soon as someone finds out what you can do, they immediately start thinking about how it can benefit them. That's called human nature.

And there were other limitations. For starters, I learned that I could only make suggestions that the other person was at least *open* to. Jason Merin *never* shared the cinnamon-chip muffins his mother sent him, no matter how much I prodded. He couldn't even *entertain* the idea. But Davey "Plopper" Plimpton—who I soon discovered was game for just about anything (including, apparently, dropping a deuce in his second-grade teacher's desk drawer, which was the straw that landed *him* in St. Mary's)—had *no* problem sneaking into the trunk by Jason's bed while everyone was asleep and swiping me two.

Still, whatever it was, it had to be within reason. In a world surrounded by mantras—do unto others, turn the other cheek, cast the first stone—somehow *within reason* became mine. "You can't push too hard," my dad later taught me. "You can't just go up to some random guy on the street and tell him to give you a million dollars, or even a thousand. He won't go for it. It's outside the realm of possibility. *Fifty* dollars, on the other hand . . ."

It was only a matter of figuring out who could be manipulated and to what degree. Thankfully, most of the sisters were open-minded. And my life at St. Mary's was bearable—even, at times, pleasant. But it wasn't enough. I was an outsider. I was named by a committee of nuns after some of *their* heroes. The other kids looked at me differently (unless I told them not to). They didn't trust me. And I didn't blame them. We were all outsiders. Satellites. Leftovers. We were the uneaten onion rings of the world, and nobody but God wanted us.

And there were days I wondered about that, too.

I know what you are thinking. "Hel-*lo*, dipwad. Why didn't you just use your little mind trick on some poor, unsuspecting couple and convince them to adopt you?" After all, St. Mary's was in the business of shucking kids off onto nearly anyone who would have them. The beds were full. The donations scarce. If you were willing to feed a mouth, St. Mary would give you one, even walk it out to your car and help you buckle it in. But there were three reasons I didn't go for that plan.

Reason one: Almost nobody ever visited St. Mary of the Woods School for Wayward Boys except parents who already had boys there—and usually then only on the holidays when the boys would plead to go home and the parents would remind them of all their past atrocities under the watchful eye of a half dozen crucifixes.

Reason two: Those few who *did* visit were always in the market for the one or two snot-nosed toddlers or soggy-diapered babes who still sounded cute when they burped. The would-be parents cooed, and gooed, and gaaed, and made ridiculous faces, and any of us older boys who saw them pointed and laughed out of jealousy. If you were over the age of five, you were used goods.

And the most important reason of all: I didn't want to. I didn't want to con some poor, hapless couple into adopting me. I wanted someone to choose me because they wanted to. Not because I looked deep into their eyes.

Which is why I stared down at my shoes the day Dad came to St. Mary's, looking, he said, for someone who could help him take over the world.

By the time he showed up, I was nine years old and practically had full run of the joint. I knew who could be manipulated and who couldn't. I knew exactly what I could get away with. I had almost come to terms with the fact that I would be stuck there until I was eighteen, at which point I would probably get a job at JCPenney persuading women to buy overpriced perfume. I had big dreams. But I never dreamed of working as part of a criminal enterprise. The thought simply hadn't occurred to me. Maybe it was all the stained glass.

He wore a Hawaiian shirt that day, like all the other days. Pink and orange—two colors that have no business mingling anywhere but a sunset. It didn't help that his hair was orange as well, both the spiked mess on top of his head and the overgrown shrub on his face. He was tall and skinny—not toothpick skinny, but Popsicle stick, easy. His big green eyes always seemed to be looking at everything but the person he was talking to, meaning it would be hard to get his attention, even if I wanted to.

Yet there was something magnetic about him. This man was different from all the other adopting parents who were trolled through the school—yuppies and DINKs in dress shoes with designer purses tucked under their armpits. This man had awful taste in clothing and was too cheap to get a decent haircut, and you could tell he didn't get enough sleep by the dark half-moons beneath his eyes. He walked with a shuffle, as if he was afraid to completely lift his feet. And he chewed his lip. The top one with the orange mustache hairs cresting it. Sister Katheryn introduced us.

"Michael, this is Mr. Edson."

"*Professor* Edson," the man corrected.

"Excuse me. *Professor*. He'd like to talk with you for a bit. Would that be okay?"

I looked at the man, and he looked at his tennis shoes. He was fiddling with a smooth black box that he quickly stuffed back in his pants pocket. I nodded, and Sister Katheryn led us into a small room with an old oak table and three or four high-backed chairs. Then she turned and left the three of us alone. Just me, the orange-maned man in the Hawaiian shirt, and the Holy Spirit. He spent a minute funneling his beard through his hands before he spoke.

"Hello," he said.

"Hello," I said.

"My name is Benjamin Edson. Have you heard of me?"

If he wasn't a saint, a president, or an *American Idol* contestant, I hadn't heard of him, and I knew right from the start he wasn't a saint. "Should I have?"

"I hope not," he said, looking around the room. "Did you hear Sister Katheryn and me talking about you?"

I shook my head out of politeness, then thought better of it. There didn't seem to be any point in lying to this man. I *had* heard. I had heard her say the words "Really? Michael? *Our* Michael?" when he asked to see me specifically.

"Are you really planning on taking over the world?" I asked.

"No," the man said. "That was just a joke. Why? Are *you* interested in taking over the world?"

"Are you kidding?" I cringed. "That's like asking to have everyone's problems dumped on you all at once."

Professor Benjamin Edson pounded on the table with hairy-knuckled fists, causing me to jump out of my seat. "That's *exactly* what I keep telling *them*, but they never listen to me."

I said I didn't know who *them* was. He said he didn't either. This man was bizarre. I kind of liked him.

"You don't need to take over the world to make an impression," he said.

"Oh," I said.

"Power is recognizing that you have a choice and then having the courage to make it."

"Uh-huh," I said. I had no idea what he was talking about. He asked me a few questions, normal interview stuff. If I

19

had lived here at St. Mary's all my life. If I enjoyed reading and learning about new things. What my favorite flavor of ice cream was. If I knew anything about my parents. If I got along with everyone at the school.

Yes. Definitely. Cherry cordial. No. More or less.

"I hear you are interested in magic," he probed. I nodded self-consciously. He seemed to know a lot about me already.

"Just a few card tricks. I'm not very good," I said.

"My great-grandfather was a magician. He *was* pretty good. But don't worry. We all have something that makes us special. I have a few tricks I could teach you."

He asked about my friends at St. Mary's and if I had any other hobbies. I made up some things. I could tell he wasn't convinced, and I wasn't trying as hard as I could have. Finally he folded his hands in front of him.

"Can I ask you a rather personal question, Michael?"

I nodded.

"Do you believe in God?"

I'm sure I must have looked even more confused at that point. I glanced around the room to make sure we were sitting in the same place. There was a cross on three out of four walls. There was a chapel down the hall where alabaster angels loomed over you. The whole place smelled like incense, except for Father Gabriel's breath, which smelled like communion. Maybe it was a trick question.

"I was raised by nuns," I said.

"Just because you are raised by accountants doesn't mean

you can balance a checkbook." He laughed a little at his own joke, but then his smile retreated back under his mustache again. "I take your point, though. So I assume you believe in good and evil, then?"

I wasn't used to anyone talking to me like this. As if there was more than one way to answer a question.

"I guess so."

"So," he pressed, leaning across the table so that I could see traces of gray in his flaming orange beard, "which are you?"

His breath smelled like butterscotch.

I just sat there, speechless. Legs crossed. Arms crossed. Crosses all around. I *wanted* to say good. I really did. I wanted to say it because I knew it was the right answer. But the more I thought about it, the less sure I was. I had done some mean things already, and I was only nine. I once convinced Jalen Scott to let me eat his entire birthday cake and then convinced him to clean up the mess after I threw up all over his bed. I had convinced poor sixty-year-old Father Howard to bend over backward and try to kiss his own butt, causing him to topple and nearly break a hip. I had done several things I wasn't proud of. And I had done some of them to nuns.

Then there was the whole "*all* of us are sinners" thing that had been drilled into me since before I even knew what guilt felt like. So I knew, even then, what the answer *couldn't* be.

"I guess," I began, ". . . I guess I don't know."

Professor Edson leaned back in his chair and exhaled deeply, like a man who has just finished Thanksgiving dinner. He looked around the room.

"You have a big family here," he said, his voice tinged with regret. "Lots of brothers and sisters. Fathers and mothers. A whole host of people looking out for you."

"I guess," I said, though *watching you* might have been more to the point.

"It's a safe place," he mumbled to himself, looking around. "But I said I would, and I will." Then, before I could ask him "Would what?" he turned back to me. "Do you want to see a magic trick?"

I nodded. None of the teachers at St. Mary's ever performed any magic tricks, though Sister Juanita sometimes seemed like she could appear from out of nowhere. Benjamin Edson showed me his empty palm. "I learned this from my father," the man said. Then he reached behind my ear and produced a penny, tarnished green so that Abe's face looked to be covered in mold. He set it on the table between us. Then he stood up and reached out to shake my hand, and I knew our conversation was over.

"It was nice meeting you, Michael Marion Magdalene Morn."

"Yeah, you too," I said, feeling my stomach sink, thinking that the interview was over too quickly, that I had screwed it up somehow, probably my one shot at getting out of here. That I wasn't going home with this strange man in the hideous pink-and-orange shirt who really had no intentions of taking over the world.

And then there was an opening. Benjamin Edson shoved his hands into his pockets and looked me right in the eyes for the first time, almost as if he was looking through them, snaking his way into the folds of my brain. And I could have said it. Could have returned his stare easily enough and planted the seed.

"Get me out of here," I could have insisted.

"Take me home."

But I didn't.

He slipped on his coat and walked to the door where Sister Katheryn was already standing. Then he turned and glanced down at his chest.

"What do you think of this shirt? Too much?"

I shrugged. The professor nodded, smiled, and turned. I watched him sign out and then escape through the front door of the building without another word to anyone else.

"He seemed to like you," Sister Katheryn said, emphasizing the *he* way too much. I didn't bother to smile politely. I had blown it. I looked Sister Katheryn in the eyes and suggested that I should take the afternoon away from my studies to reflect on the meeting I just had and God's great plan for me. She agreed that was a great idea.

Instead I spent that afternoon eating cupcakes that the school cook had baked for Father Matthew's birthday and feeling sorry for myself. "You have a big family here." He had said it softly, sadly, as if he knew, as if he could see the little pit that had opened up inside me. And then he left.

23

I had to face it. I was stuck at St. Mary's for the next decade or so. If that was the case, I was going to see just how far my power could take me. I couldn't take over the world, but maybe I could take over the school. If I could get Sister Beatrice to attempt a backspin, I could probably get everyone in the place to bend to my will.

I was still planning my takeover of St. Mary's three days later when the professor showed up again, wearing the exact same shirt as before. He had a stack of papers tucked in his armpit and two ice-cream cones in his hands. One of them looked to be chocolate. The other was cherry cordial.

"I've come to show you another magic trick," he said, then bent down and whispered, "I'm going to make you disappear."

THE INSTRUMENT,
NOT THE CROSS-DRESSER

What I've done since escaping St. Mary's . . . it's criminal. In the past year alone, I've robbed banks. I've robbed people. I've robbed people standing outside banks. I've committed a handful of cons. I have resisted arrest, though the officer didn't know I was resisting, so maybe it doesn't really count. I have broken and entered, usually into some university laboratory to swipe dangerous chemicals or a cutting-edge prototype. I have loitered extensively. I once ordered a water at a restaurant and then filled the clear plastic cup with Sprite. I am thirteen years old and I already have a history that would land me on *America's Most Wanted*, provided anyone actually knew who I was. But Dad makes sure we escape without a trace. He keeps us safe.

If I was a supervillain, my name would be the Influencer or

Mr. Manipulative or Dr. Suggestive—though I guess that last one's got more of a late-night cable television ring to it. I would wear an all-black bodysuit with a picture of a skull on the front, except instead of eye sockets there would be those little swirlies that hypnotists and magicians use, the ones that seem to spin forever like a bathtub that won't stop draining. And I would also have rocket boots, because why not.

Except I'm not a supervillain. Not even close. Supervillains are beyond me. Not to mention most of them are totally bat-crap crazy. Stalin was a supervillain. Genghis Khan. Vlad the Impaler. Then of course there're the ones everyone usually thinks of, with the flashy costumes and the spiked gauntlets and the never-ending maniacal giggles like a chronic case of evil hiccups. Guys with names like Doombringer, Dealer, and Doctor Apocalypse. General Xog. The Nihilist. All those deranged demagogues in their secret lairs with their legions of henchmen and their laser death rays and demands for total subjugation. The ones you hear about on the news terrorizing *other* cities. Making their ridiculous ultimatums. Planning to alter the moon's gravitational pull in order to sink Iceland or infiltrating the United Nations with a Ban Ki-moon cyborg. To be a supervillain, you *really* have to want it; you have to let the ends justify the means.

I'm not even sure what my ends are yet. Dad thinks I'll go to college someday. I think it would be cool to go scuba diving off the coast of Australia. It would probably behoove me to get kissed by someone who isn't a nun somewhere that isn't my cheek. I have goals, but they're not exactly the stuff of world domination. Like I said, I'm no supervillain. I'm not even that bad a guy, really.

And Dad's not either. He's more of your mad-scientist type. He knows a crap ton about engineering and math and chemistry and physics, and history and literature, for that matter. He devours books like bonbons. He's always spouting quotes at me the way the sisters used to do at St. Mary's, but his at least come from more than one book. I'm fairly certain he's a genius. Dad says the word *genius* originally meant "guardian spirit," in which case he's definitely a genius. He's scatterbrained. And odd. And he *dresses* like an escaped mental patient. But he's not insane. And he's not really evil. Dad doesn't believe in dichotomies, in one or the other. It's not a line where you fall on one side or the other. It's a great big circle, and he and I are in the center of it.

He once told me over a box of melty bonbons there are *three* kinds of people in the world: those who don't believe in anything, those who believe in the *one* thing, and all the rest of us schlepps in the middle who don't know what to think. Dad says the first two are dangerous, the one because you have no idea *what* they are going to do next, the other because you *know* what they're going to do, and they are going to do it no matter the costs. But us, we're not dangerous. We're just survivors.

Of course, Dad also says it's important to believe in something. Even if it's wrong.

"Hand me that soldering iron, will you?"

We are sitting in the basement—sorry, the *lair*—complete with its secondhand map of the world where the U.S.S.R. still takes up half of Asia, and its secondhand sofa with coffee stains the size of a sumo wrestler's butt cheek. We have an $87,000 scanning electron microscope, but we get most of our furniture from curbs -Я- us. There are rows and rows of metal shelves stacked with bins of hardware—tiny screws and bolts and fuses and transistors and enough silicon to fill two valleys. A bank of computers, most of them oversized and ancient looking, lines one side. On the opposite wall there is a calendar and a poster of a white fluffy kitten dangling from a windowsill, eyes wide with fear, urging us to HANG IN THERE! In the other corner sits the hollowed shell of an FIM-9 Stinger missile that Dad once scavenged for spare parts. We use it as a wastebasket now. One of my jobs is to empty the missile.

Dad is at the workbench, hunched over another of his inventions, a bowl of pistachios beside him. He's fond of nuts. I am sitting on the stool next to him eating greasy potato chips and doing my homework, even though it's the middle of June and the sun is blazing and I'd much rather be helping him with his current contraption or just sitting in the backyard with its eight-foot privacy fence, zoning out to some tunes. But I'm on the Professor Edson year-round homeschool schedule, which means I spend half my summer tucked into a book or drooling over imbalanced chemical equations.

I understand why. Putting me in school would require filling out certain forms, forms asking for personal information. Forms that could lead to questions that could lead to men in black suits knocking on our door, flashing credentials and asking if my father is home. Men who wear sunglasses even in the wintertime. Dad's not a real big fan of the FBI. Or the CIA. Or anyone with an acronym and a badge. Hence homeschool, and world literature on a June afternoon. I can practically smell the fresh-mowed grass, and it's making me itch.

Today's assignment is *Crime and Punishment*, a thick Russian novel that I'm barely slogging through. Dad's a sucker for the classics. *Crime and Punishment* is about a man who murders an old woman in his building and does his best to not feel guilty about it—a pretty good hook. So far the only conclusions I've come to about it, though, are that the writer was depressed and that axes are a messy way to kill old ladies. Some days I wish I could just reread Harry Potter.

"Pass me that chip," Dad says. Mozart is playing in the background. Like I said, sucker for the classics. I look over at his waiting hand and give him the half-eaten one I'm holding.

"No, the *micro*chip." He sticks the first chip in his mouth anyway, then takes the second, soldering it in place with nimble fingers. The three buttons on the black box in front of him flash for a moment, then stop. Green, white, red. I hold my breath, like always, and wait for all the halogen lights above us to go out. Or the microwave upstairs to explode. Or the radio that we keep down here to start picking up signals

29

from some alien race. But nothing happens. The box apparently isn't finished yet.

"What's it supposed to do again?" I ask.

Dad beams. He gets that way about his boxes. They are his other children.

"It's supposed to be a sonic disrupter, but I'm having a little trouble with the magnification. The focus array keeps resetting to the default modulation," he says, speaking a language that I am still learning. My father's hope is that someday I will be trilingual, capable of speaking English, Spanish, and Mad Scientistese fluently. "Would you like to see the math?" He holds up pages and pages of scribbles that look even more incomprehensible than a Russian novel. I shake my head. I enjoy helping my father with his work, but there are some days I wish we could just lounge on the couch and watch Animal Planet reruns instead. "Do you see any more of those loose screws lying around here somewhere?"

"I'm looking at one," I say, waiting too long for him to get the joke, then giving up and looking for them anyway, finding them scattered all over the floor. I gather them up, one by one. "So I was wondering if I could go the mall with Zach today," I say, handing him his screws.

"The porcupine?" Dad asks absently. The man has a hundred nearly identical little black boxes gathering dust on the shelves down here and knows exactly what each one of them does without looking at the labels, but he can't seem to keep up with my anemic social life.

"His street name is Spike," I remind him.

Zach, aka Spike, is a henchman—one of Tony Romano's knuckle rollers and pretty much my best friend—and he and my father have met at least two dozen times. Usually when my father finishes a project that the big man commissioned from him, Zach comes by to exchange it for a fat envelope of cash. Zach is like me in that he's a little bit *different*. He can bristle his skin with three-inch quills and then make them shoot out by, I don't know, tightening his butt cheeks or something. Hence the name Spike. All henchmen have street names, kind of like aliases. Not me, though. I'm just Michael.

Of course, I'm not a henchman either. I'm something else.

"Spike. Right. Sorry." Dad pulls away from his box and looks at me. His bushy orange brows are caving in, universal sign of fatherly concern. His lips work around the words a few times before his tongue utters them. "It doesn't bother you, does it?" he says at last. "Not having any normal friends?"

"What do you mean by normal?" I ask, licking the salt from my fingers.

"You know, people who go to a real school and pass notes in class, who go bowling on the weekends. Who don't shoot thorny barbs out of their pores."

"I don't think anyone goes bowling anymore," I say.

Dad frowns. "I used to like bowling."

I snort. I can't help it. I can't picture my father bowling. "So does that mean I can go?"

He turns and rifles through some parts on the workbench.

He can't seem to find what he's looking for. I reach over and take a guess, handing him an eyeglass screwdriver that had snuck behind a bin of bolts. He smiles and nods. "Sure. Go. But only if you stop and pick up another one of these circuit boards." He points to a part he's already soldered in, then writes the model number on a Post-it note and I stick it in my pocket. He tells me to swipe sixty bucks from Charles Dickens to pay for it. We pay cash for everything. Checking accounts require forms and . . . well, let's just say that there are a lot of things in the world that require forms. "Give Aziz my best," Dad says.

I look at the unfinished black box. They all look the same, even on the inside. Circuits and chips and a whole lot of imagination. It's not the pieces, I know; it's the way they fit together. My father just has this knack for making something extraordinary out of the everyday. There's really nothing the man can't fit into one of those things. I stand there for a moment, just staring at him, impressed even though I'm still not sure what it does. I feel the itch. "Would you rather I stay and help?" I ask. I can tell what he wants to say. I see it in his eyes, his need to have me here where he can keep an eye on me. Dad opens his mouth, lets it hang there for a moment, then snaps it shut.

"No. I've got it," he says. "Go to the mall. Play with the porcupine. Be back by dinner. It's taco night."

He smiles warmly, and I see how hard it is for him, to lend me out. But Dad wouldn't be caught dead in a mall. He doesn't understand them. Wonders why you have seventeen different stores all selling basically the same pair of jeans. Wonders why people go to a store just to look at things they can't afford and don't even need. But it's not just that. He can't imagine being one of them. The bystanders. The ones who spend their whole lives holding their breath, waiting for something remarkable to happen.

"Thanks, Dad," I say. "I'll see you later." I stuff a bookmark in Dostoyevsky and wipe my hands on my pants, then head to the surface, to sunlight.

"Wait," he says, stopping me on the stairs. "Tell me who said this: 'I am a man because I err! You never reach any truth without making fourteen mistakes and very likely a hundred and fourteen.'" He glances down at the dog-eared copy of *Crime and Punishment* sitting on the corner of the workbench.

I shrug. "I don't know. I'm not to that part yet, I guess," I say.

"Oh. Well. You'll get there," he remarks, then turns back to his work, and I gallop up the stairs before either of us changes our mind.

The walk to the mall winds me through the neighborhood. It doesn't really have a name—like the ones in the burbs, Oakcrest or Willowwood or Admiral's Landing—though everyone knows it's Romano territory. I pass the corner deli and the Happy Dragon, provider of Take-Out Tuesday. Mr. Hyung waves at me from the window. Past the pizza place with the cracked windows and the Laundromat where the old

33

ladies congregate to smoke. I know some of them by name. They know me as the professor's kid. The two checkers-playing geezers at the park give me toothless smiles. It's not really a park, just the only patch of green for miles. The old men bring their own lawn chairs and set up the board on an overturned trash can. The park's not much to look at; it's decorated by empty bottles planted along the curb—green glass flowers with jagged petals—but it's kind of pretty how they reflect the light. Nobody gives me a second look as I pass by. I know a lot of people wouldn't even *drive* through this neighborhood, but they don't belong anyway.

I meet Zach outside the Sears and we bump fists and then make fun of each other's hair. I'm still working the wind-swept, unbrushed mop of limp brown wisps I've cultivated since Dad rescued me from St. Mary's. Zach's got a streak of green running down the middle of his buzz cut, looking as if someone spray painted a line to show where he could best be split in two. He says I look like a skater, and I say he looks like a thug. We both know I'm right.

Zach and I met last summer, when he was hired on as a bodyguard and gopher to the Romano family, doing what-ever Big Tony asked. Tony Romano is one of the few really big guns left in New Liberty after the Great Migration, when the well of villains dried up and all the heroes left for greater glory. He runs a wide-reaching crime syndicate with fat, greasy fingers stuck in every conceivable pot. Gambling. Extortion. Money laundering. You name it, Tony's in it. He's also my father's number-one customer and the reason we get a 50 percent discount on our heating bill. Most of the boxes Dad builds sit on the shelf in the lair, but the ones that do make it out of the basement usually end up in Tony's meaty hands, and he pays pretty well for them. Dad says he doesn't know what Tony Romano uses the gadgets for and doesn't want to know—it's best that way. But in New Liberty you need to be on somebody's good side to help protect you from everybody else's bad side, so Dad makes it a point to pick up the phone whenever Tony calls.

It's not like this anywhere else. In places other than New Liberty, just about the time the cops get pasted, some tight-panted freak with a mask on will come swooping in to turn the tide. Guys like the Judicator, with his giant hammer and flashy silver boots, or Miss Mindminer, who always knows what you're thinking. Or the Gemini Twins, who can combine their DNA to mutate their shape. You hear about them all the time on the national news. But they are the defenders of other burgs, pledged to protect other citizens from other evils. New Liberty doesn't have a champion, and hasn't had for as long as I've lived here. There was that group of rich business types who dressed up in stupid costumes with fiberglass wings and pretended they could fly a year or two ago, but one run-in with a power line was all it took to end their short careers as vigilantes. It's a Super-less town, and though he's never said it out loud, I suspect that's one of the reasons Dad likes it here.

Instead, we have people like Tony, who is exactly what you think he is. Everything about the boss screams hyperbole, from his pinstripe suit and four-hundred-dollar Oliver Peoples sunglasses to his pasta-bred belly and the golden wolf's-head cane he pretends to need to walk. Tony provides the walls. The imaginary lines that separate the bad from the worse. He has dozens of people in his employ, most of them bruisers with hairy chests, leather jackets, and below-average IQs, but a few of them like Zach and me. Talented. Zach says his stint with the Romanos is just an apprenticeship, that he hasn't made a permanent commitment to the family or anything, but it's clear by the designer labels on his clothes that he likes the perks of the job.

Zach is an orphan like me. We both got adopted into this world. I guess that's one of the reasons we get along. That, and we like the same grungy music, and we both think "deep fried" and "chocolate covered" are food groups.

"How's your dad?" Zach asks as we shuffle by the stores, letting the mall walkers and stroller rollers pass us. Liberty Square is one of two malls in the area, sitting right on the equator between the side I'm from and the side I'm not. The whole place has a dingy halo to it, like the film of scum ringing the bathtub. The overhead lights flicker on occasion. The waste bins are usually overflowing. Even the plastic ferns seem to wilt. But it has one of the few dollar stores in America where, surprisingly, everything is still only a dollar, and a halfway decent place to get chili dogs, and a photo booth for teenagers to make out in. The other mall is at least thirty miles north, in the burbs. I've never been there, but I've seen pictures.

"You know him," I say. "Head stuck in a box."

Zach nods. He makes it a point to ogle every high school girl we pass, though none of them look back. This is the reason we come to the mall. It's pretty much the only reason we ever go anywhere. To watch them. Teenage girls are like precious gemstones: they sparkle and shine, and we just stare at them with breathless wonder. Being homeschooled has its disadvantages.

"I still don't know why you two just don't go on a crime spree and get it over with," Zach says. "I mean, seriously, with his little inventions and your, you know . . ." Zach makes his eyes bug out of his head in a poor imitation of me using my power. I give him the shush-it look, afraid he's going to just scream it to the rafters. Zach knows all about it, my little mind-control thing. He's one of only four people who do, myself included, and he's the only person *I've* ever told. I was forbidden to, of course. One of Dad's few absolutes, spouting the axiom I had actually learned already at St. Mary's: that people are drawn to power, that they will latch onto it and find a way to use it to their own ends. But I slipped. Call it a moment of weakness, but I had to tell somebody. Somebody my own age. Somebody who could appreciate what it was like growing up different. As soon as I said it, I swore Zach to secrecy. Bad guys don't worry about hiding their powers from other people, I know, but like I said, I'm not a bad guy.

"You could steal millions in a matter of days and then retire in style in Aruba or Venice or something," Zach continues.

"I don't think Dad wants to retire," I say. "He likes it here. He likes his work. I think he's building up to something special."

Zach shrugs. "Does he ever even leave the house?"

"Sure," I say. "All the time." If by all the time you mean once every month or so—and usually then to go rob something. We even have our groceries delivered. To the empty house next door.

Zach looks at me skeptically. "But don't you ever get tired of being a lab rat?" he asks. "Caged away in that basement of yours, building those little boxes?"

I give him a dirty look, which is as close as I ever get to getting mad at him. Zach is quick-tempered, and when his anger flares, so do his spikes, which could cause a scene. He's not as concerned with hiding his power as I am. I look at Zach's two-hundred-dollar high-tops and frown.

"I'm not a lab rat," I say.

"Squeak. Did you say something?" he says, scrunching up his nose. "I don't understand lab-ratese."

"You're a jerk."

Zach holds out his hands, wrists together, ready for a pair of invisible handcuffs. "Dude. I terrorize local businessmen, then I take their money and spend it on video games. Of course I'm a jerk." That's one thing about Zach. He's comfortable in his own thorny skin. Makes me feel better about myself.

We stop by the candle shop to smell everything they've got until we annoy the old ladies who work there and get kicked out.

"All I'm saying is that you should aim bigger," Zach says as we head to the food court. "You could come work for us, you know. The boss could use someone with your skills. Normally when Tony has to be convincing, he uses a baseball bat. Or a pair of pliers." I'm about to tell him TMI when his hand suddenly presses against my chest, stopping me. Being held there, looking at the bulge in Zach's arm with its scaly black dragon tattoo, reminds me that this was the summer I was going to start working out.

"Don't look. Over there. Pizza place. Front table," he says in a hushed voice.

I look.

"I said don't look!"

"You can't say 'over there' and 'don't look' at the same time," I tell him, but I see exactly who he is talking about. Two of them. Just finishing lunch. They look about Zach's age, maybe a little older. I can see why they got his attention. They're cute. Of course, most girls look cute to me. I grew up in an all-boys school and have spent the rest of my days in a basement with a man who looks like a washed-up fishing boat captain. All girls are a beautiful riddle. But these two are quantifiably attractive, the dark-haired one especially.

"I think they see us."

He's right. They are actually looking our way. I smile and am completely surprised when the girl with brown hair smiles back. That never happens. Twenty-plus trips to the mall and never a smile back. Suddenly I am overly conscious of the ketchup stain on my jeans. Zach grabs my arm, pinching hard.

"Dude. You've got to do it."

"*Do* it?"

"You know . . . your thing . . ." He stares deep into my eyes, pressed so close I'm afraid he is going to kiss me, which is even more horrifying when I think about what can pop out of his skin. I wince and push him out of my face.

"Yeah, see. That's what I meant when I said I need you to keep that a *complete and total secret*. Besides, I'm not supposed to use my power unless Dad tells me to or it's like a life-or-death thing."

"This *is* a life-or-death thing," he says. "I spend twenty hours a day cooped up with a bunch of poker-playing, cigar-chomping, overweight old men who curse at each other in Italian. I *need* this." His eyes are saucers now, the big bad wolf eyeing the little girl who just walked through the door. "Come on. They like us. They keep looking this way."

I chance another peek. The two girls *are* casting furtive glances in our direction. It could be flirting. Or maybe they think we are stalkers and are calculating how close we have to get before they call 911. After all, I can pass for boy-next-door, but Zach . . . not so much. I brush Zach's hand off my arm, which is a little dangerous; he's funny about being touched, ever since his cat jumped on him in the middle of the night and had to be buried the next day.

"All right." I sigh. "What do you want me to say?"

"You know. 'Hi. I'm Mike. This is my friend Zach. You

think he's hot and want to make him your new boyfriend.' Or something."

I groan, long and loud so that my displeasure is noted. But the truth is, I want to go over there too. "No promises," I say, and he punches me playfully on the shoulder. We walk over, Zach leading the way. The two girls exchange meaningful looks, and I wonder if there isn't some website I can go to that would help me break the code. I'm sure there is an app for it, but Dad won't let me have a cell phone.

"Hey," Zach says, running one hand a little too obvious-casual along his new green stripe.

"Hey," the blond girl with the tritone nail polish and the exposed belly button says. She is dressed in clothes that cling to her and show off her bony shoulders and flat stomach, clothes with labels I don't recognize, which probably means they come from stores you won't find around here. A north sider, probably. I see she has glitter on her lips *and* on her eyelids. The other girl hasn't looked up yet. A couple of really awkward seconds pass before I realize that "Hey" is as far as Zach is going to get.

"Do you mind if we sit here?" I ask, pointing to the two empty seats at the table. It's a question, not a command. I'm not about to use my power, despite Zach's pleading glances. The blonde looks at her friend and shrugs. Then the other girl—the one with walnut hair cut pixie short and dimples like quotation marks, the one dressed in a tight black T-shirt and cardigan—finally looks up at us as she moves to the other side of the table.

I look away. I'm secretly relieved when Zach goes for the now-empty seat beside the glittery one in the miniskirt.

"I'm Zach," he says.

"Becky," the blonde says.

"This is my friend, Mikey."

"Michael," I say, shaking Becky's hand. The other girl sips her Coke. She's a straw chewer, you can tell; her cheeks pucker with the effort of sucking through the collapsed opening, causing her dimples to vanish. Zach says something I don't quite catch, but Becky laughs, so I'm guessing he doesn't need my help anymore. I move around the table and sit down.

I'm suddenly more nervous than the time my father put a lead vest and protective goggles on me, saying, "You might feel a little jolt."

The girl finishes her sip, then holds out a hand cold and wet with condensation. "I'm Viola," she says. She smiles again, and whatever I was thinking of saying next vanishes. I rack my brain for something clever to replace it.

"Viola," I repeat. "Like from Shakespeare?" Dad makes me read him, too. The comedies *and* the tragedies. I remember Viola being a cross-dressing hero in one of them.

"Like from the orchestra," she says.

"Oh, right. Of course."

"My mother plays in one. My sister's name is Cello."

"You're kidding, right? Is your brother's name Timpani?"

"Trombone, actually. But we just call him Bone."

I laugh. She doesn't. So I stop. "You *were* kidding, right?"

42

She's still not laughing. I figure somehow I've blown it already, and I start to blame my father for teaching me way too much about physics and nineteenth-century literature and absolute jack about talking to girls. Then, finally, her smile reappears.

"Of course I'm kidding." She rolls her eyes. "I don't have a brother. Or a sister. But my mother does play in the orchestra." She takes another sip. Her bangs fall into her eyes, and she leans over and sweeps them away. I try not to look at them—the eyes, that is. Lead us not into temptation. I try instead to focus on the buttons of her cardigan, realize that might be misinterpreted, and give up and stare at the table.

"So is it Michael or just Mike? Or do you have, like, some cool nickname or something?"

Henchmen have streets names. I'm something else.

"Michael's good," I say.

"Got any brothers or sisters, Michael?"

I look back up, suddenly wondering what I was thinking even sitting here, talking to this total stranger. This totally gorgeous total stranger who has instantly struck up a conversation, as if we'd known each other for years. This totally, captivatingly gorgeous stranger whose ears, I've just noticed, are a little on the pointy side, just a shade elfish, studded with sapphires and curved like conch shells. What do I say? Do I make something up? The problem with making stuff up is that you have to remember it later.

"Actually I'm an only child, orphaned from birth and eventually adopted by a mad scientist who builds top-secret

43

gadgets in our basement." It comes out too fast for me to stop it. I smile my that-was-the-punchline smile. She gives me a strange look, arching one thin eyebrow.

"That is *so* fascinating," she says, playing along. "So is he your sidekick or something?" She points to Zach, who is already whispering something in Becky's ear. The other girl pushes him away, playfully, I hope. I don't want her to accidentally get pricked.

"Sidekicks are for wusses," I answer. "Zach and I just hang around the same circles."

The girl named Viola nods and smiles a coy smile. A smile with something else on its mind. "And you two just wander the mall on a summer day, looking for a couple of girls to tell your stories to?"

"Actually I'm just trying to get out of doing more homework," I say. I lean back in the chair. This is me trying to be charming—at least without using my power. I'm pretty sure I'm overdoing it. She takes another long slurp of soda. It's mostly ice left, but she doesn't seem to mind the obnoxious noises she makes.

"Maybe somebody forgot to tell you. It's June. School's officially closed for the summer."

"Not for me. I'm homeschooled."

"By your dad, the evil scientist?"

"I never said he was evil," I say. "Just mad."

"Mad like crazy."

"More like enthusiastic."

"Homework in June," she whispers. "Sucks to be you. Want a breadstick?" She holds up the last one from her plate. She has already taken a bite out of it.

"No thanks," I say, wondering what kind of girl offers half-eaten food to a boy she's only just met. She shrugs.

"So what does *your* dad do?" I ask her.

"He hunts down people trying to take over the world and puts them in jail."

"Really?"

"No, not really," she says, thrusting the breadstick in a tub of congealed cheese dip, where it stands at attention. "You *are* gullible. I guess you don't get to talk to girls very much, if you are a homeschooled orphan with no sisters and an enthusiastic father."

"Does it show?"

"Only a little," Viola says. "I mean, we've been sitting here talking for, like, three minutes and you haven't looked me in the eyes yet." She kind of drops her head to get my attention, and I can't help it. I'm sucked in. I look. Amber with flecks of brown. Honey dusted with cinnamon. I know I shouldn't say anything, but I can't help myself.

"They're remarkable," I whisper, then watch, horrified, as her pupils blow open.

"They are, aren't they?" she replies mechanically, and I can tell by the way she says it that she never really thought so until now. Until I said something.

My cheeks flush, and I look down at the table again,

breaking the spell. That was a mistake. I should have just kept my mouth shut. She shakes her head a little. Across the table I see Becky's hand move to her phone. I wonder what Zach has said or done to bring their conversation to an end so soon. Wonder what I can say next that might give me chance to talk to this girl who is not afraid to share her half-eaten breadstick with me even though we only just met, but all I can come up with is "So—do you hang out here a lot?"

As soon as I say it, I regret it. An entire spring getting schooled in the Romantic poets of England, and *that's* the best I can do?

"No. Never," she says, jangling the ice cubes in her cup again. "This was a total fluke."

"Like a stroke of good luck?"

"Like a chance occurrence," she amends. She and Becky exchange another predetermined signal from the codebook. I look at Zach, who gives a what-did-I-do? shrug.

"So we should be going, I guess," Becky says.

Viola stands up, and I stand with her. We are less than three feet away from each other. I try to find any excuse to touch her, just a graze, a shoulder, an elbow, anything. Instead, I just stand there.

"Right. So I promised my Aunt Clarinet we'd be home early," Viola says with mock exasperation, rolling her eyes at me.

"That's funny," I say. "Tell Cousin Oboe I said hi."

And finally she laughs. And it's musical, like an arpeggio. "I will," she says.

I meet her eyes once more, just for a sec, determined not to say anything this time. Then she brushes those bangs aside again before turning away.

"It was nice meeting you," Becky says, trailing after and turning to wave.

Zach and I sit at their abandoned table and watch them whisper and giggle their way down the corridor. I wait and wait and wait for her to look back, just once, like they always do in the movies, but she never does.

Suddenly a pizza crust sails in my direction, splattering sauce on my shirt, a stain to match the one on my pants. "What the heck!"

"Where was the voodoo, dude? The whole Jedi mind thing?" Zach scoffs.

"You seemed to be doing fine without it," I say.

"Sure. Until she told me about her *boyfriend*," he replies morosely. Then he smiles. Or sneers. "Got *his* name, though. We could hunt him down and convince him to dump her."

I shake my head, watching the girls get swallowed by the crowd. "Convincing some guy I don't know to dump some girl you just met so that you can have a shot with her? Now *that* sounds like a worthwhile use of my power."

"Who said anything about using *your* power?"

Zach raises an eyebrow, and a row of thorns about an inch long springs from his forehead, then just as quickly retreats. I look around to see if anyone has noticed.

"Let's go to the Kernel Cart," I say, hoping that somewhere

along the way I might run into her again. Viola. Whose mother plays in the orchestra and whose father does not put people in jail. By then, hopefully, I will have thought of something else clever to say, and this time, when she laughs, she'll put her hand on my arm for a couple of seconds, like they also do in the movies. Zach gets up, but before we leave the table, I pull the abandoned breadstick from its quagmire of congealed cheese and take a bite.

"*Oh . . .* that's totally *gross*, dude," Zach says. "You don't even *know* that girl."

It *is* a little gross. I know it. But I'm a sucker for symbolic gestures; I grew up taking communion, after all. And part of me thinks that maybe I do know her, just a little. Like maybe it isn't just a fluke. And that maybe, if I look hard enough, I will find her again.

I don't. See her, that is. Like the heroes that once protected New Liberty, she has disappeared. That doesn't stop Zach from teasing me about her. He's only two years older than me, but he has already had three girlfriends—though the moment they get to the kissing part, things get prickly and he gets dumped.

"You talked to her for all of three minutes."

He's right, of course. But that doesn't keep me from glancing in every store window.

Once the giant bag of caramel corn is finished—paid for by Zach and mostly consumed by me, as most things are between us—we leave the mall and the promise of meeting even more girls and head south, back toward our side of town, veering a little to fill my father's order. Though it's out of Zach's way, he says he wants to come with me to the Techno Tree—the electronic supply store that my dad spends most of his not-so-hard-earned cash at. The owner of the store—a skinny, high-strung Indian named Aziz—is a contributing member of the Romano Family Urban Renewal and Resources Fund. In other words, he pays for people like Zach to check up on him every now and then and make sure he's safe from roving hooligans and competing criminal elements.

"You don't think he's got one of those night-vision infrared implants, do you?" Zach asks as we shuffle along the broken sidewalk, kicking beer cans and pausing now and then to read the new graffiti, marks for lesser gangs, the ones content with pushing drugs and popping tires. The cars parked along the street transition from Suburbans to beaters the farther we get from the mall. You can tell you've crossed back over when all the Starbucks disappear and the yellow caution tape comes out.

"Or maybe I'll get some kind of laser hidden in an ink pen or something," he adds.

"He's not James Bond," I remind him. Aziz doesn't sell weapons, though he could sell you everything you needed to make one of your own. As we walk, I point to the various symbols painted on the stone and ask Zach to interpret them for me, but he doesn't even know most of them. "Small-timers," he says. "Most of 'em just kids with crap parents and too much time on their hands."

We stop just outside the store and wait for the one customer in there to leave before going in. I know I'm just picking up a circuit board, nothing illegal or even suspicious, but it's still best to have the place to ourselves. Aziz is standing by the cash register, dressed as usual in a sweater and slacks, his graying hair pulled back into a ponytail, peering at us through his half-moon glasses like a shaman.

He doesn't look happy to see us. Normally he greets me with a smile. He and my father are kindred spirits of a sort; they have known each other for years, before I was adopted. They have even worked on a few projects together. When I come in alone, Aziz usually offers me tea, but Zach's presence changes the dynamic. Aziz circles around behind us and locks the door, flipping the sign in the window from OPEN to CLOSED. He has nothing to worry about, of course. The cops don't mess with Aziz. Tony pays most of them not to.

The shop looks the same as always. Aisles of wooden shelves stocked with every kind of gadget, gizmo, and electrical whichamajigger you could imagine. Transistors and resistors. Batteries of every size and shape. Servos and motors, fuses and gears. Photoreceptors and motherboards. My father sometimes comes and spends hours wandering the aisles, the cogs in his own overstuffed head meshing together.

"Misters Madison and Morn," Aziz calls out. "What can I do for you gentlemen?"

I say hello and show him my father's Post-it with the circuit board's model number on it. He moves his head from shoulder to shoulder, which I've learned means either "no problem at all" or "could stand to be spicier."

"How is your father? I haven't seen him in a few weeks," Aziz says, consulting a catalog behind his counter.

"Keeping busy," I say. Zach squeaks at me and makes his little rat face, but I ignore him.

"And Mr. Romano? I trust he is doing well?" Aziz inquires, coolly cordial.

"Actually," Zach says, suddenly very serious, putting his hands behind his back, "that's what I've come to speak to you about."

Aziz quickly loses his polite smile and grips the counter. I shake my head, but the store owner can't take his eyes off Zach, who is moving toward him, chest puffed like a gorilla. "It seems your account is overdue, Mr. Aziz, and Mr. Romano sent me to give you a reminder. . . ." Zach curls his fingers into a fist, and a dozen three-inch spikes shoot out around the knuckles, so it suddenly looks like some kind of wicked sea urchin swallowed his hand.

"But I paid for this month," Aziz starts to mumble, backing away from the counter. I figure that's far enough.

"Stop being a jerk," I say, kicking at Zach's heels. The spikes get sucked back in. Zach laughs and puts his hands up in surrender.

"Just messin' with ya," he says. "The boss is fine. Thanks for asking."

Aziz looks at both of us, back and forth, back and forth, and then lets himself smile weakly. "You had me going there for a minute," he says, swallowing hard, and I kind of hope Zach will apologize, but I know it won't happen. For Zach, power is that look in Aziz's eyes—the one that still hasn't gone away. Aziz glances over at me once more, frowns, and then escapes into the back storeroom to find my father's part.

"That wasn't funny," I snap.

"It was a little funny," Zach says, but he doesn't push it. Instead he starts wandering the aisles, touching everything. I glance around the room. I know that this stuff should interest me. That it should speak to me on some intrinsic, geeky, inspirational level. That I should see in this giant collection of parts a vast creative universe waiting to be tinkered with, soldered together, transformed. I think of the look my father gets every time he comes in here. But whatever he has, I don't have it yet. I lean back against the counter, and my eyes fall on a little black box with three buttons on it, sitting on a top shelf, pushed back as far as it will go. Probably a security device. An alarm or a motion detector, maybe. My father could cram anything into one of those cubes.

Eventually Aziz comes back with a small brown bag and hands it to me—he saves the brown bags for special customers. When I start digging in my pockets for the cash, he puts up his hands and moves his head back and forth, shoulder to shoulder. I thank him and head to the door, glad to get out of here without Zach showing off anymore. "Tell your father I said hello. And give my regards to Mr. Romano,"

Aziz says behind us, flipping his sign back to OPEN.

"I will." I'm guessing I will be back here in a couple of days. Maybe I can have some tea then.

We turn up the block, headed toward my house. As we walk, Zach points out all the stores and restaurants that Tony has a collar on, making me wonder why the whole street isn't just named after him. Big Tony Avenue. Or better still, Romano Way. You could probably parse out the whole city if you had a map; take a big Sharpie and outline the neighborhoods. This is Tony's. To the west is Maloney territory. Even farther south you've got rival gangs fighting over trailer parks and burned-out apartment complexes. Then there're all the neighborhoods north of the mall. The ones with private security systems and wrought-iron fences.

"I mean, it's New Liberty," Zach continues. "Nowhere is *really* safe. But Tony makes sure everyone here stays in business, at least." Then he starts going on and on about how nice the bathrooms are in Tony's house—gold-plated faucets and sixty-inch flatscreens. I start to tune him out. I can't stop thinking about our little run-in at the mall. She was right. I don't get to talk to girls enough.

I interrupt Zach in the middle of some spiel about how Tony Romano is probably the most feared man in New Liberty, ever since the Harbinger—pretty much the city's last great supervillain—slipped up and got himself disintegrated. "It just goes to show, you don't have to have superpowers to be respected, you know?"

"Yeah, whatever," I say. "Hey, you know how in the movies the chick always goes for the dangerous guy? Do you think that's true? I mean, do you think girls like that kind of thing?" I had seen a lot more movies since I'd escaped St. Mary's. Friday night is movie night. My father's attempt at normalcy. Taco night. Movie night. Game night. A series of typical family nights to balance out our rob-a-bank and test-out-this-new-superconductor days.

Zach snorts at me. "You're not dangerous," he says.

"I didn't say *I* was dangerous. I just asked if they really fall for the dangerous guy, or do they go for the good guy."

"You're not the good guy either," he points out. "You're goon number three. You're the guy that gets his neck broken when the hero shows up under cover of darkness to infiltrate the bad guy's lair in the finale. You get to say something stupid like, 'Hey, did you just hear something?' and then, *snap*, you're a mound of Play-Doh on the pavement."

"That's not me," I say.

"Fine, then *I'm* that guy and you're the guy that says, 'Nope, I didn't hear nothin'. Did you?' and then has *his* neck snapped."

I wonder if he's right. Wonder if she even gave me a second thought or just left me with a half-eaten breadstick. "You're just jealous," I say.

"Jealous?"

"Because I have a cooler power than you."

Zach stares, incredulous. "You think so? Tell me, Mister Mindflop, when was the last time you used that little trick?"

I had to think back. Besides the accidental use today, it was probably a month ago, when I parked myself by the ATM machine at the Piggly Wiggly and convinced some guy in a sweater vest to withdraw a hundred dollars from his checking account so we could pay the power bill.

"I don't know," I say.

"Exactly what I'm talking about. Even *if* your power is cooler—and I'm not admitting that it is—you're too scared to use it. If you weren't, you would be walking home with that chick from the mall right now instead of arguing with me. Come to think of it, we could both—"

Zach's rant is cut short by the crackle of gunshots, a not entirely unusual sound in New Liberty, except these are coming from very close by. I can feel him bristling beside me, his instincts triggered. Two more gunshots follow, then some screaming and an alarm.

I duck just as the windows of the jewelry store in front of us explode.

A COMET SIGHTING

The detonation tears through the city streets, one sound blanketing all others. Zach and I crouch there and watch the glass fly. We should run and scream like all the people around us, but we don't even move. Paralyzed and mesmerized both. I get a strange prickling on my skin, then another sound, like a dial tone or a dog whistle, a constant buzz. My instinct tells me to turn around, double back, find another way home, but Zach grabs my hand and pulls me behind the dingy glass of a bus stop, mostly hidden from view. Smoke belches from the jewelry store windows, obscuring our line of sight. A mother of three runs past us in the opposite direction, two of her kids trailing behind her, the third crying in her arms. The little one drops a stuffed bear he is holding and wails even louder as they duck inside a nearby apartment building, slamming the door behind them.

I wonder if I shouldn't follow them. If they would even let me in.

"Look," Zach says, pointing as three men emerge from the jewelry store, large black duffel bags stuffed. Zach's eyes are large. Clearly impressed. These aren't hooligans or thugs. They don't belong to any of the graffiti gangs we passed on the way here. They are professional criminals, the likes of which New Liberty hasn't seen in a while. The men, dressed in matching black leather jumpsuits and armed with assault rifles, step through the hole in the window, walking with steady, determined strides. Silvery metal masks hide each of their faces, wrapped halfway around their skulls, with three rectangular slits where their mouths and eyes should be, like a toddler's first jack-o'-lantern. They look almost like robots. They even move in sync.

"Those aren't your guys, are they?" I ask Zach, though I already know the answer. Tony's men don't wear masks. Nobody in New Liberty wears masks except for dental hygienists and hazmat crews. Zach shakes his head. I can see the bristles already peeking through the taut skin of his cheeks. "Could be Mickey Six Fingers's goons," he says, "but they wouldn't dare mess with this neighborhood, and they mostly use bats and pipes. That's expensive hardware."

The men in the silver masks fire into the air, making sure the bystanders give them a wide berth. Each shot makes me jump. I can't help but feel like I should be doing something. Running, probably. Or maybe calling the cops, crazy as that sounds. I say as much to Zach, who already has his phone out and is recording video of the whole affair.

"Trust me," he says, "somebody is already on the way."

I stop and listen, and in a second I can hear the sirens. The three men in silver masks stand in a huddle outside the jewelry store, aiming their rifles in every direction. Zach turns and points to an approaching cop car, wailing and flashing, screaming to a sideways stop before being riddled by an assault-rifle onslaught. The officer leans out and squeezes off a couple of wayward rounds, then ducks back into the car just as his windshield shatters under a spray of bullets. The siren lets out one last pathetic whimper. Three metal faces whip around as a white van appears from around the corner, T-boning the first police car, knocking it out of the way, the cop still stuck inside.

"Hope he's not on our payroll," Zach mutters.

There are more sirens from down the block. An old man pokes his head out the door of the shop directly behind us, spits on the street to let us know how he feels, then slams the door shut again. In all the buildings you can see people peering through parted curtains. They haven't seen anything like this for a long time either. Nobody's quite sure what to do anymore. I look around, half expecting to see Tony himself walking up, brandishing his cane, demanding to know "What the hell is goin' on heah?" But the lines have been drawn, and Tony wouldn't get caught in the middle.

Another police car careens down the street toward the scene

of the crime. The side door of the van opens, and a fourth steel-faced man pulls what appears to be a rocket launcher up onto his shoulder.

"Ba-zoo-ka," Zach marvels, his voice almost cartoonish. I plug my nose from the acrid smell of smoke and look through the slits between my fingers. It's like watching a lion take down a baby gazelle. The laws of nature at work—that whole circle-of-life—but it still kind of makes your skin crawl seeing it. The squad car squeals. The man in the van fires, and the rocket sizzles through the air, planting a crater in the street for the cop to drop into, landing with another plaintive cry. A third police cruiser slams into it from behind, goes airborne for a moment, and then flips over on its side.

I think I've seen enough.

"Seriously, man. Time to go," I say. I wonder what my father would say if he knew I was just sitting here, watching. Suddenly I desperately want to be back home.

"No, wait," Zach says, pulling me back down next to him with his free hand, still recording with the other. "Here comes the cavalry."

Zach points his phone at the SWAT truck charging from the other direction, plowing through abandoned cars on an intercept course with the white van, its reinforced bumper knocking sedans away like Ping-Pong balls. For a moment I think it's going to make it, but Rocket Man reloads and fires just in time. The missile scores a direct hit, and the truck rolls twice before landing on its back like a flipped turtle. The officers try to scramble out of their vehicles, but a barrage of gunfire keeps them pinned down as the masked robbers pile into the back of the white van.

"Who said crime doesn't pay?" Zach whispers.

I look around to see if anyone else is coming. More cops. Maybe some of Tony's men. I don't know. *Some*body. I forget where I am for a moment. These men, with their metal masks and their machine guns and their van clearly fitted with bulletproof glass, they are out of place, and the effect is disorienting. I am suddenly nauseous. I peer through the haze as the van screeches backward, clearing a space, then pulls out into the street. Beside me, Zach stands and bristles as if he's going to do something, though I know he's not. His thorny hide is no match for a rocket launcher. The tires squeal, trying to find purchase on a street studded with broken glass. The fire in the jewelry store snorts, and another window shatters. Zach turns to say something to me, but I can only see his lips move as his phone suddenly drops from his hand.

I can't hear anything over the sonic boom.

I topple backward, barely catching myself on the edge of the bench as the sound, curled into a tight fist of singular force, slugs me in the gut. Everything is muffled, like I've shoved Q-Tips in my ears clear to my brain.

I think of my father. And the box he was working on today, the sonic disrupter. Maybe this is his doing. Maybe he's come to save me. I look around. Then, suddenly, a streak of blue light comes shooting out of the sky, whatever's at the tip of it landing on the hood of the armored van, which catapults straight up into the air on impact, doing two perfect somersaults before crashing down back on its wheels. It's the kind of thing you are used to seeing in slow motion in the movies, so in real life it happens way too fast.

"What is *that*?" Zach says, stupefied. He points to the guy dressed in blue—perfect blue, the kind you only see on color wheels and postcards of the sky in Wyoming—his black hair spiked out like some Japanese graphic novel cover boy, a blue mask covering his nose and ringing his eyes. Black boots rise up to his knees, and the form-fitting outfit he wears ripples with muscular implication. He's at least six feet tall. Maybe closer to seven. There are no symbols or emblems on his chest. Whatever he is, whoever he's with, he's not advertising, but judging by the gymnastics he just made the van do and the fact that he fell out of the sky at two hundred miles per hour and landed on his feet, there's little question he's more than just NLPD or SWAT.

He's the real deal.

Beside me, it looks like Zach's about to soak his hundred-dollar jeans, hands clutching the bench with white-knuckled ferocity. We should *really* leave now. Both of us. But I can't take my eyes off the guy. After all, I've never seen one before. Not in person.

The blue-costumed figure approaches the disabled van in measured strides, ripping the back doors free as if peeling a tangerine. There is another explosion of gunfire as he disappears inside. Some shouting as the van rocks back and forth on what's left of its wheels, looking as if it is having a seizure.

Then silence. No more gunshots. No more explosions. Behind me, the man who spit on the sidewalk opens his door again and stands there with one eye closed. Zach whistles to himself.

"What . . . in the world . . . was *that*?" he asks again.

I still don't have an answer, but whatever *it* is emerges finally, holding four full duffels of stolen jewels. When it steps off the back of the van, the whole thing lurches. The jewel thieves must be inside, but it's clear they aren't coming out. The masked stranger drops the bags at the feet of what must be the terrified store owner, who now stands outside in the pool of shattered glass. One by one the innocent bystanders emerge, peeking their heads out of windows and through cracks in doors, shimmying out from underneath cars like mice. A few officers manage to pull themselves through their smashed windows, clearly wondering whether or not to even bother aiming their guns at this new arrival, but before they can get the chance, the mysterious figure raises one hand toward the sky and, in a blink, launches himself toward the clouds. I clutch at my ears as the boom hits me all over again, then look up at the streak of blue light left in the man's wake. Some of the bystanders begin to cheer, but most just stare at the sky like zombies, like me.

Zach's gone ghostly, face drained of all color. "Tony's going to flip when he hears about this," he says, bending over to retrieve his phone.

I nod. It's true. And not just Tony. Forget the people in the silver masks, whoever *they* were. Forget Tony and Mickey

"Six Fingers" Maloney and the NLPD and all the other small-timers looking to make their marks on the city.

New Liberty apparently has a new "hero."

Whether it likes it or not.

"Come on," Zach says, pulling me away from the smoke and the carnage and the wailing of more sirens, ambulances and fire trucks and who knows what else bearing down on us. I follow him a few steps and then stop, bending over and picking up the stuffed bear that had been left behind—its fur smelling of smoke, one black eye popping loose—and setting it on the step of the apartment building where it belongs.

Hoping somebody will come to rescue it.

Zach and I split, and I sprint home and pound through the door into the empty main floor of our house, beelining for the lair, taking the stairs two at a time, nearly tumbling down them, catching myself on the railing. Dad's in the same spot I left him in hours ago, the bag of chips empty beside him, humming to himself. Bach, I think. I stop at the bottom step to breathe.

"How was the mall?" he asks without even looking up, ignoring, apparently, the fact that I am doubled over like an asthmatic finishing a marathon.

"You'll never . . . *believe* . . . what just happened!"

"Did you get my board?" he asks, nose still pressed down into his little black box.

The board. I curse under my breath. I've completely forgotten about the package from Aziz. I must have dropped it or set it down back at the jewelry store and neglected to pick it up. I make a production out of slapping my forehead. "Yeah. Okay. I forgot the board, but listen, I have to tell you something—"

"You forgot to *get* it? Or you forgot to bring it *home*? Or you forgot that I even asked you to buy it in the first place?"

"The middle one, I think. Dad, seriously, I think we have a problem."

"Of course we have a problem. I need that board if I'm going to finish this," he says.

"No. A bigger problem. A big . . . blue . . . bulletproof problem."

Finally I've gotten his attention, at least enough to pull him out of his box. My father sits back in his chair and pulls off his goggles; there are red raccoon rings around his eyes matching the red-and-white pineapples on his shirt. He has potato-chip crumbs in his beard. He regards me with a skeptical eye, as if he suspects I'm about to try and sell him something. I take a deep breath, trying to calm myself. Go slow, I think. Let it all sink in.

"So Zach and I were walking home from the mall when suddenly there were these gunshots, right? And all these guys showed up, dressed up in black with silver masks and machine guns and I had never seen anything like them before, and they knock over a jewelry store, and then they were like *blow! kablow! ka-ba-ba-blow!*, blowing up everything in sight, and the cops came, but they got totally toasted, and the dudes with the masks, they pull out this rocket launcher and the SWAT team's like, *kaboosh!*, and I was all ready to run, but then the sky suddenly rips apart, like *keeyrack!*, and this guy, I don't know, he's like eight feet tall and dressed in this blue bodysuit with this mask and everything, he comes falling out of the sky, and *thoom!*, just pummels the van, like *crunch!*, and then disappears inside, and it's all like shaking and stuff, and when he comes out, he's got the jewels, and he just sets them down on the ground and *kazow!* shoots right back into the sky, and if you go look outside you can still see the streak of blue where he flew away. . . ."

I take another breath to keep from passing out.

"Are you hurt?" my father says, slowly eyeing me up and down.

"No. I'm not hurt," I say, shaking my head. Did I look hurt? I glance over myself, looking for any trace of blood. There is a spot of tomato sauce on my shirt where Zach hit me with the pizza crust.

Dad nods. "And these men . . . the ones in masks . . . what were they like?"

"I don't know, Dad. They were all the same. Just, you know, a bunch of men in black suits with guns. Like clones, almost. But this guy, the other guy. You should have seen it. He just dropped out of the sky—"

"And these men, they were just going about their business, robbing this store, when this other individual flew in from nowhere and interrupted them?"

This other individual. Who, like, just happened to drop in

from a little glide through the neighborhood. "He's not like a random passerby, Dad, he was a superhero. And he didn't interrupt them. He totally vanquished them."

I can see him chewing it over, the little gears in his head spinning. It's a lot to process, even for me. I can't imagine what he must be thinking.

"I see," he says finally. "And what did *you* do?"

"What?" I blink, maybe, fifty or sixty times, trying to comprehend how, with everything I just said, this is somehow about *me*.

"Aside from *not* getting my circuit board, what did you do while these masked and tighted men clashed? Did you help the bystanders? Interfere with the cops? Did you sneak into the jewelry store while everyone was distracted and find a nice gold watch for my birthday? What?"

I sit on the bottom stair, exhausted, shaking my head. "I didn't *do* anything. I hid behind a bench with Zach and watched."

"That's it?" he asks, one eyebrow arched. "Just watched?"

"Yeah. That's it," I say. Some Super freak of nature shows up out of nowhere with a swath of blue panty hose across his face and makes mincemeat out of a posse of heavily armed goons, and all that matters is what *I* did about it. "I think you're missing the point, Dad." I'm not entirely sure what the point is, but I'm sure he's missing it. It probably has something to do with the fact that there is now someone in town who can fly and deflect bullets *and punch holes through freakin' cement*. Of course I didn't actually *see* him punch holes in cement, but he certainly *looked* like he could. But Dad's expression is blank, impossible to read. "I thought . . . I don't know, that maybe you'd be a little *concerned* or something! I mean, this guy, he's like nothing else I've ever seen. He put a hole through a van's engine with his *foot*! He's strong. He's fast. He's powerful. He really could be trouble."

He nods at this, at least. "And so . . . ," my father prods, but I'm not sure what he's looking for. It's his teaching style. Fish for answers until he gets the one he wants. And so? And so what?

"And so . . . we need to be *careful*?" I venture.

"Yes," he says. "'A man cannot be too careful in his choice of enemies.'"

He pauses, waiting for me to say something.

"Oscar Wilde," he finishes.

"Right," I say. "Oscar Wilde."

Dad turns back to his box. "I guess I could probably make do with one of the older boards for now. No sense going back out there. Not with all this excitement. Besides," he adds, slapping his hands on his knees, "it's taco night, isn't it? I do love taco night."

Dad closes the lid on his box and makes for the stairs. He pauses next to me.

"I'm glad you're safe," he says.

While he boils the rice, I turn on the television and sit on the torn corduroy-covered loveseat. We don't technically have cable, though the little black three-buttoned box by the

67

wall can hijack over two thousand different channels from whatever satellites are pointing our way. I find the first news station I can and sit with a throw pillow clutched to my chest. I can hear Dad singing in the kitchen.

The thwarted robbery is all over the local news, going viral. Reporters are swarming the scene. Five would-be burglars were found inside the van, tied together with electrical wire ripped out of the vehicle's guts, their metal masks torn off and stacked in a neat pile beside them. Their identities are not being released to the public, but they are not believed to be affiliated with any of the known gangs or organizations currently operating in the city.

Which means New Liberty has a new criminal element.

But even these metal-faced goons with their machine guns and rocket launchers aren't the headline. The banners running along the bottom of the screen read NEW LIBERTY'S NEWEST SAVIOR and BLUE HERO HALTS WOULD-BE ROBBERS. Fuzzy snapshots of the man in the blue tights flash every other second, and every person interviewed gushes like a squeezed grape, eyes wide as they describe him rocketing out of the sky.

". . . like a canon. I had to cover my ears . . ."

". . . split the earth when he landed . . ."

". . . punched right through the door . . . with his bare fist!"

". . . couldn't get a look at his face, but I'm almost positive he smiled at me. . . ."

Wow. The guy makes one appearance, hangs around for five minutes, and he's already a celebrity.

I flip through stations, taking it all in, over and over again.

Nobody knows who he is. Nobody has seen him before, at least not in New Liberty. Channel Six dubs him the Cobalt Comet, for the streak he left across the sky. The fact that he can fly has everyone's undies in a bunch. Fliers are rare. Only one out of every ten Supers can do it, apparently. Even Captain Marvelous couldn't fly. It's clear the Cobalt Comet has super strength as well. There is wide speculation about what other powers he might have, where he came from, whether he is even human, that sort of thing. Can he shoot fire? Call down lightning? Is he a divine being? Does he gain his powers from celestial bodies? Is he a secret government weapon? Every news station in New Liberty seems to be scrambling to find out anything it can—and just making stuff up when it can't—yet nobody asks *why* he's here. Maybe I'm the only one wondering it, but I doubt it.

One channel is devoted to playing the event over and over again. I sit and watch the footage pieced together from a dozen phones, hoping *not* to catch a glimpse of Zach and me camped out by the bus stop. If my face shows on the news and Dad finds out about it, I'll be grounded for a year. Thankfully, all lenses were locked onto the action, just like Zach's was. I'm somewhere in the background, impossible to recognize.

Dad calls out from the kitchen that dinner's ready and I should turn off the TV.

"It's on every station," I say, taking the seat across from him at the table. He's cramming a taco shell, layering it with the skill of a mason, topping it with a flourish of cheese. He enjoys the act of fitting things inside other things. Compartmentalizing, he calls it. I slop a taco together, though I know I'm not going to eat it. The jolt of the afternoon still has my stomach twisted. "They are calling him the Cobalt Comet," I add as an afterthought. It feels funny, talking about a superhero the way you might talk about the neighbor's new dog. But my father's stony face keeps my own voice in check.

"Kind of a stupid name," he muses, picking lettuce out of his beard. "Why not the Azure Avenger? Or the Cerulean Crusader? Comets are just balls of dirty rock and ice. They're really not that remarkable, if you think about it. We make a big deal out of them, go out and watch them, but I've never known one to do anything special."

"I don't know," I say, pushing a kernel of half-frozen corn around on my plate. "It was pretty . . ." I fish for the word. Amazing? Frightening? Awful? It was all of those. But even that doesn't capture it, that feeling that everything around you has suddenly gone into motion, that you can actually feel the earth spinning on its axis. ". . . unsettling," I decide.

Dad shrugs. "It's not the first hero New Liberty has ever seen."

No, but it's the first one *I've* ever seen. In the flesh, at least—provided his skin is actually *made* of flesh and isn't some strange mutant alien polymer or something.

"Comets pass," he says.

"And the men in the metal masks?" I ask.

My father pauses, half-eaten taco in hand, and finally it breaks, just a little, that marble facade of his. The corners of his mouth crack, and I can see the shift in his eyes, like a curtain pulled, revealing at least a hint of concern. I've never seen my father scared before, not even when we are robbing banks or sculpting plastic explosives in the lair, but it's obvious that the thought of these silver-faced thugs spooks him a little, maybe even more than the superhuman freak who wears his underwear on the outside of his pants. He starts to say something, then backtracks into a wan smile.

"We've seen their kind too," he says. "Tony will look after us. And *we* will look after each other." He reaches across the table and puts his hand on my shoulder. Then he glances over at my barely touched plate. "Ready for dessert?"

Dad overnukes a couple slices of cherry pie and then launches into a lecture on how rice is the single most important food in the world and how the Spanish explorer Cortez was probably the first European to have taco night. Afterward, I finish clearing the table, thinking maybe I'll call Zach, when Dad asks me over the plate he's rinsing, "So, did you see anything you liked at the mall?"

And suddenly I remember. Black sweater and short brown hair, chewed straw and piano laugh. Funny how a sonic boom and a hundred gunshots can make you forget. But now, thinking about her, I feel the warmth spread to my cheeks. I turn away so he won't see me.

"No. Not really," I say.

I'm not sure why I don't mention her. Maybe because, here, in this neighborhood with its potholed streets and its hollowed-out cars, in this house with its flaking paint and this kitchen with its peeling linoleum, sitting above a secret lair full of black black-market boxes, something like her can't exist.

Dad nods, satisfied with my answer.

"Of course," he says. "We have everything we need right here."

I finish clearing the table, then excuse myself and go sit on the porch. The air is thick with the expectation of rain. Half the porch lights are burned out, up and down the street. You can hear a car alarm bleating like a lost sheep two blocks away. On the corner, three teenagers are grouped around a streetlamp, whispering to each other. I see one of them make a gesture with the flat of his hand, making it soar into the sky. Up and away. They sense it. So do I.

So does Dad, but for some reason he doesn't want to admit it. Or he just doesn't want to talk about it. But it's obvious. Something changed today. A shift. I can hear him putting the dishes back in the cabinets. Compartmentalized. I think maybe I missed something. An opportunity.

Viola, Dad. Her name was Viola. The instrument. Not the cross-dresser. And she was beautiful.

I look up at the stars, at the streak of blue light fading against the darkness, and wonder why she didn't look back.

And what I would have done if she had.

GREAT CHAIN OF BEING

When I was ten years old, I stepped on a spider. I noticed it skittering across the kitchen floor toward the table where my father and I were having breakfast. I watched it scurry to within striking distance. Then I casually lifted my slippered foot and smashed it before taking another bite of Cheerios.

My father, sitting across from me, put down his copy of *Popular Science* and gave me a serious look. Not angry, exactly, but obviously displeased. The kind of look that lets you wish you had the last ten seconds of your life back to do over again.

"Why did you do that?" he asked.

"It was a spider," I said, thinking that maybe he just saw me stomp and didn't know why.

"I know it was a spider," he said. "What I want to know is why you killed it."

I looked at him, confused. Then gave the exact same answer.

"So just because is a spider, it demands to be annihilated?" he pressed. He crossed his arms over the blue fronds of his shirt and leaned back in his chair.

Annihilated. That seemed kind of extreme. I just stepped on it. "Well, no, but . . ."

"Was it attacking you? Are you hurt?"

"No, but . . ."

"Was it poisonous? A brown recluse, maybe? Your life was in danger, perhaps?" he pried.

"No. I don't think so." I had no idea what a brown recluse spider looked like. Moreover, I had no idea what my father was freaking out about. It was just a spider. Now it was a splotch on the floor. I would clean it up, if that was the problem.

"Perhaps you were bitten by spiders as a little boy back at St. Mary's, so you've developed a phobia?"

"Phobia?"

"A deep-seated fear of spiders that you can't control," he explained. "Do you have arachnophobia, Michael?"

I couldn't remember ever being bitten by a spider before. This one hadn't been any bigger than a nickel. I don't think I was afraid of it. Maybe a little grossed out. The more questions he asked, the more confused I got. I shook my head.

"What was it, then?"

"I don't know," I said. "I just saw it and I stepped on it."

"Hmmph," my father said. He buried his nose back in his magazine. I should have let it go, but I didn't. I couldn't. I never can.

"What?" I asked him.

"I just think you should have a reason, that's all."

"For squashing a spider?" I almost said killing, but that sounded almost as bad as annihilated. Squashing sounded innocent. Or at least accidental.

"For everything," he replied. He peered at me from over the top of his magazine, like a prying neighbor nosing over a fence. "I don't care that you killed it, so long as you had a *reason.*"

He stared at me for almost a minute more, waiting, I guess, for the right answer. But there was nothing I could tell him. I didn't know why I did it. So I looked down at the smeared spot that had gotten me into this mess. Then I reached down with my napkin and wiped it up, wrapping it gently in the folds before tossing it in the trash can. I sat back down at the table and waited for my father to turn the page. I pushed away my bowl of cereal and thought about it some more.

"Does it have to be a *good* reason?" I asked.

My father put down his magazine again and took a sip of his coffee. Then he smiled at me.

"That all depends on what you mean by *good*," he said.

That was the last spider I ever squashed.

The day after his arrival, the news stations are still salivating over every little scrap of story they can peel off the streets regarding the Comet. Apparently the *Cobalt* was dropped in the middle of the night, to save ink and conserve headline space. Besides, the Comet sounded cooler by itself, and half of

New Liberty had no idea that cobalt was even a color.

They interviewed as many witnesses as they could find, even the mother of the little boy who dropped his bear. And of course everybody saw something a little different. One person swears that he saw flames coming from the Comet's boot heels. Another claims that there was electricity wreathed around the hero's eyes. Yet another insists that she had seen the Comet the night before at a bar and took him home to her apartment but wouldn't tell the rest. "Not till I get a book deal," she teases. No one says anything about two teenage kids taking it all in from a bus stop on the corner.

On the morning news, experts in the area of vigilante justice and superhuman phenomena dissect the film footage from the crime scene, speculating on the nature of the Comet's powers, trying to work backward to determine his origin. Is he a supernatural being from beyond the grave? Does he derive his powers from nuclear energy? Is he a genetic mutation? One expert postulates that the Comet is just an ordinary man like the rest of us, except he's been augmented with a titanium endoskeleton to enhance his strength and a pair of kick-butt antigravity boots to help him fly. He is compared to others like him. Corefire. Sartorian. Archon. Another channel features an impassioned local preacher declaring the Comet the second coming of Christ, quoting, "And they shall see the Son of Man coming in the clouds of heaven, with power and great glory." But I, for one, don't buy it. I've seen plenty of pictures, and in none of them is Jesus wearing spandex.

Still, I can't say that I blame them. The innocent bystanders of New Liberty had lost their faith in capes. And now here it came, rocketing back to them on the Comet's big blue tail.

There is some speculation on the men in the metal masks as well. One channel dubs them the Silver Syndicate. Another claims that they might be the same group responsible for a rash of bombings along the West Coast a few years back. An expert in criminal psychology and organization insists that they are mindless soldiers—you can tell by their movements, their coordination—and that, as soldiers, they must naturally have a general. A leader. What follows is endless speculation on who that might be, with one expert going so far as to suggest it might be the Comet himself.

My father calls for me from the basement. I can barely hear him over the TV.

"Michael, come down here for a minute."

I reluctantly flip it off and shuffle to the door, pattering down the stairs to find him in his usual spot, one of his unfinished inventions sitting on his lap.

"I need your help," he says, motioning to an empty chair.

I slump into it, nodding toward the box that he moves to the workbench. "What is it?"

"Something I've been working on for a while now," he says.

He woke up this morning as if it were any other, grabbed his coffee, and retreated to his lair without a word on what happened yesterday, as if nothing remarkable did.

"For a while? You mean like since this morning?"

"I mean like since before I met you."

"Oh," I say. The lair is full of half-finished projects. One shelf holds figures and blueprints for at least a dozen inventions not yet started. My father's ideas come much faster than his hands, or our ever-fluctuating income, can keep up with. Still, it sometimes comes as a blow to think about how much life he lived without me, how much I still don't know about his past. I look over to see that the missile is overflowing with crumpled paper. He takes the little black box and sticks it on top of what looks like a metal colander turned upside down, little blue and yellow wires crisscrossing over it.

"Isn't that the spaghetti strainer?"

He nods and attaches a few more wires. The whole thing looks like a prop from a bad science-fiction movie, the kind with rocket ships on strings and flashlights for ray guns.

"Here, put this on," he says.

"You're kidding, right? Like on my head?"

"Not kidding," he says. He rifles through the pile of parts he's collected on his bench until he finds two suction cups with little metal coils on the ends. He licks them each once, then sticks them on either side of my forehead, just beside my eyes, feeding the wires to them.

"Ew. That was your spit," I say. Then I see him reaching for the button on the box that is currently resting on the metal bowl on top of my skull. I instinctively grab his hands in protest.

"No, no, no, no," I say. "Not until you tell me what it does."

78

I've been in this chair before. I need to know what I'm getting myself into.

Dad smiles his innocent smile. "It's an amplifier . . . basically. It captures a person's brainwaves and intensifies them, increasing them both in terms of power and range. Or at least it's supposed to, though it's still in its infancy. But don't worry," he tells me. "It's perfectly safe. The red button isn't even activated yet."

"It's not the *red* button I'm worried about!" I say. He would never hurt me on purpose, I know, but this isn't the first trial run I've been a part of. "Remember the time you tried to give us both X-ray vision?"

My father shrugs it off. "A minor setback."

"We couldn't see for two hours!"

"You're exaggerating," he says. "It was thirty minutes. Forty, tops. Besides. This is not like that. I promise. This doesn't do anything you can't do already. It just does it better. Hopefully. Maybe. As long as everything works perfectly for a change, and your head doesn't explode."

I give him bug eyes. He says he's only kidding.

Then, before I can offer up more examples in protest, Dad reaches over and presses something. I hear the box above me hum and feel the colander on my head start to vibrate. I brace myself for the electric shock. Wait for my brains to be scrambled or my hair to catch fire, or my tongue to go numb, but nothing else happens. I don't feel any different at all, save for a little more idiotic now that I have a vibrating metal bowl on my head. My father checks a few things on the computer screen beside him, columns of numbers that I can't even begin to understand, then turns back to me and says, in all earnestness, "All right, Son. Tell me to pee my pants."

"What?"

"Go ahead," he prods. "Make me pee my pants."

I can't help it. I look down at the front of my father's khakis, then back up at him. His face is completely earnest. This is stupid. "Do you *want* to pee your pants?" I ask. I feel like I'm talking to a three-year-old.

"I most definitely do *not* want to pee my pants," he says emphatically.

I shake my buzzing head. There are so many things wrong with this scenario already. For starters, we have a rule that I'm not supposed to use my power on him. And he knows that I have a hard time convincing people to do things they aren't at least somewhat open to. Plus he knows it's coming. He's prepared himself against it. There's no way it will work.

"Dad, I really don't feel comfortable . . . ," I start to say.

"That's the whole point. Just look in my eyes and tell me to spend the penny."

Spend the penny? Now I don't even know what he's *talking* about. I reach up and rub the suction cup on my forehead, which is starting to itch. The colander is still humming. I look at my father, meet his eyes.

Fine, I think, if it will get this over with. I stare back into his eyes.

"Pee your pants," I say halfheartedly.

"No," Dad says immediately. "With gumption."

I'm not sure I have any gumption, and if I did, I'm guessing I wouldn't use it to make my father wet himself. "Fine. Pee your pants, *please.*"

My father looks back at the screen. Shakes his head, then turns back to me. He puts both hands on my cheeks. His hands are freezing.

"Concentrate," he says.

"Seriously, Dad? There's a humming metal bowl on my head and these suction thingies are uncomfortable, and you," I say, sniffing, "really need a shower."

"Just do it. For me. Just one more time."

"Fine," I say, exasperated, fixing him with my gaze, latching onto those sparkling jades, trying to ignore the buzzing. "Pee your stupid pants!" I command him.

The colander suddenly hums louder, and I instinctively look at the front of Dad's pleated slacks, waiting for the bloom.

But nothing happens. On the screen, all the numbers suddenly disappear and the box on top of my head powers down. Dad frowns. Slumps. Shakes his head. Then he reaches over and takes the colander off my head, and I can see a little wisp of smoke escaping from the top of the box.

"It should have worked," he says.

"Maybe you just need more coffee," I say.

He looks at me, still scowling at his failure, but the coffee comment gets him, and soon he is snorting. And then we are both laughing, leaning back in our chairs. The mad scientist and his son, secreted away in their hideout, trying to make a tinkle.

"I guess it was pretty ridiculous," Dad says in between breaths. We let the laughter peter out in a series of coughs and sighs. Dad recovers with a shuddering breath, wiping his eyes, and then stares across the room at the calendar pinned to the wall. Each month showcases a famous scientist or inventor. June is Sir Isaac Newton month. a guy who got famous just for watching stuff fall out of the sky. My dad could so kick Sir Isaac Newton's dad's butt in a science fair any day of the month, even if all his inventions don't work right the first time.

Dad mumbles the date to himself. His face goes white for a moment, and then he smiles.

"What?" I say. "Do you think you really have to go this time?"

The mad scientist turns and gives me a wink.

"Yes," he says. "Let's go."

An hour later I am staring at a baboon's shiny pink butt.

How my father went from not peeing his pants to going and watching other animals whiz wherever they wanted to is beyond me. But as soon as the idea hit him, he was sold on it. We *had* to visit the New Liberty Zoo.

"Yeah. See. I'm not sure that's such a great idea now that there's a *masked vigilante crimefighter on the loose*," I remind him, but he dismisses the thought and tells me to grab my sunglasses;

we will go incognito. He even pulls on his only non-Hawaiian-themed shirt, a muted green polo I bought him one year for his birthday under the stipulation that he try to wear it whenever we were seen together in public. With his hair mostly brushed and shoes on his feet, he looks almost ordinary.

"To the Edsonmobile," he cries, pointing one finger in the air, stopping to put the Scrambler in his pocket. We are going incognito, but there's no sense getting our faces on security cameras if we can help it.

The New Liberty Zoo is exceptionally crowded, it seems. Last night's rain cooled things off, and the animals are prowling. All around us, soccer moms drag their broods from cage to cage, buying their happiness with promises of face paint and overpriced souvenirs. The carousel screams an accordion waltz. Escaped balloons ride the wind, strings fluttering beneath them.

It feels weird. Being here. Part of the crowd. But it's a good kind of weird. Dad looks content for once, the normally furrowed brow of concentration finally ironed out, his hands stuffed into his pockets, whistling arias to himself as he walks. He looks carefree. Or careless. Maybe there isn't much difference.

I, on the other hand, find myself glancing over my shoulder every ten steps.

"Michael. Look how busy it is. Do you think any of *these* people are afraid of a blue man coming out of nowhere and beating them up?"

"I don't think these people are wanted criminals building bombs in their basements," I whisper back.

"I'm not building bombs," Dad replies. "I have never built a bomb . . . unless you count the self-destruct mechanisms, in which case I guess I've built several."

Maybe he's right. Maybe it's fine. Maybe I'm just being paranoid.

"Besides," my father adds, "aren't you always saying I should pull my head out of the box and go appreciate nature?"

"Yes, but . . ."

"Well, there you have it," he says, "What could be more natural than visiting wild animals trapped in artificial replications of the environments they were ripped out of to be put on public display?" The baboon in front of us scratches his hindquarters. "Just try to relax and have a good time."

So I try. I decrease the over-the-shoulder glances to every minute, then every five, and then I forget completely. Dad's right. We are unknowns. Not like Tony, who would part the crowd like Moses if he were here. We can blend if we need to.

We say good-bye to the baboons and then make our way through the other ecosystems, traipsing through jungles and oceans, trying to ignore the aroma of elephants that settles over the plains. My father feeds the giraffes and mimics the lions. In a moment of wild abandon, he takes off his sunglasses and tells me to do the same. We are safe, he says. He gives a short lecture on the evolutionary link between primates and human beings. He hoots when the gibbons start howling at each other. He buys us both cotton candy, huge tufts that come apart in soft, feathery wisps that threaten to fly away. I let him ruffle my hair without smirking.

He drags me over to the ice-cream stand. "Dad. Really. I think this is all a little much."

"Nonsense," he says, ordering us two cones full of torna-doed soft serve. "It's a special occasion." And it takes a moment before I realize what the occasion is. Just this. Just him and me. Out. Together.

We finish our dessert on our way to the desert, passing a zoo security guard who is obviously more interested in a group of college girls by the cougar cage than he is in us. The girls are cute but way too old for me. Besides, every girl I see just reminds me of yesterday. And then almost everything does. The pizza crusts in the trash bins. The soda straws on the ground. Every short-haired brunette I walk behind looks like it could be her, and I find myself walking faster sometimes just to get an angle, just to take a peek, just to make sure it's not.

It's not.

Inside the desert pavilion, I crouch down to watch a pair of lizards chasing after each other. My father crouches next to me, arm around my shoulders.

"Which one is the boy?" he asks.

I can't be sure, but I've seen enough nature shows to know that the male is usually the one doing the chasing.

"Wrong," he says.

It was fifty-fifty. I point again.

"It's a trick question. There is no boy."

I look again. They look like your typical desert lizards to me. Beady black eyes. Dry scales. Beige and brown spots running in a pattern along their leathery little bodies. Only their tails seem unusually long, thrashing quickly back and forth as they skitter among the rocks.

"They are all females," Dad explains. "They are whiptail lizards. There are no males of this species. They are capable of reproducing asexually, essentially creating clones of themselves."

"Oh," I reply. Now I'm thinking about men in silver masks.

"They aren't the only ones. Komodo dragons can do it as well. And hammerhead sharks. Then there are pond snails. Fascinating creatures." I try to think of the last time I heard anyone talk about a pond snail with such esteem. "Of course this kind of reproduction is probably not good in the long term," Dad continues. "Doesn't do much to promote diversity. Plus you'd have to grow up without a father."

"Could be worse," I say, and I hear his sharp intake of breath. Dad looks at me with an odd expression, as if I've just said something completely profound when I was only pointing out the obvious. He settles on his haunches, hands folded in his lap. The crowd moves around us, oblivious. "I didn't mean *you*. I just meant . . ."

"I know what you meant," he says. Behind the glass, the lizards crawl over each other. Insulation. Safety in numbers.

"You don't remember anything about him."

It's not a question. He's asked me before. More than once. The answer is always the same. I was less than a year old when St. Mary's got her hands on me. No birth records. No ID. Even a DNA test didn't match any of the records the local authorities had on file. I was completely disconnected. A free soul, Sister Katheryn said.

"I know he was a jerk," I say. After all, what kind of man leaves his kid in the corner of a White Castle? I mean it as kind of a joke. You know, how absurd it all is. But Dad frowns, his face darkening.

"There are some choices that are made for us." He takes a deep breath, then stands up. "Come on," he says. "Let's go see the llamas."

We leave the desert and head toward the petting zoo in the back. I walk a step ahead of him, his shadow mixing with mine, still thinking about Viola and the Comet, but now also thinking about llamas and cloning and White Castles, and lizards who are just like their moms and kids who never knew their moms, and how I should be thankful to have a father, and not just any father, but a certifiable genius who can explain the laws of thermodynamics but will also sit and laugh at your stupid jokes, who thinks snails are fascinating and insists that dessert is not a sometimes thing.

I turn my head, ready to thank him for bringing us, for all of this, and walk straight into the back of a stranger. A man in a gray sport coat, a touch formal for a trip to the zoo. I take a step back, tucking myself back beneath my father's arm. Insulated.

"Sorry," I mumble as the man turns and looks at us. Dark haired, wearing a white button-down shirt and a pair of black jeans. He looks very well put together, tucked in, trim, and smooth. His eyes are gray to match his coat. People I've seen with gray eyes usually have a hint of another color, flecks of bright blue or green. But his are gray as a rain cloud.

"It's all right," the man says. "It's crowded today." He curls his lips into a polite smile, then squints at my father, head cocked. "Hold on a sec, do I know you?"

"I don't think so," my dad says curtly, furrowing and squinting back. I chance to look at the man's waist. Looking for a badge or a gun, any sign of danger, but the slim black belt is empty.

"You look familiar, though. Maybe I've seen your picture somewhere. In the paper, perhaps?"

My father shakes his head; I can sense him tensing, winding up. Our pictures have never been in the paper. Dad makes sure of it. I wonder if we are about to make a run for it. Wonder if I should step on this man's toes or pull his shirt up over his head or something.

Or maybe just ask him to leave us alone. The way only I can.

The man with the gray eyes turns to me.

"Is this your son?" he asks.

"No," my father says immediately. I make the mistake of

turning and looking up at Dad, but then quickly turn back to face the man. "This is my nephew, James."

"Hello, James," the man says. "Nice to meet you."

I don't reach out to shake the man's hand. We don't shake hands with strangers. We don't tell anyone our names. We don't fill out forms. We don't use credit cards. We don't go places like the zoo. For this very reason.

"James," my father says softly, "we've never met this man before, have we?"

I shake my head. I catch the look in my father's eye, and I realize he's giving me permission. I turn back toward the stranger. I take a long, hard look into those frozen gray pools, watching his pupils stretch.

"We have never met," I say, moving even closer so that I can smell peppermint on his breath. "You don't know us at all."

I can't be sure if it takes or not, but the man nods, then looks at me—a little foggy, as if he's just remembered something long forgotten. Or the other way round.

"Excuse me. So sorry," he says, giving one last odd little smile. "Enjoy your day," he says.

"No problem," Dad says, then reaches down to my shirt and pulls off my sunglasses, opening them and handing them to me—my cue to put them on as he steers me by the shoulders around the gray-eyed man, walking in measured steps past the desert pavilion and the ice-cream stand, staying on the edge of the crowd, up against the wall.

"Do you know that guy?" I ask, glancing back over my shoulder to see if we are being followed, though it doesn't appear that we are.

My father shakes his head. "No idea," he says. "But I think that's enough appreciating nature for one day."

In our study sits a game table of sorts, gouged cherry in need of restaining, inherited from one ancestor or another. After dinner—Chinese night—Dad invites me to a game of chess. I lose for the fortieth time in a row, though I at least make a battle of it, capturing his queen and leaving a bloody field of crippled pawns before I'm cornered. Never am I more tempted to use my powers on Dad than when we are playing chess. "I think you'd rather move here," I'd say, setting his king up for the kill. But I don't. So I lose. Again. We shake hands, as gentlemen do; then he retires to his bedroom, book in hand. Something on neurophysics. Even thicker than *Crime and Punishment*.

He pauses at the door.

"Don't stay up too late," he says. "I may need your help tomorrow."

I nod and he turns, but before he can shut the door, I stop him.

"Dad?"

He peeks his furry orange head out through the crack, looks at me with his liquid eyes. I feel a weight, a pressure to say it all, everything I'm thinking. Like a logjam in my head. But it's too much for today. So instead I just say, "I had a really good time today."

. "Me too," he says, and I can tell he's thinking the same thing. We look at each other for a moment, but neither of us wants to be the one to go first. So he just waves and shuts his door, and I tiptoe to the living room and flip on the television, keeping the volume down.

Breaking New Liberty news. The men in the metal masks have struck again. And again. And again.

Three banks, all at once, according to the grave-faced news anchor on Channel Five. Apparently there are more of them than originally thought—these men with the black uniforms and permanent expressions. They struck in force, using explosives to breach the doors and more explosives to breach the vaults. They didn't worry about the alarms—happy to trigger them, it seemed. Dad says there are a dozen ways to rob a bank, and most of them don't require bombs or guns, but these men took the direct route. They broke in and loaded their bags, disdainfully flashing their hollow metal grins at the security cameras as they strolled past. Save for the differences in build, they seemed identical. Whiptailed lizards in black suits.

But the three banks were nothing compared to their biggest target, the one that the news cameras were all focused on.

Approximately fifteen minutes after the first rash of robberies, ten steel-faced criminals crashed through the outer wall of police headquarters. They used a garbage truck, the kind with the forklift in front, pouring out the back of it like it was the Trojan horse, machine guns spitting, sending a dozen cops scattering for cover. Surveillance cameras captured every moment. The initial shootout was intense but over quickly. The cops tried to hold their ground, but the masks and suits were all bulletproof, and with most of the police force speeding to three knocked-over banks with triggered alarms, it didn't take long for the masked men to take over the building.

The attackers moved in unison, swarming like ants. Just watching their hollow faces on the screen gives me the creeps. There could be anything behind there, grinning skulls or alien bloodsuckers or swirling black holes. Or maybe they are just blank. Oval heads without faces.

They didn't release any criminals from the cell block. They weren't there for comrades. They were there for ammunition. And to show New Liberty what its police force was good for.

Three banks and a police station. No way anyone could stop them all. But the ticker marching along the bottom of the television says otherwise.

THE COMET STRIKES AGAIN!

He got to three out of four, that's how fast he was. Four masked men were found unconscious inside the vault at Old National Bank and Trust, bound together with telephone cables, wrapped like garlands around Christmas trees. Two more were found in the Dumpster outside the Forum Credit Union, knocked out cold with garbage bags for pillows. It couldn't have taken him more than a minute at each place before he was back in the sky again. He couldn't make it to the third bank. He barely made it downtown in time.

He landed at the police station just as the men finished emptying the armory, loading the truck and another white van with enough weapons and ammunition to outfit a militia. A clip from one of the outside cameras showed the garbage truck pulling out just as the Comet came rocketing in. You can hear the sonic splinter of his arrival, the staccato of the gunfire, the growl of the truck's engine barreling toward him. Even though I know it's recorded video—that all this has already happened—I still hold my breath as I watch.

The garbage truck plowed right into him, ten tons of metal at forty miles an hour. The camera showed the Comet turning just in time to be caught in the headlights, bringing up one hand to shield his eyes, bringing up the other in the sign to halt. But the truck didn't stop. At least, not until it hit the wall of blue muscle, its back end lifting off the ground, men in masks, stolen guns, and boxes of bullets tumbling out like a popped piñata. There were more shots. A brief scuffle. The video is spastic. You can make out one of the men flying at least twenty feet through the air. You can see the white van screeching away. Can see at least eight of them surrounding him, but they were no match. The Comet didn't bother tying them up or even taking off their masks, just left them in broken heaps strewn across the police station's parking lot. Then, before the cops could question him, arrest him, or thank him for saving their hides, he vanished back into the night sky, leaving his telltale mark behind.

The camera fixates on it for a moment, that blue streak, then switches back to the news anchor's haggard face. "We take

93

you now, live, to a statement offered by New Liberty's chief of police."

The camera cuts to a barrel-chested man with a horseshoe mustache and a clear desire to be anywhere else. He is standing on the steps of his still-smoking headquarters. He opens with assurances that everything is under control and that they are not at liberty to share the information they have, which is another way of saying they have none. Then he says something that strikes me.

"It is clear we are dealing with new and very dangerous threats."

Threats. Plural. Officer Mustache knows what kinds of people there are in the world, too.

"Who's winning?"

I jump, nearly slipping off the loveseat, then turn to see my father standing in the entryway. He is staring at the television as well.

"Sorry?"

"Who's winning?" he asks again.

I look at the bullet-pocked walls of the police station; the smoldering remains of the truck, its front end smashed so hard that it looks like it's smiling; the lingering scar of blue light stitched across the sky in the background; the little piles of men collapsed on top of each other.

"Good guys, I guess?" I'm not sure how else to put it.

Dad nods thoughtfully. "When you are winning a war, almost everything that happens can be claimed to be right and wise."

It's a quote. Einstein, probably. Or Lao Tzu. Or Lady Gaga. I can't keep tabs. He waits for me to guess, but instead I ask, "What's that supposed to mean?"

Dad stares at the image on the screen the way he stares at his columns of figures, at the complex equations he scribbles on paper towels sometimes, or on the bathroom walls. Scrutinizing it, dissecting it, reconfiguring it into something that makes sense to him and sometimes only to him.

"It means that if they are winning, they are the good guys, whether they are or not."

As I fall asleep that night, I imagine I am back at the zoo, back in the desert pavilion. There is a man standing by the whiptailed lizards, dressed in royal-blue spandex with black boots up to his knees. His back is to me, but there is no question who he is. Everyone else in the place is gawking at him. Snapping pictures. Pointing and whispering. I walk up to the man and stand next to him, keeping my eyes on the lizards, not daring to look. Finally I can't take it anymore. I turn to see his face.

But there is nothing to see. He is wearing one of those silver masks. With the dark hollow eyes and rectangular mouth.

"Excuse me," I say. "Do I know you?"

The man reaches up and removes the mask with one blue-gloved hand.

And my father stares at me blankly, as if he's never seen me before.

THE MAGIC TRICK

I remember the day I learned who my father, Benjamin Edson, really was. The day he unlocked the door. It wasn't a big surprise. There was no grand revelation. I had my suspicions. The men in long, dirty raincoats who would come to the door at night and ask to see him, armed with briefcases, the butts of pistols peeking from waistbands. The hours he would spend secreted away, leaving me upstairs with my mountains of homework. The occasional explosion that shook my plate and my chair as I sat in the kitchen eating a PB and J while he rushed up the stairs, hair smoking, mumbling to himself and smiling at me as if to say "That could have gone better."

And I had asked. A hundred times. A thousand. Ten thousand. But the answer was always the same: "I'll tell you when it's time."

And then finally, after two years of living in the same house as a man who spent most of the day in hiding, my father put his hands on my shoulders and asked if I was ready.

He walked me to the basement door, closed and locked as always, the only key tucked into his pocket. Then he took out a small stack of photos.

"What I'm about to tell you is just between us, do you understand?"

I nodded.

"You can't tell anyone, not without my permission. Got it?"

More nodding.

"Swear?"

"I swear." I remember crossing my heart and not my fingers. I could tell what was coming. I didn't want to blow it.

"All right, then," he said, showing me the first picture. "You wanted to know who I am and what I do. Well, *this* is who I am."

The first photo was about half the size of the others, old and grainy, blurred yellows, blacks, and grays. It showed a man with a long curving mustache like a scimitar, wearing what looked like thermal underwear, standing beside a wooden crate with a lock on it. He wasn't smiling. In fact, he looked pretty miserable. His hair was cropped close, and he had no shoes on.

"I come from a long line of box makers," my father said. "My great-grandfather was a magician in London. His name was Robert, but he called himself Marvelo the Magnificent. He was a trickster and a hack, for the most part, performing parlor tricks on street corners, pulling cards from shirtsleeves and scarves from ladies' bonnets. But he had this one bit that he would do for his finale. A magic box, three feet square. And he would somehow cram himself into it. Of course he wasn't a very large man, as you can see, probably about my size, but still, to shove oneself into a box of that size is impressive.

"And that wasn't even the trick. An assistant—some hulking brute he had pulled off the street and paid a shilling—this accomplice would put a lock on the box, one of those ancient padlocks that you always imagine hanging from dungeon doors, and drop the whole thing into the Thames River. The crowd would hold its breath, waiting to see if Marvelo the Magnificent would surface, if he would break free from the box and escape the icy claws of death. Sometimes the women would faint. Sometimes they would beg their husbands to dive in after him. They would rush the banks and shout for help. It was a spectacle.

"Of course the box had a trick bottom—my great-grandfather had designed it that way, though it still took some effort to squeeze himself free, especially underwater. He would emerge, dripping and gasping but undoubtedly alive, begging them all to drop another coin in the hat.

"He escaped from that box ninety-seven times, my great-grandfather. On the ninety-eighth, the bottom tricked him back."

I pictured the man in the photograph trapped inside his wooden crate, pounding and kicking against the sides, sinking to the floor of the river, drowning in his three-foot-by-three-foot coffin. It gave me a shudder and I wondered if I was ready, but Dad took the picture of Marvelo the Magnificent and handed me another. This one was of better quality, though still washed-out, mostly browns and grays. It showed a man standing outside a large brick building, presumably a factory of some kind. A wagon stood to his right. Two giant stacks reached up out of the building, their smoky breath clawing its way into the sky.

"Robert's son, Reginald, my grandfather, took up the family love of woodcraft and started making boxes of his own, though his were larger, three feet by eight feet, mostly. They were fine works of craftsmanship, made of rosewood, cedar, and mahogany, lined with velvet and lace—though admittedly no one was *too* eager to buy them. Still, he developed a reputation for his artistry."

I looked again at the photo, at the wagon that was stacked three high and six deep with the boxes. I wondered if they were empty or if there were already people inside them.

"For a while, being laid to rest in an Edson coffin was a sign of prestige. But then the war came. And the blitzkrieg. And my grandfather switched from rosewood to pine and opened a factory to mass-produce those boxes of his. Demand was high. The ships brought hundreds of men who needed one immediately, or would soon enough. Whenever the air-raid sirens cried out, Grandfather would huddle with his family in the cellar, praying for their safety—but secretly hoping that not everyone in town would make it through the night. You can profit from death." He took the picture back.

A drowned magician and an undertaker. I wasn't sure where Dad was going with all this, but I hoped it got better.

The next photo was a snapshot, like from one of those old instant cameras, showing a man in a white coat like a dentist, glasses perched on his nose, arms crossed in front of him, standing in a lab of some kind, other white-coated men with glasses and short haircuts scurrying in the background.

"He made a lot of money off the war, my grandfather. Enough to send his own son, my father, off to college. This man, the late Anders Edson, traveled the world earning his education, learning everything he could about computers and engineering before he was hired by our good friends at the United States government to make . . ." He waited for me to fill in the blank.

"Boxes?" I guessed. I figured it wasn't chocolate bars.

My father nodded. "Little metal ones like so." My father made a box with his hands, not much bigger than those lining the shelves of our basement, though I didn't know that yet. "They contained little computers, very sophisticated, the cutting edge of technology, and they became the guidance systems found on nuclear missiles—the little brains that would someday help obliterate Moscow or wipe China from the face of the earth, or so the government thought. Turned out all those boxes would sit inside all those missiles inside all those silos just gathering dust. Still, they could have destroyed mankind if they'd wanted to. And my father would have been partly responsible. Unfortunately, my father had *his* father's

100

entrepreneurial spirit but lacked his common sense. He sold his secrets to the Russians and likely found himself at the bottom of a river, just like Marvelo, except without the audience.

"I never knew any of them, of course," Dad said. "My grandfather died before I was born, and my father disappeared when I was only three, but I somehow inherited their fondness for boxes."

The third picture was snatched back, and the three men disappeared back into my father's pocket.

"What about the last one?" I asked as the pictures vanished. There had been four photos. He had only shown me three.

"Just an old friend," he said. Then my father reached into his other pocket and pulled out the key, a little coppery thing with nubby teeth, and held it between us. I started to reach for it and he pulled back, just a little. He looked me dead in the eyes.

"Boxes are marvelous things, Michael. There is a moment, just before you open one, when a box contains anything, when it could *be* anything. And even though you know it's not true, you still imagine that one day you will find a box that holds the exact thing you've been looking for, the thing you've wanted most of all."

I remember nodding. Hearing what he said, but not really listening. Just looking at that key. Opening that door and finally figuring out what he *did* down there all day—that's what I wanted. I reached for it again, but he still held back.

"That's the other thing about boxes," he said. "You don't

have to open them. It's your choice. You can stay up here as long as you please. But you should know that if you *do* open that door, if you look at what's inside, things will never be the same. And you won't be able to turn back."

I looked up at my father. The man who had rescued me from St. Mary's School for Wayward Boys. Who had brought me ice cream and bought me my first pair of tennis shoes and taught me how to play backgammon and what it's like to sleep in on Sundays, the way God supposedly did. And I knew that no matter what was down there, it wouldn't change the way I felt about him. I nodded, and he handed me the key.

I opened the door and flipped on the light.

And made my descent.

For three days, nothing happens. Not nothing, nothing. Just nothing remarkable, nothing. The sky is blue, not streaked blue, just plain blue, with the occasional wisp of cloud for garnish. The kids are out in force, even along our street, playing stickball and tumbling off skateboards, sitting on front steps and smoking, occasionally looking up at the sky.

Don't misunderstand. There are still crimes. This is New Liberty, where the police blotter gets its own section in the daily paper. Purses are snatched. Six cars are stolen. Four houses are broken into. A convenience store is held up, but the suspects hide their faces with ball caps and sunglasses. The police arrive well after the perpetrators leave.

No sign of the Comet, though. Or the men in masks.

The news choppers flitter all around the city like humming-birds, hoping to catch a glimpse of him. I can hear them pass over our neighborhood, and I watch my Dad's nose twitch. Apparently a group of high-school kids calling themselves the Comet Chasers tools around in a truck spray-painted with blue fireballs, hoping to catch him on camera to post to their web-site. One man actually sticks his own cat in a tree and sits on a folding lawn chair in his front yard with his camera, waiting to see if the hero will come and rescue it. After four hours he gives up and calls the fire department. They don't come either, but a news reporter does. They are working every possible angle.

There is speculation that he is gone already, the city's new blue defender. That he was just passing through, like one of those rough-shaven gunslingers who show up in town just long enough to take out the trash before flying off into the sunset. That he has already taken care of the Men of Steel, as the bank-robbing, police-headquarters-smashing posse is now being called, and has moved on.

I spend too much time upstairs watching television. Less time down in the lair. I get behind on my homework. Occa-sionally Dad resurfaces, coffee cup in hand—the one that says QUIET. GENIUS AT WORK. "You really ought not be watching this," Dad says when he sees me. But I watch him watching, stuck there momentarily, sucked in the same as me. Then he shakes his head and fills his mug with lukewarm coffee and tells me I'm welcome to come join him. I want to say the same but don't.

And yet for three days I'm told to stay close to home, where he can see me, though he immerses himself in his work until it's time for dinner and then pretends like it's just another night. Sandwich night. Spaghetti night. Fishstick night. I sit at the table and listen to lectures on electromagnetism, pre-Raphaelite poetry, and Kant's categorical imperative. The fishsticks are freezer burned. The helicopters pass overhead and Dad pauses again, a spoonful of peas at his lips. We both wait for the *tchk-tchk-tchk* of their rotors to fade.

It's these times, when nothing is happening, that you become absolutely certain that something is happening.

I call and talk to Zach, but the conversation is short. Tony is still cleaning up some messes—the Forum Credit Union was under his protection—and tightening security. He says the same thing. Everything is all right. Don't watch the news. They've got it all wrong. But then I look out the window and see a black SUV roll past one afternoon and know it's Tony's men checking up on us. Making the rounds.

This morning a package arrives on our doorstep, hand delivered—the post office doesn't even know we exist. My father snatches it up and takes it into the lair without a word.

The door's unlocked, of course. I could follow him down. But instead I finish *Crime and Punishment*. The ending sucked. This guy, Raskolnikov, goes all *The Shining* on some old lady, chopping her up like kindling, and all he gets is six years in prison. Sure, the prison's in Siberia and he will die of frostbite, but that still seems like a small price to pay for coldblooded murder.

Not that I care. Far be it from me to judge. What gets *me* is that he still gets the girl at the end.

Even the ax murderer gets the girl.

I close the book. I trace back the days. Today is Saturday. A good day to go hang out at the mall. Dad might let me if I promise to go with someone. A little added protection. I call Zach.

He picks up on the first ring. I can hear a lot of noise in the background. At first I figure it's the TV turned up too loud, but then I can tell it's shouting. A party at the Romano residence. "Who is that yelling?" I can't make out most of the words, but those I do are all of the four-letter variety.

"That would be Tony," Zach says. "He's in a mood. He's got me stuck here as added security. I'm not allowed to leave the compound."

"You said there was nothing to worry about," I remind him.

"There is nothing to worry about," he tells me again.

"Then why is he yelling?"

"Probably because everybody's still worried," Zach explains. I sense he's not telling me everything, but I don't push it. Instead I tell him that I'm headed to the mall anyways and promise to pick up an extra bag of caramel corn for him.

"You shouldn't go by yourself," he says.

"Thanks, Mom. I think I'll be all right."

Zach snorts. "Whatever. I'm just looking out for you. Besides. She's not going to be there."

"That's not why I'm going," I say back, then add, "and you don't know that for sure."

The shouting increases in volume, and Zach says he needs to go. I hang up and then go brush my teeth and tame my hair and snag two twenties from the hollowed-out copy of *David Copperfield* on the top shelf. It's not stealing. Dad says the money is for both of us, for whenever we need it. I notice there's only a couple of hundred bucks left in there. Maybe Dad has more stashed away somewhere. Or maybe it's almost time for another ATM run. Or maybe the thing he's working on right now is almost finished, and Tony's men will be by with another fat envelope soon. I hope so. I could really use a new pair of shoes.

I grab my sunglasses and head to the door, pausing by the basement.

I should tell him, should really *ask* him, but I'm afraid he'll say no. If Zach was coming with, maybe, but I don't want to lie about that either, and I've got to get out of the house for a while. I open the door a crack and stand there, listening to the sound of power tools and Vivaldi. One foot hovers hesitantly over the top step and then retreats. Maybe I'll just write him a note.

I leave it magneted to the fridge. If he comes up, he will see it. If he doesn't, he won't even know.

"Be back in a little while," I call out in just above a whisper, soft enough that I'm certain he can't hear me. Then I close the basement door and slip out the back one.

Zach was right. She isn't here, though I walk up and down each wing of Liberty Square seven times. It's summer Saturday lunch hour: a smorgasbord of tank tops and tight shorts and too much cherry lip gloss, but nothing catches my eye. I am a man on a mission. I'm sure I look suspicious, scouting every store. I almost have her paged over the intercom—"Would the cute brown-haired girl whose family is actually not all named after musical instruments please come to the courtesy desk?"—thinking that if she were here, then maybe she would find it funny, though more likely she would be embarrassed and never speak to me again. So instead I wander, a roulette wheel spinning endlessly in my head, landing on nothing in particular: Why did I possibly think she would be here? Why won't my father talk to me about what's happening? What has gotten Tony Romano's boxers in a bunch? Where did all these crazy people even *come* from?

What am I doing here?

I look down at my shoes, toes peeling, splitting along the seams, thinking about what Zach said. About being too afraid to even use my powers. I kind of hate it when he's right.

I head to the Starting Block and breathe in the smell of new leather, flipping price tags on the cross-trainers, all of which cost fifty bucks or more. Dad says it costs about five dollars to make a pair of tennis shoes. He says the world is full of robbers and thieves but that most of them wear loafers and neckties. I look over at the counter to see the store's sole employee, a forty-something man with almost no hair. He has a small gold ring on his finger and a much larger doughy one around his middle. He looks impressionable. I find my size and settle down on a bench to try them on.

Beside me, two kids about my age start whispering to each other. They are staring at a display of new high-tops. Those fancy ones probably cost fifteen dollars to produce, which I guess is why they cost a hundred twenty. One boy takes a box and just holds it, reverently, as if it's some golden idol and he the brazen archeologist who unearthed it. I slip one foot inside my new shoe and wiggle my toes to make sure there is room.

"Just take 'em," one of the boys hisses.

"Is he watching?"

The short kid—the one not holding the box—glances over his shoulder, and I do the same. The sales guy is ringing up a mother with three toddlers. "*Naw*, man. Just *take* it."

I shake my head. I shouldn't get involved.

Then I hear my father's voice and think about the last time I sat and watched and did nothing.

With a sigh, I lean over and hiss at the kids to get their attention. "I wouldn't, if I were you."

They both turn and glare at me, realizing they've been overheard, their intentions revealed, and uncertain what to do next. If I was an adult, no doubt they would drop the box and take off running, but I'm one of them. Just another punk kid.

"Come on, man," Shorty pleads, but the kid holding the shoes doesn't move, just stares at me.

"Mind your own damn business," he says at last.

It's good advice. I know it is, but I can't help it. I shrug. "Fine," I say. "Do whatever. But you *will* get caught. Probably before you even leave the mall. The store has cameras." I nod toward the dark half globes hanging from the ceiling, thinking how maybe I should start bringing the Scrambler with me everywhere I go. "And the shoes have security tags. You'll trigger alarms. The mall cops will be waiting for you by the front door. Odds are you'll be taken downtown. Your parents will have to come pick you up. You'll go to court. Pay a fine. Do some community service. That is, unless you've done something like this before."

Shorty purses his lips and blows me off with a wave, but I look at the kid holding the shoes, and I can tell by the look in his eyes that this isn't his first time. He's been caught before.

"In that case," I say, "they might ship you off. Somewhere they can watch you better. Maybe military school. Or juvie. And all for a pair of shoes?" Shorty tugs on his friend's arm, but the other kid doesn't move. He just stares at me with his big brown eyes getting bigger by the second. I shake my head and then snap my fingers, breaking the trance.

"Give them to me," I say.

"What?"

"Just give them here and wait for me outside."

The kid looks like he can't decide between taking a swing at me and making a mad dash for the exit. Finally he hands over the box.

"You're sure this is your size?"

He nods. I nod back. Then I take both of our boxes up to the counter.

The clerk looks at me a little strangely and asks me if I found everything all right. I nod, and he scans both pairs, removing the security tags and stacking them one on top of the other. "Your total is one hundred seventy-three dollars and eighty-three cents," he says mechanically. I can sense the two kids on the other side of the glass. I take the money out of my pocket and set it on the counter.

The man smiles. His name tag says he's Chad. He looks like a Chad.

"One hundred seventy-three dollars . . . ," he repeats.

"And eighty-three cents," I finish for him. "I know. Except you forgot about the buy-one-get-one-free special." I look into his eyes. They are mud colored, though I've found it makes absolutely no difference what color the eyes are. Blue, brown, green, hazel, they all impress the same. He hasn't shaved in a couple of days, and there are acne scars on his forehead. Probably had a rough go of it in high school.

"Buy one get one free?" he says, confused, his pupils widening.

"The promotion just started today," I remind him.

"Oh," the clerk says. He lips are twitching. One finger starts to tap on the counter. Involuntary resistance. I get it all the time. The body reacts when the mind can't.

"And you forgot my frequent-shopper discount, too. I'm in here all the time. It's fifty percent," I say firmly.

"Fifty percent?"

"I'm a preferred customer," I whisper, as if it is our little secret. I've actually never stepped foot in this store until today. There is a pause, and I feel the sweat beading on my back. This shouldn't be that hard. I've done worse.

"You are," he agrees finally. His finger stops tapping. I can tell he's locked in. I try to ignore everything else around me and just stay focused on those muddy brown eyes. The man smiles and winks. Rings up my purchases. I notice he rings up the cheaper ones as free and I correct him. "No, Chad. The *high-tops* are free." Chad apologizes and recalculates. The register claims I owe twenty-seven bucks. I could probably get out of that too, but I'm already starting to doubt myself, so I fork over what's due.

"You are a good man," I say, taking the bag from him as he closes the register and hands me my change. He rubs his temples with his fingers and stares at the display for a moment. He knows something doesn't add up, but he gives me the receipt anyway.

I meet the two boys just outside the store. I take the bigger box from the bag and hold it out to the taller one, but he just stands there.

"Just *take* 'em, man," Shorty says again, and I wonder if that will become his mantra. If he will grow up to be one of those thugs spray painting his symbols on the brick walls outside the Techno Tree, stealing loose change out of unlocked cars, no ambition at all. Nothing to believe in except the shoes on his feet. I push the box into the other kid's stomach, and he instinctively grabs hold. I don't let go yet, though.

"A box can be almost anything," I tell him, but I don't bother to look him in the eyes. I don't have to. I've got his attention already. "But once you open it, things will never be quite the same."

The kid nods—as if he has the slightest clue what I'm talking about. Even I don't know what I'm talking about. I just know a kid on the edge when I see one.

I start to leave, but the kid with the new pair of hundred-dollar high-tops reaches out and grabs my shirt.

"Dude, are you some kind of magician or something?" he asks. I realize I've gone too far.

I look him in the eyes this time and tell him he has no idea who I am. That he's never seen me before in his life.

I step outside and check my watch. It's only two o'clock. I should head back. It's pizza night. Except, for some reason, I'm in no real hurry to get home. The breeze has taken the edge off the sun and my new shoes hug a little tight, constantly reminding me that they are there. I decide to break them in by taking the long way home.

I detour away from the cracked pavement that would lead me back and head north, walking in almost the opposite direction from my house. I don't know why. I'm drawn by the smell, maybe. The air is fresher up here. Trees will do that for you. After a while I pass by a string of shops specializing in junk normal people can't afford: custom framing, a bakery just for dogs, a store that sells nothing but scrapbooking supplies. The sidewalks are made of terra-cotta tiles painstakingly laid by hand. I think about the shoes I bought. Nearly two hundred dollars on the price tags. Twenty bucks total to make. I paid nearly thirty. Someone somewhere was cheated.

I make another wrong turn on purpose and soon find myself in a neighborhood I've never even seen before.

It looks surreal. Too artificially perfect. Like a paint by number. The dogs sit docilely behind invisible fences. The lawns are all carefully manicured, and equally well-groomed kids run through sprinklers while their mothers plant marigolds in window boxes. The privacy hedges are neatly trimmed, there only for decoration. They won't keep any masked men out. I take another random turn, relishing in the fact that I am more than a little lost, the incessant chatter in my head quieting to a dull rumble. I feel like an explorer discovering El Dorado.

Or a thief breaking into a high-security vault.

Eventually I come upon some community baseball diamonds. Today they are filled with softball teams dressed in uniforms sponsored by local butchers and banks. I figure I still have a little time, so I find a seat in the back row of some bleachers, behind a host of moms and dads and whining brothers, plucking away on pads and phones, only half watching the game. It feels weird sitting here, doing something so ordinary, when just last week I sat and watched a SWAT van swallow the business end of an RPG just a few miles away. Though it seems like much longer than a week from where I'm sitting now. I take an exaggerated breath of suburban air and watch.

The game is close. Already the last inning, according to the chatty couple below me. I can feel the buzz even though I have never played organized sports (forms required). The girl at the plate hunkers over, her blond locks fanned out from her helmet, her pants crusted in dirt. She rockets a pitch deep into right field, over the heads of the opposing team, scoring the girl on third and winning the game. I clap and cheer with the rest, doing my best to blend in. Somebody's mother turns and gives me a high five. It's uncomfortable and strangely comforting at the same time, touching this stranger. The girl runs and leaps into her team's arms, triumphant.

There is a moment—a perfect moment—where I sense this is how things should be. I close my eyes.

Then it's over. I just sit there as the bleachers empty. The families full of siblings and tag-team parents gather their daughters and deposit them in their hybrid cars. I'm alone again. And I suddenly realize I have a very long walk home. If I can even find my way. I deflate, hunched over. Then I feel a tap on my shoulder.

I spin and look, and everything locks up inside me.

Honey and cinnamon. Dark hair dipping just past her ears, slightly golden tinged in the sun. Blue jeans ripped at the knee. White shirt with top two buttons undone. I'm staring at an impossibility.

She smiles.

I must be hallucinating. The heavily oxygenated atmosphere has gone to my head. Yet there she is, standing right in front of me.

"Come here often?" she says.

I'm speechless.

"Michael, isn't it?"

"Um. Yeah," I manage to squeak out. "You're . . ."

"Viola," she says, pretending to be offended. At least I hope she's pretending.

"Sorry," I blurt. "For a moment I thought maybe I was just imagining you."

She looks at me like I'm insane. Or an idiot. Or both. I should convince her that I'm not insane—just start with that. "Yeah, no, I mean, I don't really, you know, come here that often. Ever." No. Not insane. Just an idiot. "You, you know, come here often?"

"I play," she says, looking out over the field. "I mean, I used to. Before I got busy with other stuff. I still like to come cheer on my friends."

"Yeah. Me too," I say, wondering when was the last time I cheered Zach on for anything. Probably the time I dared him to see how many marshmallows he could stick to his face.

Viola's face narrows into a smirk, and I see the dimples working their way to the surface again. "You're not stalking me, are you?"

Oh, god. She *does* think I'm insane. I put up my hands, backtracking. "No. I swear." But she makes an exaggerated production of looking around anyway, as if she expects a posse of henchmen to leap out of the dugout and kidnap her. "I was just walking home and got turned around and stopped to watch the end of the game. I had no idea you were here. Seriously."

She squints. "So you expect me to believe that we just met each other again by *accident*?"

"Chance occurrence," I say, shrugging.

"Total fluke."

Dad says there's no such thing as fate. That what we ascribe to fate is just dumb luck, a fickle wind steering your ship through the ambivalent seas of chaos. But I start to question if everything Dad says is true. Viola smiles and waves good-bye to some of the other girls in uniforms, all walking off with their families. Some of them wave back.

"Are your parents here?" I ask.

"My dad's at work and my mother's at a wedding."

"And you weren't invited?"

"I hate weddings," she says, stuffing her hands into the back pockets of her jeans. "So fake. Everything is planned, down to where people can sit, what they can wear, what color the bow on the toothpicks in the little sandwiches are going to be. It's a big illusion."

"The wedding?"

"All of it," she says. "Wedding. Marriage. This idea that it's going to be perfect. With everybody smiling all the time."

"How do you *really* feel about it?" I ask.

She smirks at me again. "I *feel* like I should probably get back before my father gets home," she says. She looks over my shoulder.

"Is it far?" I ask.

116

"A few blocks."

The next part comes out without a pause, which is good, because if I had stopped to think about it, I wouldn't have said it.

"Then I'll walk you."

Viola shakes her head. She seems nervous. "I'm not supposed to walk home with orphan boys with crazy dads bent on taking over the world." Her hair falls in her face again. When she brushes it away, I look into her eyes. I can feel it coming. The urge to push just a little. It would be so easy. Just once. Nothing criminal. Just make her let me walk her home. That's all. And maybe hold my hand along the way.

But I do what I think is the right thing and look down at my new shoes instead. Viola puts a finger under my chin, tilting me back up.

"But maybe I'll let you buy me a snow cone," she says.

"So you used to play softball and then you got busy with other stuff," I say as we pass yet another playground, uncracked plastic slides awash in primary colors and actual swings attached to rubberized chains. No beer-bottle flowers here.

"I do a lot of community service," she says.

"You mean like helping people and stuff?" The way I say it makes me look like a total jerk, I know. As if I've never entertained the idea. Which isn't at all true. Only an hour ago I helped a kid get a new pair of shoes.

Viola shrugs. "I like to be involved," she says; then she

points to a little shack hiding behind the playground. A large woman with a golden beehive on her head and stains under both pits sits on a stool beside two ice-shaving machines and a row of brightly colored bottles. She is wearing sunglasses. I realize I am not. I took them off back at the mall and never put them back on. I have no disguise.

The menu board only has one item listed.

"Go ahead," I say, pointing. "Get whatever you'd like, though I hear the snow cones here are to die for." She laughs again, and in that instant I wish I could capture her laughter and store it away somewhere. Little jars that I could keep on a shelf and open whenever.

"You first," she says.

I order half cherry, half watermelon. She orders something called tiger's blood mixed with suicide, and I suddenly feel boring. I pay—the whole amount this time—and point to the only empty bench, taking a seat as close as I think I can without making it obvious. She offers me a bite of tiger's blood, and I have to admit it tastes much better than mine. We don't say anything for a while. Just slurp syrup and crunch ice, watching the kids spiral down and crawl back up. St. Mary's used to have a playground. It wasn't much. Just an old wooden swing set with four seats and a tinfoil slide that burned the backs of your thighs in the summer. It was a piece of junk, but I still smile thinking about it.

"So let's have it," Viola says, snapping me out of my daydream.

"Have what?"

"I don't care. Something. You know what neighborhood I live in. Know I played softball. You even know my views on matrimony. All I know about you is that you're homeschooled and I'm the first girl you've ever talked to."

"That's not true," I say. "You're just the first one who ever talked back."

She crosses her arms and waits. I try to think of something interesting I can tell her, but most of the interesting things about me I probably shouldn't share. That I robbed a bank, twice. That I once had my eyebrows singed off by a temperamental flame thrower that my father really thought was aimed the other way. That I am, in all likelihood, the only thirteen-year-old eligible for the FBI's most-wanted list. That my father once built a device capable of reversing the earth's gravitational pull within a five-foot radius but accidentally crushed it when both he and it smashed into the ceiling. None of these seem like first-date material.

And this isn't even a date. It's a chance encounter with snow cones. Finally I think of something.

"I was raised by nuns."

"You're kidding, right?"

"Nope. Until I was nine years old." She seems impressed. Or maybe just surprised. "I know. Doesn't seem to fit, does it?"

"So you haven't known your dad all your life? The enthusiastic one?"

"No, but I guess I lied to you the first time. I had a lot of sisters growing up. Sister Josephine. Sister Margaret. Sister Katheryn—"

"I get it. Was it like in the movies? Do they really hit you with rulers? Do they sing and dance?"

Only if you make them, I think to myself. "They don't use rulers. They use whips. Like in the Spanish Inquisition." She cocks another eyebrow at me, and I recant. "They're really very sweet most of the time," I amend.

"So you must be really religious or something."

"Or something," I say. I try to quickly change the subject. "What else? Let's see. I have green eyes."

"I can see that."

"And I like pizza."

She makes a sound like a buzzer in a TV game show. She has red snow-cone juice dribbling down her chin and wipes it off with the back of her hand. "Try again. Everybody likes pizza. Say you like sushi. Or haggis. Or monkey brains. Don't say pizza. Pizza is boring."

"Okay, I hate pizza," I say. "I'm allergic to it, in fact. What I really like is bald-eagle-egg omelets cooked in unicorn blood." She laughs arpeggios again.

"I'm not sure I can believe anything you say."

"That's because I'm a compulsive liar," I say.

"Yeah, me too."

"Really?"

"No. I'm lying."

I finish off the rest of my snow cone, dislodging the little gumball that they stick at the bottom to keep it from leaking. I try to bite into it, but it's rock solid, so I spit it out and then look down at the ground where it rolls. Abraham Lincoln looks back at me.

"Wanna see a magic trick?"

Viola turns and looks me in the eyes and I get lost there for a moment, forgetting what I just said.

"Yeah. Show me," she says.

I nod and bend over for the coin, spinning it in my palm a little for effect. I think about my Dad's great-grandfather sinking to the bottom of the Thames. I change my voice, make it deep and dramatic. "I will now make this penny disappear."

She looks at me with one raised eyebrow. I mumble some magic words and then wave my arms around. She is smiling, but I watch as her eyes trace my every move, determined to catch me in the act. But it's too late, I've got her. She blinks just once, and the coin is gone.

I show her my empty palms.

"Where is it?" she asks, reaching up, tucking a loose strand of hair behind her ear. "Show me your pockets." She bends over and looks underneath the bench.

"It's magic," I say with still-open hands.

"I guess it is," she says, and applauds me with three claps. Then she reaches into her front pocket for her phone, which has started to buzz excitedly.

"Dad's home," she says. "Wants to know where I am. I should get going."

We walk up the block, transitioning seamlessly from one pristine neighborhood into another. Not a single broken window.

"So are you going to be a magician when you grow up?" she asks.

"I'll probably end up in sales," I say. "What about you?"

"I don't know. I mean, I *used* to know what I wanted to be," she says.

"And . . . ," I press.

"I can't tell you."

"You can. You should," I say.

"You'll laugh at me."

"I won't. I promise."

"You will. It's *so* first grade."

"Try me."

Viola sighs, shoots me a warning with her eyes: if I laugh, I am a dead man. I nod my understanding. "All right. When I was seven years old, my parents drove me out west on this long, boring family vacation. You know, Grand Canyon, Old Faithful, all that touristy stuff. But we stopped at this planetarium. One of the huge ones with the telescopes that can see whole galaxies and meteor showers and distant planets. Well, my father knew somebody who knew somebody, and they let us in after hours, and I got to look for as long as I wanted."

Suddenly Viola's face lights up as she looks at the sun-blanched sky. "I never realized how much is out there, you know? Everyone thinks of space as this cold, empty place, but it's not. It's filled with light, and heat, and movement. With possibility."

Staring at her lost in the clouds, I understand. I almost reach out to grab her hand. "So you always wanted to be an astrono-mer," I say.

"Anyone can be an astronomer," she says, coming back to earth. "I wanted to go *out* there."

"An astronaut," I say, nodding. "Ah. Every first grader's dream."

She punches me playfully on the shoulder. I'm a little sur-prised by how much it hurts.

"You said you wouldn't laugh."

"I didn't laugh," I say. "I think it's terrific, actually. It's important to have dreams."

Viola sighs. "I have a telescope at home, but it's not much good in the city." She kicks a rock, apparently the only loose rock on the entire sidewalk. It vanishes into the grass. "You can't see them here like you can out there."

"So what's the coolest thing you've ever seen?"

"I've seen Neptune. And the moons of Saturn. And I got to watch the Perseid shower up close. How about you? Ever been stargazing? Ever seen anything cool?"

I try really hard not to look at her.

"I saw a comet once," I say.

We walk a half block more and she stops, pointing to a large white house at least twice the size of mine. Sunroom. Deck. Lights up and down the driveway like a landing strip. "Nice digs," I whisper. She points to a room on the second floor.

"My parents let me have the master bedroom because it has the biggest closet." I start to accompany her to her door, but she stops me. "Probably best if you stay here," she says. "If my dad sees you . . ."

I tell her no problem. I understand. Fathers can be like that sometimes.

"Maybe I'll see you around again?" I say. "You know. Run into you. Chance occurrence or whatever."

"Or whatever," she says, walking backward for a bit before turning and walking up to her door.

This time I don't wait for her to turn back around and look at me again. "Hey," I call out. "Look in your pocket."

"What?"

"Your back pocket. Check it."

She pauses on her porch, then reaches in and pulls out the penny. I take a flourishing bow, the way I imagine Marvelo the Magnificent used to do the first ninety-seven times.

And then I hide behind some bushes as her father opens the door.

I get home nearly two hours later to discover Dad still shut in the basement. Beethoven is blaring, actually loud enough that I can feel it through the floor. Dad obviously can't hear the front door close. I check the fridge to find my note is still there. He probably hasn't even been upstairs. He gets that way sometimes: so transfixed, so submerged in what he's doing that he forgets to eat, to sleep, so that when he finally does try to stand, the blood rushing back to his feet causes him to curse. I will have to go rescue him, pull him out, order the pizza using our fake name, the Richardsons—but first I go to my room to do a little research. Dad at least believes in the power of the internet, even if I'm not allowed to have an email account or anything; our shelves can only hold so many books, and even Dad needs to go online to catch up on the latest research in particle physics sometimes.

I glance at the headlines—the Nautilus rescues an ocean liner crippled at sea, the U.S. reengages North Korea in nuclear talks, there's a big prison bust near Justicia—nothing I care about. I find what I'm looking for and print it out, writing down the general specifications for what I need in the margins. I hear sounds coming from the kitchen. Cupboards and can openers. The professor has emerged.

When I step into the kitchen, he is standing over the stove. That's the first sign that something is wrong. It's supposed to be pizza night. He's messing with the system. A can of double noodle soup boils away in its pot. He doesn't bother to turn around, though I know he knows I'm there.

"You're home," he says with his back still to me, and I can't tell if he means it like "and thank goodness" or "where the hell were you all this time?" Judging by the sound of his voice, I'm going with the second.

"I left you a note," I say, pointing to the fridge.

He glances at the scrap of notebook paper. *Went out,* it says. *Be back soon. Love, Michael.* In retrospect maybe I could have been more specific.

"I needed new shoes," I add, even though that wasn't at all

my motive for going. But you have to have a reason, and I'm not sure I could explain the real one.

"It's not a good idea," he says. "You going out by yourself like that. Not with everything that's happening."

"Depends on what you mean by *good*," I say, then instantly regret it. I'm sure he's frowning over his pot at having his own words thrown back at him.

I hesitate to tell him that I wasn't by myself. I'm not sure he would understand. In the three years that I have known him, my father has not expressed one iota of interest in women. Occasionally I will make a sidelong remark about an actress during one of our Friday-night film sessions, someone I think might be his type, Jodie Foster or a Naomi Watts, someone attractive *and* intellectual, and then watch his expression. Nothing. The closest he has ever come to talking to me about girls was describing asexual reproduction three days ago at the zoo. I try to imagine what an ordinary father might say. "You met a girl? What does she look like? What's her name? Where did you meet? Is she pretty?" And I would say some cheeseball thing like, "Oh, Dad, man, she's a knockout." And he would cuff me in the shoulder to let me know that I had just been initiated into the world's oldest secret society.

But my dad is extraordinary.

I look down at my printed sheet, taken minutes ago from one of those stargazer websites. It shows a panoramic view of the summer sky in the Western Hemisphere—at least what it might look like on a perfectly clear night with no skyline and a great pair of binoculars. On the back I've made a little drawing, a plan. It's nothing like what he would come up with, but I've seen enough of his blueprints to get the basics down: where the lens might go, labels for the power source and the microprocessor, the buttons on the top, a paragraph explaining what it should do. I imagine a box that could show the stars to anyone at any time, day or night. I'm not even sure it's possible, but if anyone can shove a planetarium into a pocket, it's my father. And when he asks me what I want it for, I will tell him all about her. I put a hand on the paper, ready to make my request, but he speaks first, his suddenly stern voice stopping me cold.

"You broke your promise," he says.

I take my hand off the paper and curl back up into my chair. The tone in his voice gives me a chill, and suddenly I'm spinning, trying to remember all the promises I've made him over the last few years, trying to figure out which one he has in mind. Did I promise him I would never meet a girl at the mall? Did I promise him I would never sneak out of the house? Did I promise him I would tell him everything, always? I don't remember saying any of these things. For starters I never actually even thought I would meet a girl.

"I'm sorry," I say, meaning I don't understand, but also as a preemptive apology for whatever it is I've done, or whatever it is he *thinks* I've done. Dad carefully upends the pot, siphoning the soup into two bowls. Then finally he turns, and I can get a good look at him, gnawing on his lip, two steaming bowls of mostly mush in hand. He sets the bowls down and carefully settles into his seat, as if he expected to sink right through it.

"You were careless, and irresponsible," he says, as if he knows already. As if he's been spying on me the whole day long. If this is what I get for buying a girl a snow cone, imagine how he'd react if I actually kissed one, though that thought just makes me even more jittery.

"Dad, listen," I say. "It was no big deal. I didn't say anything."

Actually I said quite a bit; I don't even remember half the nonsense that came out of my mouth. But she probably didn't believe half of it either. How could she?

Still, he's right. I was being careless. I couldn't help it. It was her. She just made me feel like I had nothing to worry about.

"Didn't *say* anything? You told him everything, apparently."

Him? Obviously my dad has a very mixed-up sense of where my interests lie.

"Him?" I say out loud.

"Yes, him!" Dad says, pounding on the table, broth sloshing over the sides of his bowl. "Your friend. The porcupine. *One* secret. I ask you to keep *one* secret, for your own good, and you can't."

Oh.

So that's what this is about.

"You talked to Zach?" I ask meekly.

"No," Dad says. "I talked to Tony. Less than twenty minutes

ago. Apparently your thorny little friend let slip about your talent, and now Tony has asked a favor of us."

Of us. He means of *me*. I collapse into the kitchen chair, overcome by too many emotions at once. Anger at Zach for telling Tony. Anger at myself for telling Zach. Anger at Dad for insisting I keep the secret from everyone in the first place. Anger at Tony for wanting to take advantage of it. I guess the emotions are all the same; I'm just having trouble choosing a target.

"What kind of favor?"

Dad takes a deep breath, gathering what's left of his composure. He grabs a napkin and wipes up a spot of soup that spilled. "He wants you to go with him. Tonight. To meet Mickey Maloney. They are having a discussion of sorts, and he wants you there."

A meeting. Between the heads of the two most powerful criminal organizations in New Liberty. "And you *agreed* to this?"

"The Romanos keep us safe, Michael. They keep the cops out of our business. They help put the food on the table." He gestures to the quagmires of oily noodle slush sitting in front of us. "He's not the sort of man you simply say no to."

No. Of course not. We all have responsibilities. We all owe somebody. I owe Dad. Dad owes Tony. The transitive property of New Liberty. I have to go. But a meeting with Mickey "Six Fingers" Maloney sounds about as much fun as rubbing lemon juice in your eyes.

"Tony has promised me that you won't get hurt," Dad says.

Of course. But I doubt Mickey Maloney made the same promise. I know what the Maloney crew does to people. I get the gritty details from Zach, that prickly little snitch. I picture myself floating at the bottom of a river. Except instead of a box, I've got rocks tied to my ankles. Or is it cinder blocks?

"What time is he coming?" I ask, looking at the clock above the stove.

"They will be here to pick you up in twenty minutes," Dad says glumly. "They said not to bring anything."

"But they asked me if you had a suit."

I wore a suit only once in my life. When I was seven years old, some wrinkly philanthropist held a benefit on behalf of St. Mary's School for Wayward Boys, and the whole gang was invited. He even rented tuxedos for all of us to wear, the whole lot of delinquents decked out in black and white to match the nuns and priests who accompanied us, ambling through the ballroom like puffins on parade. The benefit was a smashing success. People who were rich enough to raise twenty children apiece but had none of their own watched as the boys of St. Mary's put on a talent show over glazed chicken and limp asparagus. Several boys played the piano or sang something from the hymnal. One boy tap-danced. I remember Davey Plimpton reciting the Gettysburg Address.

I was just discovering my real talent at that point. I hadn't quite gotten it down, or I might have done a little hypnotism onstage. Maybe gotten Father Gabriel to squawk like a chicken or one of the nuns to do a suggestive dance on the buffet table. Instead I performed one of the card tricks I had just started to learn. I screwed it up twice, but the crowd applauded anyway. Nobody booed, even though I was terrible. They were much too polite.

I learned two things that night. One: rich people give to charity to feel better about all the money they waste on themselves. And two: most people would rather lie right along with the crowd than tell the truth on their own.

Except for criminals. Say what you want about them, at least they are honest with themselves. They know what they want and aren't afraid to take it.

Tony Romano wanted my power, if only for one night to convince Mickey Maloney of something. I owed it to him to try. He was a part of our family, for better or worse. And you don't say no to family.

SIX FINGERS
AND A HELPING HAND

I t all starts with a favor.

My dad. Son of a bomb maker. Son of a son of a coffin maker. Son of a son of a son of a flea–bitten magician in the back alleys of London who should have stopped with grand finale number ninety-seven.

Or maybe he shouldn't have gotten started to begin with. After all, he had to know it couldn't last forever. Eventually the bottom would drop. Or in my great-grandfather's case, it wouldn't. You can't escape from the box forever. Death can be cheated only so many times.

It's a question I've asked myself before. When to stop once you've started. It's not as if you can take it all back. Not in this world, anyway. I know a thing or two about absolution, saying penance, sitting in confession, the giant erasers we use to wipe the slate clean. St. Mary's taught me that it all catches up to you eventually. Maybe one or two times you can get away with something. Get a free pass. Be excused. But at some point, there really is no turning back, and the only question becomes how to quit while you're ahead.

The first time it was a favor. Someone had heard about my father's work in college with nanotechnology and applied microparticle physics and wondered if he might be able to construct a little something. Not a weapon, exactly. More like a *shield*. For a client who had a dangerous occupation and needed some additional protection. Of course such technology already existed, but it was cumbersome and unwieldy—designed for missile defense systems and the like. This person needed something small. Something that could repel bullets and resist fire and even explosives, but that could fit into your pocket. A kind of personal force field. My father said it was possible. With enough time, resources, hard work, and ingenuity, anything was possible. This man, Ogden Black, provided the resources. My father provided the rest.

It took him six months to build. It was the first black box he ever sold, and he was paid a hundred grand for it as a return favor. It was a spectacular success—a personal deflector shield in a five-inch cube, worthy of the cover of *Scientific American* or at least *Guns & Ammo*.

Instead it found its way onto the cover of *Newsweek*, under the bold red letters proclaiming a SUPERVILLAIN RAMPAGE.

For a hundred thousand dollars, Ogden Black, small-time

bank robber, became Mr. Impenetrable, one of the most successful villains in New Liberty history. He used my father's invention to go on a crime spree that netted him millions, laughing as the bullets disintegrated before they could reach him, taunting the Diamond Dame as her focused light beams simply bounced right off. Then he retired on some unmapped island where no one could find him, shielded by a fortune stolen from others.

A year after Mr. Impenetrable's disappearance, my father got a postcard in the mail. It said, *Happiness is seventeen million dollars and a little black box. Thanks. O.M.B.*

My father tried to keep it a secret, of course, but word spread about the force field and the genius who made it. More requests were made. A device that could project a lifelike replica of its user. A machine that could send out a magnetic pulse that disabled all electronics in a three-mile radius. A box that could harness the power of marvelantium, concentrating it into a beam. The money was nice, but it was secondary. Every request was a challenge. A chance to prove himself. To show his father and his father's father what a box maker could *really* do.

Benjamin Edson had found his calling. He was a genius. A criminal genius, but a genius nonetheless. But, like so many geniuses, he was lonely. He wanted somebody to share his genius with. Someone to follow in his footsteps, to keep the line of box makers going. A desire, I guess, that brought him to the steps of St. Mary's.

He says he knew. The moment he first saw me, he knew that I was the one.

It's nice being the one.

The black SUV appears in my driveway ten minutes later; both of our bowls of soup sit in front of us, untouched, congealed into a thick paste that could be used for spackling. I watch the lights come up the street and shine briefly in our window. I hear the motor purr and it makes me queasy. I've seen this car a dozen times before, stopping for a pickup or delivery. I've just never been the thing being picked up.

Dad looks at the window and mumbles, "Because I could not stop for Death, he kindly stopped for me."

"Thanks, Dad. Awesome. Very comforting."

He looks at me, face full of concern. "Sorry. Emily Dickinson. Just the black car. You know, reminded me. Terrible quote. You'll be fine. Tony can handle Mickey Maloney."

Yes, I think, but that doesn't mean he can handle everybody. As if reading my thoughts, Dad glances back out the window and up at the stars. The driver of the SUV honks twice.

I leave the star-chart printout on the table and am through the front door without even saying good-bye, ignoring the hand that reaches out to me. It's partly my own fault, I know. I'm the one who told Zach, spilling my one good secret against my father's wishes. But he's still my dad, and he should take some responsibility for ruining what was, to that point, one of the best days of my life. The back door to the

SUV opens. The first face I see is Zach's.

"You," I say.

"I know," he says.

"You jerk-faced, back-stabbing, squealing little pig."

"I know, all right? I get it. You're upset. I'm sorry. But we need you, so just get in the car."

"I trusted you," I tell him.

"Okay. I'm guilty. I'm dog crap. But this is serious." He nods to the empty seat next to him. "Get in the car."

I scan the SUV. Zach is sitting beside another member of Tony Romano's posse. Two more sit up front. I notice everyone but me is dressed in brown leather trench coats. I look at my cargo shorts and green T-shirt imploring everyone to DO THE DEW.

"Oh, snap," I say. "My trench coat's at the cleaners."

"There's a suit in the back," Zach says, the note of apology suddenly gone from his voice. "You can change when we get there."

Before I can protest further, I'm pulled inside and the SUV shoots back out of the driveway. I look through the tinted windows to see my father standing in the doorway, fading fast. I should have said something, but it's too late. Maybe when I get back.

When, not if.

"You said you could keep a secret," I whisper in Zach's ear, the slight tickle of my breath enough to make three spikes jut from his lobe.

"Mike. This is Tony Romano we are talking about. He's practically my father. And you don't keep secrets from your father. Especially not with what's going on now. Besides," Zach adds, "you're in good hands. We are going to take care of you."

I turn and look at my car mates. None of them looks like a man I would want to meet in a dark alley. None of them even looks like a man I'd want to run into on Main Street in Disney World in broad daylight. But they are Tony's men, which means they are at least on my side. Or vice versa. Zach introduces me, starting with the skinny kid wedged beside me. "This is Blades McCoy," he says. We shake hands. He looks older than me or Zach, though the eye patch probably adds a few years.

"Blades, huh? Is that your god-given name or just what your friends call you?"

The young man smiles and opens one flap of his coat to reveal at least a dozen throwing knives of various lengths and designs. There are more attached to his belt and at least two in each boot that I can see. He probably has another one tucked in his underwear. If he tripped and fell down the stairs, he'd decapitate himself. At least it goes a long way toward explaining the eye patch.

Zach points to the driver. "That's Mario Andretti."

The gray-haired man behind the wheel doesn't bother to look up, but he raises a gloved hand.

"Like, *the* Mario Adre—" I start to ask, but Zach shakes his head quickly, whispering, "Best not to talk about it." Then he points to the very large black man riding shotgun.

"And that's Indiana Jones."

I can't help myself. "Because he's also an archaeologist?" I ask.

Indiana Jones turns to me. When he speaks, it sounds like a hundred bass drums thrumming inside a cave. "'Member in that first movie when he's bein' chased by that giant freakin' boulder?" I nod meekly. Indiana Jones points to himself with both thumbs. "*I'm* the boulder."

I swallow hard. "Then why not call yourself Avalanche or Rockman or something?"

The giant scowls at me. I can see he is missing several teeth. "Because I'm Indiana freakin' Jones. You got a *problem* with that?"

I definitely do not have a problem with that. I slink back in my seat and decide I should try to keep my mouth shut for the rest of the drive. There will be more time to yell at Zach later, when he's not so tense. When I'm not surrounded by knives and giant freakin' boulders.

"So tonight is pretty simple," Zach says, rubbing his hands together. "Tony's been trying to strike a deal with Mickey Six Fingers for years now, but neither could ever agree to terms. However, recent events—"

"You mean the Comet," I say.

"Recent . . . unexpected incidents," Zach repeats guardedly, "have convinced Mr. Romano to expand his list of allies. He thinks Mickey's just as concerned and needs a little extra push to join forces. He doesn't want to muscle him into it, though, which is where you come in. I told him about you, and he thought it was worth a shot."

"And if Mickey Six Fingers still says no?" I prompt, wondering what happens to me if I can't live up to my billing . . . if, like at the charity dinner, it takes me three tries to get the trick right.

"If he says no again, then we have to do it the old-fashioned way," Blades says with a sharp grin.

We drive in silence for what seems like an hour, long enough for the sun to set, before pulling up to a warehouse in a neighborhood I've never been to before, certainly nothing like the one I wandered through this afternoon. There's a line of three more black SUVs waiting for us, and everyone but me gets out. I hear the rear door open and close, and then Zach hands me a black suit still covered in dry cleaners' plastic.

"It's used. Sorry," he says. "But I think they got most of the blood out."

I peel off the plastic and inspect the contents. Pants. Socks. Shirt. Coat. Everything but the shoes. It all looks just like new, save for matching holes in both the suit and the shirt, just below where you pledge allegiance. Both holes have been expertly stitched closed with black thread. Barely noticeable.

"Fantastic," I whisper, though there's nobody in the car to hear me.

Five minutes later I'm dressed in my new suit—a little

big—complete with my now glaringly white fifty-dollar sneakers and my no-longer stylishly unbrushed hair. Another SUV arrives behind us, and four more men step out. One of them is Tony Romano.

I've seen him before. On TV, all over the news, once through a rolled-down window as he waited in our driveway. He never comes into the house. Whether that's Dad's rule or Tony's I've never been sure, but even his henchmen just stand and wait at the door, arms crossed, chins tucked into their chests. Tony is like the crazy uncle who lives in Arizona and sends you postcards every now and then, except instead of postcards, Uncle Tony sends manila envelopes filled with crisp hundred-dollar bills.

He looks just like you'd expect: Italian sumo meets Mr. Clean. What's left of his hair is combed over, a thin veil to keep the moonlight from reflecting too brightly from his crown. He's dressed similar to me in a black suit and black shirt, save his suit would fit three of me and he has much better shoes. He carries no weapons, unless you count the cane that he could beat you with, or the ten or so guys who surround him. He puts out a hand for me to shake; it feels like a dead salmon.

"Michael," he says with an accent that sounds a little backwoods. I expected Marlon Brando. I get country and western. "A pleasure to finally meet you in person. Sorry it hasn't happened before now, but your father's very protective. And understandably so."

"Yes, sir," I say.

"I've known your father for quite a while now," Tony says. "He's a genius. Knows how to keep a secret. I appreciate that."

That's a relief, at least. It's nagged me the whole car trip over, the thought that Tony might be mad that Dad never told him about me. After all, the Romanos have a habit of recruiting people with powers. I steal a glance at Zach, who kind of slinks back into the shadows. Tony reaches out and draws me closer to him, smacking his lips like he's going to swallow me whole. I can smell onions, and it makes my stomach roll. He speaks in a low whisper, making this suddenly a conversation for two.

"You understand, though, how a man in my position could benefit by having someone with your abilities," he says.

"Yes, sir," I say, keeping my voice even with his whisper.

"Though I really only have his word. Your father's talent comes packaged in a nice little black box . . . you'll excuse me if I'm a little skeptical with regard to yours."

I can see where this is headed.

"I understand," I say.

"So do me a favor," Tony Romano continues to whisper, flicking his eyes at an angle. "See that big stack of bricks behind me?" I look, hoping it doesn't look like I'm looking. "His name is Rudy."

Rudy doesn't look like a Rudy. He looks like a cement wall with steel beams for limbs and a misshapen cinder block for a head. Like with Indiana Jones, I can't help but feel Rudy's been misnamed, that he should be called Behemoth or Ogre or something. Then again, I have four names and none of them are really mine. Half of them are girls' names.

"I want you to make Rudy hit himself as hard as he can," Tony says.

I take another look at Rudy. I don't want to see him hit anything.

"Excuse me, sir?"

"Just make him sock himself, right in that big red cherry schnoz of his. Just so I know, so I can see for myself. You don't want me to look like a fool in front of Mr. Maloney, do you?"

I shake my head, and Tony backs away, smiling. I stare at Rudy's nose, a big, dark-pink fleshy thing, like the bulb of a bicycle horn. Unlike Indiana Jones, Rudy has most of his teeth, but they are all capped silver, making for one scary-looking clown face. I study my shoes, even more glaring compared to the black dress pants I'm wearing, take a deep breath, then look back up at him. I bore as deep into his murky blue eyes as I can. "Your name is Rudy, right?"

The behemoth nods. Stands oak-tree still.

"Rudy. My name is Michael." I see his pupils circle wider, mouth slacken. I try to keep my hands from shaking. "Rudy . . . I want you to hit yourself as hard as you can."

There is a moment when I think I've lost him. Where I can feel my own confidence waver and he just stands there, that same stupid, lost-puppy look on his face. Then, suddenly, his right arm whips around like a snapped rubber band, planting his fist so far up his nose that I'm afraid it might get lodged in his skull. There is a sickening sound, like smashing a rotten watermelon, and a squirt of blood, and then Rudy goes down hard on the street.

One of Tony's other thugs whistles. Indiana Jones says, "Aw, hell no." Zach shakes his head.

Tony Romano smiles and snaps his fingers, and two other men bend down and help Rudy to his feet. The bodyguard's hands are cupped to his mouth and nose, but I can see the red oozing. The look he gives me makes me wish I could turn invisible, but only superheroes get to do cool stuff like that.

Then Rudy pulls his hands away and gives both me and Tony a confused look. Then he spits on the ground, and something white, red, and silver skips up off the pavement.

I am pretty much guaranteed to have nightmares tonight.

"Excellent," Tony Romano says, still grinning, clapping me on the shoulder. "A genius. Just like your father. Just wait for my cue."

I nod, and we all follow Tony into the warehouse, me taking care to keep a fair distance from both Rudy and Mr. Jones. Zach comes up behind me, whispering.

"Bet that's the first time you ever knocked somebody's teeth out," he says.

"It wasn't my fist," I say.

"Which makes it even more impressive."

That's the thought that I carry when I enter the warehouse full of even more men in trench coats and pinstriped suits—at least two dozen of them, all hovering around Mickey "Six

Fingers" Maloney. And I realize that red-nosed Rudy is the least of my problems.

The warehouse looks like it has been abandoned for a decade at least. Half the lights are burned out, and the other half flicker sporadically. Stacks of empty crates line one wall. A few mousetraps are scattered along the floor, untriggered but baitless. A long wooden table sits in the center of the room, and only one man sits at it across from us, though he is surrounded by a couple dozen thugs standing at attention. I wonder if any of them have special powers like Zach and me, or if they are all just regular hired muscle, average joes with questionable consciences and a need to pay the bills. They make a point of hiding their guns but also make it obvious they're packing—lots of right hands tucked inside coats.

Except for Mickey. His hands are on the table. He is dressed the same as Tony Romano, except all in white, like a photo negative. And in contrast to Tony's girth, Mickey Maloney looks more like a scarecrow that has lost half of its stuffing. Gaunt cheeks, shallow eyes, long skinny neck with pulsing veins and all. The only thing they really have in common is the receding hairline. And the criminal empire.

"Mickey," Tony says, in a voice filled with fake courtesy.

"Tony." Mickey nods back, then cuts me a look. "Who's the Chihuahua with the sparkly shoes?"

I look down at my feet. In the flickering halogens, they do

kind of sparkle. Tony introduces me as his new accountant in training.

"A little young," Mickey says. "How high can he count to?"

All Mickey's goons laugh. None of Tony's do. Rudy pulls out a seat for his boss, chin still streaked red. I wait stupidly for a moment before I realize I'm supposed to pull out my own chair and sit down next to him.

"Mickey, this is Michael. Michael, this is Mr. Maloney."

I offer my hand for a shake, but the crime boss just gives me the finger.

I can't help but stare at it. "I always thought . . . ," I hear myself say.

"That I had six fingers on one hand?" Mickey finishes. "You're not the first, kid. But my name's not Eleven Fingers Maloney." He continues to hold up the finger. "Lost the other four to a Rottweiler when I was fifteen. When they went back to look, they could only find the pointer, but I made 'em attach it in the middle. That way, everyone would know how I *really* felt. Go on. Shake it." He thrusts the gnarled digit at me. I look at Tony, who nods. I bite my lip and look back at the finger just wagging at me, a giant taunting worm, laced with scars around the base. I grab hold, gingerly.

Mickey Six Fingers suddenly jerks back, hand shaking, like he's having a seizure. I nearly fall out of my seat pulling away from him. I see all Tony's men tense up, but Mickey's men just snort and shake their heads as Mickey composes himself, smoothing out his hair.

"Gets 'em every time," he says.

I catch my breath. Some joke. I wonder how many thirteen-year-olds have ever died of a heart attack. I pull myself back into my seat.

"So what's so important that we had to meet on such short notice?" Mickey says, turning his attention to Tony and ignoring me altogether.

Tony Romano leans over the table, pushing it back with his gut. "You and I both know what's so important. You've been in this town just as long as I have, Mickey. You know what it means, all of a sudden, having someone like him around."

They are talking about the Comet, of course. At least somebody appreciates the gravity of the situation. Tony gets it. Understands how someone like that changes things, alters the rules of the game.

"He's not our concern," Mickey chides. "You know that."

"Maybe not," Tony says. "But he upsets the balance. This town's crowded as it is. There are only so many opportunities, Mickey. I don't know about you, but I'm not interested in losing my share."

"Neither am I," Mickey says. "Which is why I'm having a difficult time understanding why I'm sitting here across from *you*." Behind him, one of Mickey's men sniggers, but a look from his boss shuts him up.

Tony Romano puts both meaty hands on the table, clasped as if in prayer. "Mickey. This new guy . . . he's not like us.

You've seen what he's capable of. He's not a businessman. He won't listen to reason. I've seen his kind before. He hasn't done much yet, but believe me, he is just getting started. He has plans. Guys like him, they always have a plan."

"I have plans," Mickey fires back, taking offense.

"Not like him you don't," Tony retorts. "Besides," he adds, "he's attracting unwanted attention."

"You mean . . ." Mickey whistles and looks up at the ceiling. I look up with him. I don't know what I expect to see. Peeling paint and rusted pipes. Tony nods solemnly.

And then it dawns on me. The Comet is the unwanted attention. So then who's the first guy they were talking about?

"This is New Liberty, Tony," Mickey says. "We've seen it all before. They come. They go. We hold fast. Stay out of the way. We stick around. You remember what it was like ten years ago. . . ."

"I remember," Tony says. "And that's exactly why I think we need to reassess our business strategy. It has taken us both a very long time to get where we are. I'm not going to just sit back and let some freak come in and take it all away. I'm not suggesting we start a war. I'm just saying, pool our resources and protect what's ours."

Tony Romano snaps his fingers, and Rudy produces a stack of papers from behind me. I notice most of the bleeding has stopped. Tony reaches inside his suit and pulls out a pair of glasses too small for his face, precariously perching them on his beak.

"This is an outline suggesting a temporary merger of our two enterprises. We combine everything. Business opportunities. Contacts. Muscle. Your associates become my associates. My cops become your cops, and so on. Most of it is split right down the middle, though, as you can see from the blanket statement in the first paragraph, profits from any dual business ventures are split sixty-forty."

Tony pushes the paper across the splintered table. Mickey Six Fingers pulls out his own pair of reading glasses—two wise old professors sitting across from each other—and takes the paper, tracing his one finger down the page. He nods thoughtfully, removes his glasses, folds them neatly and sets them down. Then he takes a long snort and spits, a quivering snot wad that slaps against the paper with a *thwack*. I taste bile in my mouth. Tony smiles politely.

"You think I'm an idiot?" Mickey says. "Is that what you think, Tony? That you would bring me out here, with your little punk band and your dorky-looking kid with no decent shoes, and throw this piece of garbage in my face? Is that it?"

I nervously scan the line of trench coats. I get the feeling if somebody so much as coughs, all those hands will spring from their hiding places, filling the air with lead. I'm about ready to dive under the table. But Tony just shrugs and turns to me and, in a voice calm and composed, says, "Michael, please explain to Mr. Maloney that this deal is in his best interest and that he should take it now before it is too late." Tony prods me with one raised eyebrow.

This is my moment. My contribution to the family. I flash back to the talent show: standing there in front of everyone, the cards slipping out of my sweaty hands, fanning and fluttering out all over the stage like butterflies, me on hands and knees, trying to collect them. I look at Six Fingers. He's not Rudy the obedient henchman. He's not the tired shoe salesman at the mall. He's not even Sister Beatrice. He just loogied all over the deal Tony offered him. I'm pretty sure he's made up his mind.

I remember what Dad told me. To keep it in the realm of possibility. It doesn't have to be something they *want* to do, but they can't be adamantly opposed to the idea either. For a second, I wish I had that little neural-enhancing spaghetti strainer or whatever it was Dad was building. Then I remember it didn't work. I was on my own. Tony coughs impatiently.

Mickey Maloney looks back and forth from me to Tony through buggy scarecrow eyes.

"Mr. Maloney," I start to say, knowing I'm already doomed, that my heart's not in it. I wonder what Tony will do when this doesn't work. Wonder if he will take it out on Dad somehow. Wonder how I got here in the first place. Not here, sitting at this table stuck between two crime bosses, necessarily, but here at this place in my life, where all of a sudden it matters what I do.

"I think . . . ," I say.

I stop, cock my head to the side. "I think . . ."

I can feel Rudy hovering over me, big beefy hands formed

into sledgehammers. I can hear Tony's heavy breathing. I can hear the steady tap of Mickey's middle finger on the table. It seems to have an echo, coming from the rafters above me. *Tap tap tap.* Like footsteps.

I look up. Tony looks up. We all look up.

Just in time to see the ceiling come crashing down.

Not the whole ceiling, but enough to end the negotiation. The chunk of plaster, wood, and shingles comes crashing down in the middle of the table, smashing it in two. Everyone is up on his feet, looking at the new hole in the ceiling, a dozen guns immediately drawn, expecting to see an army of FBI agents or a platoon of SWAT officers rappelling down.

But these aren't the cops. Most of the cops don't know about this place, and those who do are paid handsomely to pretend that they don't. The cops don't mess with Mickey or Tony too much—just enough to keep up appearances. Besides, if they did come, they would have to come in force. The figure standing on the roof, leaning over the new hole he's made— he's alone. That's how most superheroes work.

Tony shakes his head. "This is *exactly* what I'm talking about," he says. Then he gives a signal, and suddenly the room is filled with the drumroll of gunfire. Both the Romanos and the Maloneys swing their weapons toward the ceiling and start belching smoke. I duck behind my chair and watch as the Comet swoops down amid the hail of bullets and dispatches two henchmen with a swift spinning kick, sending them flying into their mates, then turns in time to bend the barrel of a machine gun sideways, causing it to explode. My ears split with ringing, and then the whole room is suddenly a loud, chaotic blur. Tony's and Mickey's men circle around the Comet, a seething vortex of bullets and punches and kicks. A perfect storm of thirty against one. And I am rooted in place, unsure which way to go.

"Gah!"

I feel my collar tighten and something prickle the back of my neck and turn to see a body covered in barbs—Zach the human cactus, pulling me backward toward the door. It's the first time I've ever seen him fully spiked, all quills from head to toe. He looks positively medieval, and I realize there's no way he will ever wear those pants again.

"Time to go," he says.

It's hard to hear him over the gunfire and grunts, but I follow out of instinct. Henchmen fly past me, propelled by the Comet's gauntleted fists. The superhero weaves his way through the crowd, walking like a deranged killer in a teen-age slasher flick, deflecting bullets, delivering rib-cracking kicks, tossing Tony's burly men over his shoulder like mashed soda cans. Mickey Six Fingers and his men have already given up and retreated to the back door. Zach and I are tripping over each other to get to the front, everyone scattering, try-ing to save his own hide. The Comet becomes a sapphire blur, leaping off the walls and bowling over Romano's men before they even see him coming. I've never seen anything like him. It's terrifying, but I can't help but watch.

"Look out!"

Zach points and shoves me out of the way as Indiana' Jones rumbles past, heading toward the Comet, getting larger and rounder as he goes, puffing himself up somehow like a beach ball, until he is six feet around, practically rolling, head over heels. Everyone else scrambles as the human boulder rolls past, picking up speed. I look to see the Comet crouch low, delivering a single punch. I remember what happened at the police station. Remember what he did to the garbage truck. One punch, and Indiana Jones goes flying through the air, smashing through the cinder-block wall on the other side of the warehouse, leaving a hole big enough to drive our Honda through.

The Comet turns and advances on Zach and me as we're still picking ourselves up off the ground. I look into his eyes, ready to plead for my life. I've never had to use my powers on a superhero before. I don't like my chances. His eyes are cold and calculating. All menace.

"Where is he?" the Comet barks. His voice is deep and resonant, an intimidating snarl. His square jaw juts from his mask.

I look around for any sign of Tony, but he's obviously already escaped.

"Please don't kill me," I beg.

I'm not supposed to make requests. It doesn't work if I beg. But with this freak of nature looming over me, it's all I can do.

I can't bring myself to give this man orders.

"Tell me where I can find him!" The Comet's fingers curl, and I'm pretty certain that I'm done for. Michael Marion Magdalene Morn-Edson. Born in a White Castle. Died in a warehouse. Never even got to first base. I make a list of all the people I blame for my premature death. It's not long, but it's pretty diverse. Nuns. Superheroes. Mafia heads. Fast-food employees. The Comet takes another step toward me, and I figure this is as good a time as any to remember my prayers.

Suddenly I feel a sharp stabbing in my arm as Zach grabs hold of me again, dragging me to my feet.

"Come on!" he shouts as two more of Tony's henchmen try to tackle the Comet from behind, buying us a precious second to get to the door.

I turn and follow Zach outside—the Comet still slugging off trench-coated men behind me—to where one SUV is already pulling away, carrying its lone passenger; I can see the silhouette of Tony Romano riding in the back. What's left of Tony's men pile into the other cars. Blades McCoy is riding shotgun on the one we came in. Mario Andretti is gunning the engine.

"Mike, come on. Hurry up!" Zach shouts, already climbing in. From the warehouse behind me, I hear one last gunshot, then a grunt. I leap toward the car as something small and black flies through the air just past my nose, lodging in the hood of the SUV. It looks a little like a small Frisbee, like the kind you might get in a Happy Meal, except it has a row of spikes and a pulsing orange light attached to it.

I am familiar with little pulsing lights. I've seen enough of my father's inventions to know what they mean. I drop to the ground and cover my head as the front of the SUV explodes. There is a mushroom of smoke, and I watch Zach and the others fall out the doors or drag themselves through the busted windows of the now-flaming vehicle. Mario scrambles to his feet and starts to run when a black wire or cord of some kind shoots out of the shadows and wraps around his feet, tripping him up. He lands facefirst on the gravel and screams something in a language that I can only assume is Italian. Another thin black wire wraps around Blades, dropping the kid to his knees, a knife falling from each hand. He groans, clearly hurt, and I just hope I was wrong about the underwear.

I don't wait around to see where all these things are coming from. I take off in the other direction, away from Zach and the burning SUV, away from the smoking warehouse, heading for the cornfield behind, with no other thought than to run. Legs pumping, I realize I'm the only person wearing the right kind of shoes. There is shouting. The peel of tires. I look back just in time to see something black whistling through the air.

There is a sharp pain in my knee and my legs cinch together beneath me, like pipe cleaners twisting around, causing me to fall forward. I break the fall with my hands, though it still knocks the wind out of me when I hit, causing the already black sky to grow even blacker for a moment.

I look down to find my legs wrapped tight in black cable, thin, but strong as deep-sea fishing line, at least what I imagine it must be like. I've never actually been fishing. Or seen the ocean. I struggle to kick myself free, but I'm still flat on the ground when I hear the voice coming from the shadows.

"Where do you think you are going?"

It's not exactly the Comet's voice, though it has that same gruffness, a gravelly husk that is hard to place. I look up to see someone about my size, maybe a little taller, emerge from the shadows. Dressed in a black jumpsuit with thin gold stripes along the seams, wearing a black mask that covers everything but the mouth—a pair of thin white lips set into a sneer. He's got a pair of high-tech goggles with red lenses, all bug-eyed and scary. Though I can barely see him in the dark, I'm sure he can see me perfectly. He has a black leather bag slung across his body. One hand is tucked inside, no doubt reaching for another weapon—a gun, maybe, or one of those exploding disk things that he used on the SUV.

"Please let me go," I say, realizing that here, in the dark, with him wearing those goggles, there is no way I can convince this guy of anything, no matter how badly I want to. I manage to prop myself on my elbows and try to get a better look, but his outfit has a way of blending in with the background, creating little more than an outline. I have no idea who this new guy is, but I'm pretty sure I know who he came with.

"Hey. Wait. Listen. You've got the wrong idea. I'm not really with these guys." It's a lie, of course, but it's the best I can come up with. I pull on my coat, scrunched so tight around my armpits that I can barely move. "This isn't even my suit."

"I could tell," the figure says. "It doesn't go with your shoes at all."

He takes his hand out of the bag, and I can see that it's empty. No bombs. No guns. Maybe I'll just be strangled to death. The figure in black cocks his head to the side, taking me in from a slightly different angle. Then he reaches down with a gloved hand and lifts me up without the slightest effort. He has long fingers, I notice. A magician's fingers. We stand there for just a moment, and I want to ask "So what happens now?" But before I can, there is a flash of light and the growl of a motor as another SUV comes barreling through the field at top speed, making a shower of shattered cornhusks. It's headed straight for us. The figure in black leaps out of the way just in time as the car skids to a halt, the back door thrown open. Zach reaches out and pulls me inside, then barks for Mr. Andretti to get us the heck out of there, wheels spinning while my feet still dangle out the door. There is a spray of mud and dirt as we jolt forward, ripping back through the field and toward the street.

I chance a look out the shattered rear window. At the stranger just standing there in the moonlight.

Watching me get away.

Dad's waiting for me on the porch. One hand holds a rolling pin like a club. The other holds a black box. I have no idea what this particular box does, but I can only assume it's more dangerous than the rolling pin.

The SUV jerks to a halt, just long enough for me to fall out of it, Mario still revving the engine like the green flag is about to drop. Zach says he will call me. Not to worry. That it wasn't my fault and that Tony won't hold it against me. He tells me to go ahead and keep the suit. Then the SUV speeds away, busted windshields and all.

I look up at my father bathed in the porch light, his eyes bloodshot. I take off my suit coat, torn and filthy and smelling of gun smoke, and toss it wearily over my shoulder, as if I've just come home from a long day at the office. I feel exhilarated and exhausted, the biochemical rush of nearly having my head knocked off—first by a superhero and then by his previously heretofore unknown sidekick—finally starting to ebb. I take three steps toward the door and falter. Feel his hands on my elbows, propping me up.

"I've got you," he says.

I bury my face in his shoulder, smearing sweat and snot and soot on his pink-and-white shirt, leaving my mark, imprinting all over him. I let out a shuddering breath. It's eighty degrees out here and I can't stop shaking. My father whispers to me in soothing tones. "It's all right. You're safe now," he says. "I've got you.

"I won't let it happen again."

I let him carry me to bed. Not cradled—he's never had the chance to carry me that way—but draped across his shoulder, half dragged to the room. I let him pull off my new shoes and my socks, pull the covers to my chin, feel his chapped hands on my forehead, smoothing back my hair. I open my mouth to speak, but every time I do, he tells me not to say anything. We can talk in the morning. He asks me if I want him to leave the hall light on, even though I've slept in the dark from the moment he first brought me home, as if all of a sudden I'm four again.

I nod anyway. A little light can't hurt.

Then he tells me he loves me. But he told me not to say anything.

Instead I lie there, picturing the Comet hovering over me, and the gunfire and the exploding car. The sickening crunch of his booted foot smashing into ribs, the ceiling coming down, Rudy's bloody silver grin, Zach's nettled grasp. The wire wrapped around my feet, pulling me down, all of it drawing me in. I scrunch my eyes and hold my breath and push back, past the explosions and the blood and the growling voice in my head, trying to think of something else, anything else. Until I'm back at her front door, remembering how she smiled when she found the penny in her back pocket, as if it was something she had been looking for forever.

And I feel like I've been split in half.

In the quiet I hear my father's voice on the kitchen phone,

two rooms away. It's one o'clock in the morning. My father never calls anyone unless they're going to show up thirty minutes later with food. The walls in the house are thin, with the exception of the soundproofed concrete of the basement, and the neighborhood is asleep. Even with his half whisper, I can hear him.

"This is Edson," he says. "I accept your offer."

THE MAN
BEHIND THE MASKS

My life is slowly being populated by people in masks. People in masks are not to be trusted. I learned that from a movie. Of course, in the movie, the guy wearing the mask turned out to be the hero. Come to think of it, a lot of heroes wear masks. Kind of makes you wonder what they're hiding.

I'm not a supervillain. But if I *was* a supervillain, I wouldn't wear a mask. For starters, they are hot and sweaty. And they probably make your face itch. They also make it hard to breathe—unless they are gas masks, I guess. I suppose they could serve some other practical purpose. Infrared vision. Satellite communications linkage. UV protection. Whatever. That's not why people wear them.

Think about it. A man walks into a convenience store. He's got a gun. His intentions are clear. He wears a mask. Why? So nobody will recognize him. If he takes off the mask, everyone will know who he is. Then he can be hunted down, captured, thrown in jail. With the mask on, he is anonymous. He can hide. He empties the cash register and makes it to the front door, where he is suddenly stopped by some caped vigilante with a utility belt and an overfed sense of justice or whatever.

Of course the superhero wears a mask. Why? So everybody *will* recognize him. So that his picture in the paper will put the minds of Joe and Joanna Bystander to rest and strike fear in the hearts of would-be convenience-store robbers every-where.

There is a brief scuffle. The superhero wins. The robber is hauled off to jail, his mask stripped, his identity revealed, his life changed forever.

The superhero, meanwhile, flies back to his secret head-quarters. Kicks off his boots, cracks open a beer. He pulls off his mask and looks in the mirror. Nobody knows who he is now. Not really. That's the point. He can walk down the street without getting mobbed by paparazzi. He can hang out at the mall. He can eat a ham sandwich on a park bench and feed the crusts to the pigeons.

Villains wear masks because it gives them the courage to do something extraordinary, something they might not have the guts to do otherwise. But heroes? Heroes wear masks because deep down inside, I'm guessing, they just want the chance to be normal. That's my theory, anyway.

Personally, I don't trust either of them.

I sleep in. I'm too exhausted to move even when the sun starts stabbing at my pillow through the slats. By the time I drag myself out of bed and get dressed, it's almost noon. The Sunday paper sits on the kitchen table. My printout of the night sky is nowhere to be found. I stare dumbly at the picture of the trashed warehouse. The headline reads COMET CRASHES CRIMINAL PARTY.

So it was a *party*. That explains why I'm exhausted.

I skim through the article, trying to ignore the pounding flashes in my brain. Somewhere between eight and ten p.m., blah blah blah, witnesses report seeing fire and smoke, blah blah blah, police arrive at the scene of a war zone, blah blah blah, twelve men taken into custody, seven of them hospitalized. Known affiliations to the Romano and Maloney crime families. What appears to be a business deal gone bad.

That's one way to put it.

There is a picture of the warehouse, windows of busted glass, a halo of smoke coming through its brand-new chimney, a burned-out car in the foreground. There is a quote from one of the suspects, one of Mickey's guys, picked up by a reporter before the cops could shove him into the police van. "He dropped right out of the sky. There was nothing we could do. The man is inhuman."

That's one way to put that, too.

There is more. Brief histories of the two crime syndicates. Paragraphs of speculation on why they might have been meeting.

A vague statement by the chief of police, calling for a return to order and peace. And then pages and pages on the Comet.

Just the Comet. There is no mention of a sidekick, no talk of the shorter, equally growly wraith who appeared out of the shadows toting disk bombs and grappling cords. Unlike the Super who leaves a giant smear across the sky, the person who snagged me like a trout last night apparently left no impression. I start to wonder if I just imagined it, but the bruises on my elbows and knees are fresh. There was another hero there last night. Another freak in a mask. Another thing to wrap my head around.

I put down the paper and try to listen through the floorboards. I wonder if Dad even bothered to sleep last night. I had thought maybe we could take the day off. Spend some time together. Talk about what was going on. But judging by how quiet it is up here, he is obviously down in the lair. I look over at the counter. The coffeepot holds only yesterday's dregs. Whatever he's doing, it's important enough for him to skip his morning fix. I don't remember everything from last night—there's way too much—but I do remember him saying that things would be different between us. That he was going to try harder. I remember that, and I remember the phone call.

I shuffle over to the basement door and turn the handle.

I turn again, giving it a little jiggle.

It's locked.

It can't be, but it is. I mean, it *can* be. It was for a very long time, but it hasn't been in two years. Ever since I learned about my adopted ancestors. I knock once. Then again. Then six more times, harder and harder until my knuckles sting. Nothing. No response. "Dad! Hey, Dad!" I shout. "Open up!"

"I'm right here," he says.

I spin around to see my father standing in the kitchen doorway with a half doughnut in hand, as if he's just teleported there. As far as I know, he's never built a teleporter. You'd think that would be something he'd share with his only son. "You startled me," I say.

"You couldn't hear me come in because you were shouting," he says matter-of-factly.

I point to the door. "It's locked," I say. It's more of a question than a statement. He nods, affirming my assessment. I take a deep, patient breath and try again. "*Why* is the door locked?"

"I'm working on something," Dad says, still holding his half-eaten doughnut. There is a bag of them under his armpit. "I got breakfast," he adds, as if that somehow clears things up.

"Oh, well, if you are *working* on something . . ." I have to wait sometimes for the sarcasm to sink in with him. Sometimes it never quite hits bottom, just floats there between us like dust motes in a sunbeam. But this time he gets it. I can tell by the look on his face. He struggles to find a response.

"They're cream filled," he says, holding out the bag, letting it hang there in the void.

I notice he's not looking me in the eyes. I don't reach for the bag, so he sets it down on the table and rakes his flaming bush of orange hair back. For the first time I realize how old

164

he looks. It's not the streaks of silver speckled in his beard or the sag of skin around his eyes. I've noticed those before. It's the way he stands, with one hand holding on to something, the back of a chair, the doorframe, the corner of the table, as if his own two legs aren't quite solid enough anymore. When he speaks again, the words are all spread out, as if every one of them has an anchor attached and he has to pull them forcibly from deep down inside.

"Listen, Michael. I think you should stay up here for a while."

"Up here?" I repeat. "You mean, don't go down in the basement?"

I call it a basement on purpose. A lair is one thing, but a basement? You wouldn't keep your son from going down in the basement.

"I made a mistake. You're not ready," he says. "Not for this."

"Not ready!" I shout, stepping sideways to get him to look at me. "I've been helping you for two years! You've made me rob banks. You once had me ask a cop if I could borrow his gun!"

"But I didn't ask you to shoot anybody with it," he counters.

"I was twelve!"

"I wanted you to feel included."

"Fine. Then include me!" I shout. "I'm not stupid. You said yourself that everything in life is a choice and that nobody should do something just because they're told to."

"Fathers are different," he says. "This is different. You have to do what I tell you." He tries to reach out for me. I step back.

165

"It's not permanent, Michael. A couple of days. It's just, what I'm working on right now . . . I don't want you involved."

I shake my head, piecing together the words, pulling them back apart. Don't. Want. You. He can't be saying what I think he's saying.

"Little late for that. I'd say last night I was pretty darned involved." Thirteen years old, a criminal history, weekends with the mafia running from superheroes, and I still have to use the word *darned* in front of my father.

"Exactly," he says, snapping his fingers as if I've solved the equation. "It's my fault. I thought I could protect you, that we could protect each other, but this . . . Everything's out of balance. It was unexpected. I can get it under control. But I need you to stay out. Just until I'm finished with this one thing. Then everything will be back to normal." He nearly stumbles over the word. "No. Better than normal. I promise."

My mind is racing. I look back at the basement door. What could be so terrible, so dangerous, that he's suddenly kicking me out? I've helped my father build antimatter rays. Memory erasers. I've been burned, scratched, paralyzed, temporarily blinded, and nearly electrocuted, and still the door has never been locked, not since the day I first went down. "Please tell me you're not building a nuclear weapon."

"I'm not building a nuclear weapon."

"It's smallpox, then, isn't it? You've got the Ebola virus down there? The black plague?"

"It's nothing like that," he insists.

"Then why won't you let me in?" I yell, a seething, teeth-clenched question that actually comes with a little spit and causes my father to flinch.

He finally dares to look into my eyes. His pouty bottom lip quivers. He looks pathetic, gaunt face and Popsicle-stick frame trembling under his cargo shorts and Hawaiian shirt. We stand there, staring at each other. I could do it. Could make him unlock the door, could make him tell me what's down there. And he knows it, but he still doesn't look away.

"You have to trust me," he says.

I *could* do it. But I look down, breaking the stalemate. After a moment he reaches into his back pocket and pulls out a wad of cash, peeling off two hundred-dollar bills and setting them on the table next to the doughnuts. I wonder if they came from Dickens. Or maybe he robbed the doughnut store, though that doesn't sound like something he would do without me. Of course I didn't think there was much of anything he would do without me.

"Take it," he says. "Go somewhere. See a movie. Be normal for a change. For me. For both of us."

I don't reach for the cash, shaking my head in disbelief. Yesterday he was mad at me for leaving the house. Now he's bribing me to go.

"I'm going to make things right," he says. "I just need a little time." He makes a move, like maybe he will come and wrap his arms around me again, like he did last night, but I stand there, glaring, rigid, refusing to make any move that will give him

167

permission. I'm reminded of all those chess matches I've already lost. He's never apologized for winning. There is another calculated pause, like when you're poised with the piece hovering above one square or another.

Then he heads to the door, pulling the key from his pocket.

"Sorry, Son," he says over his shoulder. Then he disappears, closing the door behind him.

I shuffle over slowly and try the handle once, just to be sure. My instinct says break it down. Grab the heaviest thing I can find, and pound away at the handle until it breaks off. But then a second impulse grabs me. To get out. To go away. I can feel the whole house collapsing, getting smaller around me. A box with no trick floor and the river all around, seeping in through the cracks.

I put on my new shoes, still caked in mud from my mad dash through the field last night, and head to the door, shutting it hard behind me, even though I know full well he can't hear it. Still, there is small satisfaction in feeling the house shudder beneath the force of a fully slammed door.

Two minutes later I come back inside, stuff the two hundred bucks in my pocket, and grab an éclair from the bag.

At the very least, it gives me the chance to slam the door again.

I walk. I do a lot of walking. When I'm fifteen, Dad has promised, he'll teach me to drive the Civic. The Edsonmobile. Of course I'll never have a license. Forms again.

With two hundred bucks, I could take the bus. I could get a cab. I could probably persuade some random guy standing on a street corner to take me anywhere in the city I wanted, even to places I know I don't belong. But I need to walk. To clear my head.

"You have to trust me," he says. And then he locks the door. I think about the phone call last night. "This is Edson. I accept your offer." What offer? What is he building down there? He can cram most anything into one of those cubes, and there are plenty of people out there who know it. Word spreads. He's not an easy man to find, but secrets can be hard to keep. Possible it was Tony. After all, he is Dad's number one customer. Except it didn't quite fit with the urgency in my father's voice. What if it was somebody else? Somebody new? Somebody I've never seen before? I'm guessing that's where the wad of hundred-dollar bills came from. Down payment. Earnest money. I wonder how much he stands to make off this thing he's building, whatever it is. Wonder if it is the thing he's building that's dangerous, or the person he's building it for

Maybe it was just paranoia that got me kicked out of the lair. Made me just another kid storming out of the house.

One run-in with a superhero, and all of sudden you are a bystander.

For six blocks, my thoughts tumble over each other till I find myself standing in front of Gulliver's Games and Grub, a dirty gray-stone building with a flashing neon sign half burned out and flyers for garage bands pasted to the windows.

It's Chuck E. Cheese for teenagers, a greasy pizza parlor with a big room full of overpriced video games and booths upholstered in torn foam padding. It's one of the only places young people can go to hang out on this side of town, and that's only because Tony looks after it. Zach and I have spent hundreds of afternoons blowing coin at this place. It's loud and chaotic and perfect for not sticking out. Dad wanted me to be normal. In New Liberty, at least on my side of town, this is as normal as it gets.

I open the door, feeling flush with the two Benjamins in my back pocket. Two hundred dollars buys a lot of Skee-Ball. There are televisions scattered throughout, showing music videos with the volume turned up loud enough to mix in with the shouting of teenagers reveling in summer break and the electronic cacophony of the arcade. Everywhere you look, there are old record-album covers plastered to the wall, artists I've seldom listened to because they aren't named Wolfgang or Ludwig.

I walk in and order a soda to wash down my doughnut, thinking that if cops or the Feds or the gangsters or the tights-wearing, sky-streaking, anvil-fisted demigods and their mysterious black-suited, red-goggled sidekicks don't kill me one day, my diet will. Then I cash in fifty bucks' worth of tokens and try to lose myself in one screen after another. Forget about my father and being locked out of the lair. Forget about Rudy's bouncing bloody tooth. Forget about the Comet growling at me, about almost being beaten to a pulp. Just zone out and mash buttons. Like any other kid.

It works, for a little while, but after tearing the heads off some ninjas, winning Daytona twice over, and fending off seven alien invasions, I'm bored. Being normal sucks. I would rather be at home helping my father defy the laws of physics. It's funny. There were days I'd be stuck down there, screwing around with a computer chip or splicing wires, listening to my father discuss the intricacies of nanotechnology or the chemical properties of Jell-O, all the while wishing I was out here, with people, other people, doing whatever.

Now I wish I was down there with him.

After an hour, I figure I'll head to the counter to order a jumbo slice for the road. I'll take it over to the park and feed the crust to the squirrels, and we can all have a heart attack together. Right after I finish this game. I lean sideways, dodging a pair of incoming missiles, and accidentally bump into someone, a girl, standing much too close to me.

"You're going to lose," she says.

She looks at me with those golden eyes, luminous and large, and then points to the screen just as my ship explodes.

Game over.

I stare in disbelief. It's definitely her. Improbably, incontrovertibly her. She is wearing one of those summery sleeveless tops, daffodil yellow, and jean shorts that I'm thinking she cut herself, by the mismatched fringe. Her sandals betray two rows of pale-pink painted nails.

"Told you," she says.

I watch what's left of my digital self scatter to the void.

"I hope that wasn't your last token."

I'm grinning like the village idiot, I know, but I can't help myself. As impossible as it is, here she is again. Standing right next to me, defying everything my father has taught me about probability during our fun afternoons full of finite mathematics. I realize I should probably say something out loud.

"You," I say. Eloquence in brevity.

"Me," Viola says, waiting for the followup.

"I didn't know you hung out here." It comes out a little accusatory, though I don't mean it to. I'm just surprised, is all.

"Why? Because I climbed over the picket fence? Is there some rule against north siders here?"

Not a *rule*, exactly. "No," I say. "Nothing like that. Just, you know, it's a bit of a hike."

"My dad dropped me off," she says. "I'm supposed to meet a friend later, but I got the times mixed up, so I'm way early. Hang on, you've got a little something . . ." She licks her thumb and reaches over and wipes a smidge of Bavarian cream off my cheek. My skin heats up where she touches it. "You got any tokens left?" she asks.

I jingle my pocket, still in disbelief.

"In that case, I challenge you to a duel. Good versus evil."

"You're on," I say. "Which one am I?"

"You can be good," she says. I don't bother to argue.

We spend the next half hour in a pixelated blur, laughing

and taunting, trying to one-up each other's score. She creams me at Alien Invasion. I barely beat her at Ms. Pac-Man. I drop seven bucks into the claw game with the hopes of winning her a cute stuffed bear, but the best I manage is a fuzzy monstrosity that looks like a chicken mated with a hippo. She names it Mikey, which I try to take as a compliment.

We spend the last twenty tokens on this motion-controlled virtual fighting game, the kind where you stand side by side and actually have to kick and punch at the screen and it mimics your movements through motion-capture technology. Three lost games of air hockey have proven that she has better reflexes than I do, but I figure I've got her on this one. For starters, I've played this game for two years solid, ever since it came out. Plus I've seen every movie starring Bruce Lee.

We play five rounds, and she beats me in each and every one of them. Mops the floor with my face. I walk out of the booth, sweating from the effort. She walks out looking fresh as a picked plum, eyes downcast, a little embarrassed, it seems, by her overwhelming victory.

"I took karate for a few years," Viola says, presumably to make me feel better.

"You might have mentioned that," I tell her. The closest I ever got to taking karate was when I accidentally smashed the living-room lamp during a reenactment of *Fists of Fury*.

"I could buy you lunch," she offers as a consolation prize, but I shake my head.

"I just got an advance on my allowance," I tell her. "I'll pay."

We snag our slices, greasy cheese for me, mushroom and green pepper for her, and sit across from each other in a booth, as far away from other people as I can manage. She immediately sticks her straw between her teeth, tenderizing it a little before entry. I offer her one of my breadsticks—one of those goes around, comes around things—and she takes it with a raised eyebrow, then drowns it in garlic butter.

"You're pretty good at video games . . . you, know . . . for a girl," I say.

"You kind of suck at them, actually," she says. "You know. For a guy." And then she laughs. And I get the same strange feeling that I got the last time we sat together. That feeling of rightness. Not rightness opposite of wrongness. Rightness like putting on a favorite pair of jeans. Maybe Dad's right. Maybe normal's not so bad.

"How's your dad?" she asks as if reading my thoughts, pulling off mushrooms and eating them one by one, sucking the oil from the tips of her fingers. "Still as enthusiastic as ever?"

Probably more so, I think to myself. "He's fine," I say. "How about yours?"

"On his way to the office. Mother is rehearsing. She has a concert coming up next weekend. You should come. It's at the arts museum."

"And watch Viola's mom play the viola."

"It's Tchaikovsky. One of her favorites. She has a solo."

"Dad loves Tchaikovsky," I say.

"Then he should come too," she offers.

174

This makes me laugh. "Yeah . . . loves Tchaikovsky. Hates people." I try to make it come off as a joke. It isn't even true, really. Dad doesn't hate people. He just has very little use for most of them. And he sometimes refers to them as mindless, uncultured, gape-mouthed zombies. He would like Viola, though, I think. If I ever had the guts to tell him about her. She's obviously smart. With Dad, that's pretty much all that matters.

"Did you know," she says, "that for the longest time, the viola played second fiddle to its more famous sister, the violin?"

"Wonder how that made the fiddle feel."

"You know what I mean," she chides. "Very few pieces were written for the viola, and it was mostly relegated to harmony in the background."

"Like the violin's sidekick," I say.

"Something like that," she says. Then she stuffs her face with pizza, crust first. She points to a spot on my head along the hairline: a scratch, barely noticeable beneath my bangs, probably from all the broken glass last night. "What happened there?"

"I fell down," I say, nonchalant. Or maybe just a little chalant.

"Ouch," she says, face scrunched.

"It's no big deal."

She shrugs an if-you-say-so shrug. "You should watch where you're going."

Too true.

On the televisions above us, they have switched to the news and are showing clips of the Comet's battle with the men in silver masks—the one at the police station. It's the fan favorite by far; I've seen it at least a dozen times already, though I have to admit it's nothing compared to seeing the man in person. Here he comes. *Swoosh*. Lands. Smashes the truck. *Cronk*. Goes ballistic. Punch. Kick. Headbutt. A mighty blue whirlwind of justice. Or something. She follows my gaze, then shrugs and goes back to her pizza.

"Seems like that guy is everywhere," I say.

"Yeah, seems that way," she replies. For all I know, Viola is a closet Comet groupie. A fangirl who runs a Facebook page about him and inks drawings of him in her notebooks. Viola heart Comet. Or not. It suddenly strikes me how little I actually know about her. And how little she knows about me.

"He's kinda cool, though," I venture hesitantly.

She deftly snatches another mushroom from its quagmire of grease and cheese, dangling it over her mouth like a victim being fed to the sarlacc. "I guess. If you're into that sort of thing." She shrugs.

"What? You're telling me that a guy who can fly and, like, punch through garbage trucks like they were made of Styrofoam—you're saying that's *not* awesome?" Even I have to admit it's awesome. Soil-yourself scary. But still awesome. "I mean, come on, how is that not impressive?"

I stop talking. I realize I'm gushing about the Comet like he's my girlfriend to the girl I kind of wish was my girlfriend. She sets her pizza back on her plate and takes her soda in both hands as if she's suddenly afraid it might blast off.

"Yeah. Sure," she says. "I mean, he's obviously very powerful."

"And the flying . . ."

"And the flying," she admits. "The flying is cool. But . . . I don't know, doesn't he, you know, freak you out? Just a little bit?"

Yes. Constantly. Every time I look at him.

"Like what do you mean?" I ask, reaching over and dipping my breadstick nub into her garlic butter, soaking it clear through so that it's dripping in iridescent yellow, looking almost toxic.

"I mean, don't you ever wonder what he's up to? Where he goes all the time?"

"Back to his lair, I suppose." But then I realize superheroes don't have lairs. They have hideouts. Or headquarters. Lairs are for villains. Or enthusiastic fathers.

"I guess," she says, not bothering to correct me. "Still, it's a little disconcerting, don't you think? Wondering when or if he's going to show up, who he's going to try and save, what he's going to do?"

"Dropping in from out of *nowhere*," I say.

"And why he has to wear that stupid mask?" Viola continues. "I mean, like you said, he's practically invulnerable. What does he have to be afraid of?"

I nod in agreement. "Exactly. Why the mask? Masks are for cowards. And the tights. I mean, really. What's up with the tights?"

"Oh, well. The tights are easy," she says confidently. "Reduces wind resistance."

"You're kidding, right?"

"Totally serious," she says. "I bet his legs are really hairy. Would slow him way down. It's either that or shave."

I suddenly get an image of the Comet in the bathtub, one leg propped on the side, running his Schick along his calf.

"Yeah, but they all wear them. Have you seen pictures of El Matador? Or who's that one guy, shoots fire out of his hands?"

"Hotshot?"

"Yeah, him. I mean, you'd think he'd go with something a little more flame-retardant. Those tights look pretty combustible. Or that one who used to be here in town . . ." I snap my fingers repeatedly, trying to remember. There is even a statue of him near the county courthouse, though that's one building Dad and I try to avoid. "You know. Long blond hair. Kind of prissy, carried that book around with him . . ."

"The Libertarian?" Viola ventures hesitantly.

"Right," I say. "*He* wore tights and couldn't fly."

"I think for him it was probably just a fashion statement," Viola whispers. She smiles, and I suddenly feel like there is almost nothing I can't tell her, almost as if she knows what I'm going to say already.

"So weird," I say.

"I know," she says.

"And what's the deal with the voices? Why is it all superheroes speak in that kind of low, gruff snarl. Like . . ." I make my voice as husky as I can and point with my finger. *"You will never get away with this, bad guy."*

Viola snorts and rolls her eyes, but she plays along, sitting up straight, getting a very serious, very stern look on her face, her voice suddenly gravelly and grim. *"Your reign of terror ends here, vile fiend."* She sneers. Then she stops suddenly. Our eyes meet, and she clears her throat. "Or something like that," she says in her normal voice.

"No. That was pretty good," I say back.

We stare at each other. Me and this girl. This girl I met by chance at the mall. By chance at the baseball diamond. By chance here at Gulliver's. Total fluke. Stroke of luck. Complete coincidence. I feel a shiver zigzag through my whole body. Viola looks back at me with those amber eyes, enveloping me in them like a bug in sap.

"Still. It must be hard," I say, glancing back at the television as she takes to nibbling her pizza again. "Being a superhero. Having to take on those guys all by yourself."

"I can't imagine," she says, chewing slowly.

"The cops can't be much help."

"No," she says. "At least, I doubt it."

"And people like us, we are basically powerless. Just innocent bystanders. What are we supposed to do?"

"Nothing," she says. "Just stay out of the way."

"Right. Exactly."

"Exactly."

"Better not to get involved."

"Better. Safer," she agrees.

"Except the city's not safe."

"No. I guess not," she says. "Not yet, anyway."

"All those guys in masks."

"You can't trust anyone these days."

There is a smack of plastic as the air-hockey puck behind me clatters into the goal. I look at all the other people around me, completely oblivious. Better sometimes not to know, I think.

"Viola," I start, but before I can say anything else, she puts up a finger, her eyes narrowing, looking over my shoulder. Gulliver's televisions are no longer streaming a bunch of music videos and news updates. Instead, every monitor has gone black.

When they spark back on, they all show the same thing. A man sitting in a high-back chair in an otherwise empty room, surrounded by plain, gray, windowless walls. He is dressed in a black uniform, military style, with polished silver buttons. To match his mask. Just one look, and I know he's trouble.

The music has stopped. Most of the video games quiet their clanging. One last Skee-Ball spirals into its hole. The man on the screen just sits there, like a teacher waiting to get every student's attention. Small crowds gather around each of the televisions hanging in the corners. I look over at Viola again, but her eyes are fixed on the screen like everyone else's.

The man in the mask is tall and well built. A sword sits across his lap—no telling if it's for decoration or if he actually knows how to use the thing. Both hands in black leather gloves. His eyes look black as well, behind the holes of the mask, and you can't even see his lips move as he talks, as if the voice comes from somewhere else or is only in your own head. His voice is both strange and familiar.

"Greetings, fine citizens of New Liberty," the masked man says. "Please excuse this interruption. Allow me to introduce myself. I am the Dictator." The man folds his hands together and sits back in his chair. "I come before you all today to inform you that your lives are about to change. In fact, at precisely six o'clock tomorrow evening, I will make an important televised announcement, one that concerns us all."

The man on the screen pauses, I'm not sure what for. For us to program our Tivos or set the alarms on our phones. Across from me, Viola is completely absorbed. Everyone in the joint is absorbed. There is something mesmerizing about this man, lounging casually in his chair with a sword in his lap, the suggestion of a threat, words pouring out from behind a frozen face as if they could come from anywhere. From anyone.

So this is the guy Tony and Mickey were talking about. I think about what Tony said. Guys like him, they're not like us. And they always have a plan.

"I have chosen you, the excellent people of New Liberty, to help me lead a revolution," the man calling himself the Dictator says. "A revolution that will soon spread from city to city, nation to nation. Together we will destroy the old world and build a new one, piece by piece, brick by brick. We will build it together. All of us, as one mind, body, and spirit, crushing all who stand in our way."

Piece by piece. Brick by brick.

"This is not a choice. This is destiny."

Build it together.

I feel a lump in my chest, pressing down, making it hard to breathe.

What exactly is he building?

The masked man holds up one gloved hand. "Until tomorrow, my loyal citizens. Adieu." Then the screen goes black, replaced an instant later with Nicki Minaj dressed like a pink-haired vampire. Viola continues to stare for a moment, then literally jumps in her seat, startled, madly fishing her buzzing phone out of her pocket. She checks the message and quickly stuffs it back.

"It's my friend," she says breathlessly. "She just canceled."

She looks at me. She's waiting for me to say something. To call her on it. Her long, thin fingers wrap around her cup. A musician's fingers, probably like her mother's. Viola. Second to the violin.

"I should probably go."

We both say it at the same time. She gives me an odd little smile. All around us, clusters of people are murmuring to each other excitedly. Viola starts to get up. Before I think better of it, I reach out and grab for her hand. It's dumb instinct, but I follow it. And I'm surprised that she gives it a little squeeze before letting go. She shows off her dimples, then snaps her fingers. "I almost forgot," she says, reaching back into her pocket and putting something small, smooth, and round into my hand. I open my fingers to find Honest Abe. The penny I picked up from the ground at the park.

"It's warm," I say.

"I've been holding on to it," she says. I go to give it back to her, but she pushes my hand away. "No, really. I want you to have it," she says. "For luck." Then she adds, almost as an afterthought, "Put it in your shoe."

"What? Why?"

"That's what makes it lucky," she insists. "An old superstition."

I reach down and tuck the penny inside my sneaker, wiggling it under my heel. There is another pause, bulging with expectation, and I can feel the question working its way to the surface, but before I can ask it, she turns for the door.

I let her get three steps from the exit before I stop her, calling out her name. There's so much I suddenly don't know, but one thing I'm almost certain of.

"I'll see you around," I say. It's not a question.

"I hope so," she says.

And then she goes.

And I let her. Because I have to get back. I have to talk to my father. Find out what, exactly, he's working on. I look back at the TV, where the local news has cut in with a special bulletin featuring the announcement we all just heard, the Dictator's face frozen on the screen. The man behind all the recent robberies and raids. Probably the whole reason the Comet bothered to land in New Liberty to begin with. At least the town finally knows who it is dealing with.

Even though I'm just starting to find out.

He's sitting at the table when I arrive, staring at the door, looking as if he's been waiting for hours, even though it is still the middle of the afternoon and he was the one who kicked me out to begin with. Maybe he spotted me from the street. Or maybe he's saddled me with a tracking device. I check my pockets for little black boxes and find only what's left of the cash.

"We have to talk," he says.

Funny. I was about to say the same thing. Except when parents say, "We have to talk," it usually means "I have to lecture you." But I'm not going to let that happen. I have way too much to say.

"You saw the announcement?"

"Yes. But that's not what we need to talk about," he replies softly, and for the first time I notice that his end of the table holds a stack of brochures, full color, neatly folded. The first one says COME EXPERIENCE THE WONDER OF MONTANA.

We don't know anyone who lives in Montana.

I walk up to the table, put my hands on the back of a chair. "Oh," I say. "All right. So you *don't* want to talk about the masked maniac who just came on television saying he had a plan for taking over the world. Fine. Let's talk about what you're working on downstairs that I'm not allowed to see."

"I don't want to talk about that either," he says, coolly adamant.

Of course not. I want to look at him, stare him down, but my eyes keep flitting back to those brochures, wondering what he has up his sleeve this time. "Fine. Then what do you want to talk about, *Dad*? Want to talk about the blue freak of nature who you keep hoping will just up and fly away or the fact that you came home this morning with doughnuts and hundred-dollar bills? Maybe you want to tell me what that phone call was all about, the one you made in the middle of the night? Or maybe you want to tell me why, if you are trying so hard to protect me, you shut me out? Because it feels like you are pushing me away. Because you are into something, aren't you? All this . . ." I spread my arms to indicate the house, the city, the universe, whatever. "All this . . . this hiding . . . it's really starting to get on my nerves. So—what? What is it that you so desperately need to talk to me about?"

I realize I'm almost shouting, but he had it coming. He brought it on himself.

Dad just sits there calmly.

"Wyoming," he says.

"What?" I'm sure I didn't hear him right.

"Or Winnipeg," he adds. He slides the pamphlets to the center of the table and fans them out like a travel agent. I see brochures for New Haven, Fort Worth, Cheyenne, Toledo. I shake my head.

"Winnipeg's in Canada," I tell him, my big heaping pile of frustration suddenly blanketed with confusion. "Nothing *happens* in Canada," I explain.

"Exactly," he says.

And then it dawns on me. He's not suggesting a vacation. He wants to leave.

Leave New Liberty. Abandon the house. The gangs and the graffiti. Zach and Tony and Indiana Jones and Mr. Hyung and the little place on the corner that sells the best pastrami sandwiches, and all the schools I never bothered to go to, and all the people I never got to know.

And the one I'm just starting to.

"Wait . . . you want to *move*?" I pull back the chair and take a seat on the edge.

"I don't think New Liberty is right for us anymore," he says. "It's not safe."

"Safe?" I choke. "When was it ever *safe*?" I mean, seriously. I could make him a list. Rattle off the string of Saturday-evening carjackings and brawls between street thugs. The kidnappings and purse snatchings and random acts that made for a New Liberty weekend. But of course that's not what he means.

"Michael, please don't make this any harder than it has to be. You're right. I should have realized sooner. I hoped maybe it would even itself out, but last night was too close, and today, and with everything else . . ."

He can't finish the sentence. And I see it finally. He's afraid. Even if he won't say it. His skin is white, his normally shrewd eyes saddled with concern. He's scared.

"When?" I ask.

"Tomorrow. Maybe the next day. Take what we need. Start fresh."

"And just leave the house?"

"More or less," he says.

I don't even want to know what that means, or I'm afraid that I already do and don't want to think about it. Dad wouldn't want to leave a trace of his work. We would leave nothing behind. "And how are we going to get there, to Winnipeg or wherever it is you think we're going? What do we do with all our stuff? We drive a *Civic*, Dad."

"We buy new stuff," he replies. "We will have money. Enough to build a new life."

Money. So all of a sudden money isn't the problem anymore. I think about what Zach said once, about Dad and me going on a crime spree. Retiring in Aruba. Or Venice. Or Wichita. I think about leaving Zach behind. And this house where I've spent the last four years. Where I learned to ride a bike and mix explosives, where I fell asleep each and every night listening to the sound of the freight trains rumbling under the South Street bridge. I can feel the penny settled beneath my heel.

"And what if I don't want to go?"

"It isn't up to you. I'm your father. It's my decision." I can see the spark return to his eyes now, summoning his courage, or maybe just losing his patience. This isn't easy for him either. New Liberty is his home even more than it is mine. The house and everything in it another of his boxes, built up over the years. He can't just pick up and leave it all behind.

"So now we have to run, because you've gotten in over your head and all your quotes and little inventions aren't enough to protect you anymore?"

"This isn't about me," Dad murmurs, fixing me with his eyes.

I point to myself. *"Me?"* I shout. "How is this suddenly *my* fault?"

"I didn't say it was your fault," he shoots back. "But you have to understand. I have responsibilities. I've made promises."

"To who?" I yell. I'm up from my chair now, fists on the table, leaning across from him, staring down at him. "To Tony? Or is it this Dictator? Because that's who you're working for, isn't it? That freak in a silver mask!"

"It doesn't matter who, it only matters why. I'm doing it for you. For us."

"I don't want you doing me any favors," I snap.

"It's not a favor. I told you, I have an obligation."

"To *who*?"

"It doesn't matter—"

"Who?" I shout.

"To your father, damn it!"

He slams the table, and the Toledo skyline slips over the edge and plummets to the floor. I watch it fall and just stare at it for a moment.

"I promised your father," Dad says again, slumping back, instantly deflated. "Right before he left you. Right before he left for good."

I suddenly feel dizzy, as if the whole floor is tilting like an amusement-park ride. And if it wasn't for the chair still behind me, I probably would join Toledo on the floor.

Turns out he was there.

The night that I was abandoned, left in the very back booth in my car seat with four hundred dollars cash and onion grease on my fingers. The night St. Mary's came to get me, Benjamin Edson was there. But not just there.

He was the one who left me.

I sit and stare out the window as he tells me about it. I sit and stare up at the shadowy sky, at the smattering of stars that are barely bright enough to pierce the haze of electric afterglow that settles like a fog. Light pollution. The reason you can't see much from here. The mask we've put on the sky to push back the darkness. Dad speaks in little more than a choked whisper as he tells me the story, spilling the one secret he's kept bottled up. As he talks, he reaches into his back pocket and pulls out the last picture, the one of "just a friend," setting it on the table between us. It shows two men leaning against each other, dressed in matching blue button-down shirts. The one I can tell instantly is a young Benjamin Edson, the professor fresh from his college years, face fuller, hair redder, freckled cheeks. The other is taller, stockier. Thick brown mane, rugged, goateed face. He looks slightly familiar. Like someone from an old commercial you watched too many times growing up. They both wear sunglasses.

"Your father's name was Renfred," he explains. "Though we just called him Renny, the few of us who really knew him. He had several others. Aliases. Kept a wallet full of fake IDs. He looked a lot like you. Same furrowed brow. Same questioning expression, never quite certain of anything. He had a great sense of humor, though. And that's not all you had in common."

Dad—Benjamin—presses two fingers to his skull and narrows his eyes.

Suggestive hypnosis. Mind control. Abracadabra.

He could do it too. My father. My real father. He was the one who passed down my gift.

"I acted surprised when you told me. I had to, of course. But you have to admit I took it in stride. Your father was admittedly a much more accomplished telepath. He was older. Had had more time to practice. He could convince a camel to part with its hump. He saved us quite a few times with his talent."

"He was your partner," I say.

The professor nods. "We started working together when we were young. Small-time robberies. We weren't interested in hurting anyone. Your father was a goo—" he starts to say, then stops, revises. "He was honorable, in his own way. Between my gadgets and his knack for getting people to see things his way, we made a formidable team. Probably could have made a real name for ourselves, but we weren't that ambitious. Renny was never interested in taking over the world. We would have been content taking only what we needed.

"But then he met your mother. Gina was her name. At least that's what she told us. She was beautiful, I have to admit, though I'm not the best judge. You've got her eyes, I'm afraid."

I think about my green eyes. Same color as the man sitting

across from me. For some reason I always thought that meant something. That maybe it linked us somehow. Guess I was wrong. About a lot of other things.

"Your mother had a history as well, had gotten her fingers dirty more than once. Our paths merged, and we became a trio. She had no powers, no talents to speak of. What she did have were connections—and an uncanny ability to get your father to do whatever she asked. She used him, Michael. Sought to abuse his power. She got us involved in more dangerous work. Kidnapping. Extortion. Said we needed to up the ante. Your father held her in check, or tried to, at least. We had a few scrapes. Mostly with the cops . . . sometimes worse. Barely escaped from Mr. Malleable once," he says, a little wistfully, "but that's a story for later. Suffice it to say we built up a sizable tab with the authorities, though they still didn't know who we were. And your mother still wasn't satisfied. She was selfish. Wanted it all. And she had cast such a spell on your father that I was sure she was using some mind control of her own. I guess love will do that to a person. Make you look past their faults."

"I guess," I murmur.

"Before long, our threesome became a foursome."

He waits for it to sink in. I point to myself.

Dad counts in his head. "Fourteen years and five days ago, in fact."

"Wait a minute," I say. "You're telling me . . ."

"That I know when your real birthday is?" Dad nods.

"We've celebrated it every year. You just didn't know it."

Five days ago. A special occasion. I think about the monkeys and the giraffes. The fatherless lizards. The cotton candy and ice cream. As close as I've ever come to having a birthday cake. No candles. Nothing to make a wish on. But it was something.

"You changed him, Michael. Renny didn't want to drag you into the life we'd fashioned for ourselves. It was a choice we made, but it wasn't one he felt he could impose upon you. So he tried to get out. Except your mother disagreed. She called him a coward. Said he was wasting a golden opportunity, squandering his talents. When he insisted on quitting, she took nearly all the money we had and disappeared."

I snatch the picture of the two of them—Benjamin and my father—from the table and stare at it. All this time I imagined my parents as total strangers. Not even real people. A couple of college kids too burdened by loans to raise a kid. A teenage mom dropped out of high school. They never had a real story. They were just extras, little more than props. And here they were: my two dads. Standing side by side.

"And you never saw her again?"

The professor shakes his head. "I don't know where she is, Michael, or if she's even still alive. All I know is that she left your father when you were still an infant. Who knows? Maybe she's even the one who turned him in."

"Turned him in?"

"You were only a few months old when the authorities caught up to him, arrest warrants for a whole host of crimes, most of them her idea. Except she had disappeared, using your father as a scapegoat to cover her tracks. The day the cops found him, he showed up on my doorstep with a diaper bag on his shoulder and a pistol in his belt. Said it was too dangerous for you. That they were after him. He made me promise, Michael. He made me promise to take care of you. But I couldn't. I was twenty-six years old. A criminal myself. What did I know about raising a child? My father built rockets. My grandfather built coffins. I come from a long line of men who knew how to package death, but none of them knew anything about life."

Dad's hands are shaking, even though he has them clasped together; his voice wavers with them.

"So you dumped me," I mutter, "at a *White Castle*?"

He frowns, guilty and disappointed. "It was close to the orphanage," he explains. "I needed you to find a better home than any I could provide. Say what you will about St. Mary's, they kept you safe. Safer than I could."

"Then why not just leave me there?"

"Because you didn't belong. You said that yourself. They couldn't appreciate what you were capable of. They were brothers and sisters, but they weren't family."

"Neither are you," I snap. Though as soon as it comes out, I regret it. I watch the words cut into him. He physically contracts. But I'm not going to take it back. Part of me wants him to hurt, for hiding it all this time. For not trusting me with the truth.

"Your father and I were very close," he whispers.

"So then what happened?"

"The night I took you, the police cornered him. I still don't know what possessed him to carry that gun. We never used them. He could have gone along with them. Waited for a moment when he was alone with one of them and performed his little trick. But they surrounded him and he panicked. Maybe he was reaching for it, maybe he wasn't. It didn't matter in the end. None of us are bulletproof."

As soon as he says it, he realizes his mistake. "Almost none of us."

I sit just there, motionless. I know I am supposed to feel something—ticked off, heartbroken, confused. But more than anything, I just feel empty all of a sudden, hollowed out, leaving me raw inside. I don't know how to respond.

"I always planned to come back for you, Michael. You have to believe me. I never let you out of my sight. I had boxes, cameras, hidden in every room of that school. I watched you grow up. I always knew what you were capable of."

I try to think back to St. Mary's. I was told every day by the sisters at St. Mary's that the Father was always watching over me. I never believed them.

"I made a promise," he says again. "I should have told you sooner. I thought that somehow I was protecting you. I didn't want you to grow up hating him. Or me. You had a name. An identity. I didn't want to take it away from you. Not until you were old enough to make one for yourself. I'm sorry."

He leans in, expectant. I know what he wants, but I don't

move. I don't say a word. I leave him there, hovering, holding his breath. The silence stretches to a minute, then three. Sitting there, in the kitchen above our lair, pamphlets for a half dozen new cities spread out over the table, I think about the last few years. About all the little black boxes we've built together and those nights spent on the couch with our shoulders pressed, propping each other up, inhaling popcorn and pretending we were part of something, something remarkable.

Those moments, they all seem diminished somehow. I can't put my finger on it. I never hated my real parents. I didn't know them enough to hate them. But I never loved them either.

Benjamin Edson was different. At least he was supposed to be.

I stand up slowly. It takes everything I have just to get my legs underneath me. What do you say to the man who promised to keep you safe and then abandoned you at a hamburger joint? I've been passed along from one father to the next to the next. At last I thought I'd settled down.

And now there's Winnipeg, and Wichita, and Cheyenne. Dad, Benjamin Edson, the professor looks at me desperately.

"It doesn't change anything," he insists. "We are still who we are. Tomorrow we can get back to normal."

And there it is. That word again.

"Do you really believe that?" I ask. I can see him floundering. He doesn't know. Not for certain. But he still looks me in the eyes; he gives me that much. I could tell him anything, and he would believe me.

Instead I push in my chair and head to the hallway, the picture of the two men still in my hand. I stand outside my room. He still sits at the table, watching me, like he has for the last fourteen years.

"Aren't you going to say something?" he asks.

I rest my hand on the doorknob. I think back to the first time we met.

"Do you want to see a magic trick?" I ask. The question obviously takes him by surprise, but I don't wait for an answer. I just go into my room and shut the door.

It takes a couple of hours, but I finally find it, in the archived issues of the *New Liberty Sentinel*. I guess at the dates based on what he told me, based on the day I was delivered into St. Mary's clutches. I scan through a thousand bulletins and articles. They don't give his real name, but it must be him. It's not much. A two-hundred-word blurb underneath a much bigger article lamenting the departure of the Vindicator, one of the last supers to watch over the city.

"Wanted criminal," it says, shot and killed in the early-morning hours by five of the NLPD's finest while reaching for a gun. A few aliases are given; none of them are Renfred or Renny. A list of outstanding warrants. No officers or civilians were injured in the confrontation. No sense that justice or injustice had been done. No mention of a three-month-old kid. Just another minor criminal leaving a chalk outline on the street. Not even worthy of a boldface headline.

And in other news, the New Liberty library reopens at its brand-new location on the city's north side.

There is no picture to go with the article, but I have one anyway. At least now I know where I come from. I know where my gift came from. I know *who* even if I'm still not entirely clear on *why*.

As I close out the window, I notice the banner headline running along the top of the current local news feed.

WHERE IS THE COMET? it says.

Next to it is a picture of the Dictator, pasted from his special televised announcement. I click on the picture and zoom in, letting the man's silver mask fill the screen. I can see myself in the reflection, and I don't look good at all.

THE LAST PIECE

So turns out I was wrong. It doesn't start with a favor.
It starts with a promise. I should know. I was raised
by nuns, and they are all about promises. The Bible's
full of them, though there they are called *covenants*, which
means *promises with pretty heavy consequence*s. If we are good, we
will be rewarded. If we aren't, we are sure to be punished. You
can chill in this great big verdant backyard of Mine, but eat one
of My apples and all bets are off.

And the big promise. The one everything hinges on. That
if we say sorry and mean it, we will be forgiven. Though to
be honest, that sounds more like an escape clause.

I didn't think Benjamin Edson even believed in promises.
They were too black-and-white for his shady gray world. He
taught me that everything was up for grabs, subject to discussion. There's nothing wishy-washy about a promise. Yet

he made one . . . to my father the coward. That's what my mother called him before *she* ran away.

I wonder if she ever promised him anything, except that she was never coming back.

I've decided: Courage is keeping your promises. Good or bad. Rich or poor. Sickness or health. Doesn't matter. You keep your promise or you risk losing everything you've ever believed in.

And then you're really in trouble.

I wake up early the next morning, finally ready to say something. I spent the whole night twisted in my covers, wrestling with my gut, trying to pin down what I was feeling. Was I more angry at my fake dad for hiding the truth, or at my real one for abandoning me? Or at my mother for leaving him? And what did it change? Would I still be here, doing the same things I'm doing now? Would my life be any different? Were there choices I would have made differently had I known? Would I still be on this same side of everything?

He's waiting for me at the kitchen table, just like before. The same place I left him. Winnipeg, New Haven, Fort Worth are still spread out, mapping the possibilities. Toledo still lies abandoned on the floor. It doesn't matter, of course. We could go anywhere. These are just pamphlets he picked up at random. A homeschooled teenage bank robber and his self-employed criminal-genius substitute father with no accounts, no IDs, no forwarding address; we are easily relocated. They have houses with basements everywhere. You can make boxes anywhere. Wednesday night can still be taco night in Wichita. It might be hard to find a supplier like Aziz, but it won't be hard to find customers for my father's wares. Somehow or another, they find you.

We could just pack up and run. Leave it all behind. Logistically, it wouldn't be that hard.

Except I'm not ready. I don't want to run.

That's what I have to tell him.

"Good morning," he mumbles. It's clear he hasn't slept. His eyes are rimmed purple. He's still wearing the same clothes as yesterday. He smells like sour milk. I think about the big promise. The covenant. I try to choke down the instant flush of anger I get just from seeing him there. It's reflex. I take a deep breath and begin my speech.

"Dad, listen. I'm not sure what exactly you're caught up in, but whatever it is, we can get through it."

This is my approach. Mend the bridge. Become a duo again. Then tell him what I want. Not *tell* him, tell him. Just tell him.

"I know," he says.

"But I can't leave. Not now. Not yet. There are still things I need to take care of."

"I know. I understand."

"So let me help you," I say. I think back to that day at St. Mary's. To our first conversation. To his question about good and evil and where, exactly, I stood on the matter. Even then he was feeling me out. At the time I thought I had answered incorrectly. Now I realize that I gave the only answer he could have believed. "You can't do it alone," I say, even though I'm not even sure what "it" is still. That's part of what I have to figure out.

"You're right," he answers with a weak smile.

I'm slightly stunned. It always surprises me a little when I'm right.

"Really?"

"Yes. I shouldn't have left you out, and I *could* use your help. I'm almost finished. There's just one last piece I need." He hands me a Post-it with a model number scrawled on it. I notice his hands are shaking, and he notices my noticing, quickly tucking them under his arms.

"And then we can stay?"

My father nods.

"And when I get back, you will tell me everything? You will show me what you've been working on and you will keep the basement . . . sorry, the *lair* . . . unlocked?"

He nods.

"And no more secrets?"

It's not meant to come out as a question, but seeing him sitting there, looking so fragile, as if he might suddenly splinter to pieces, I feel guilty. Everything he did, I know, he did to protect me. His intentions were good. Or maybe that's not quite the word.

"No more secrets," he says. "But you need to go now."

"All right then," I say, folding the Post-it and tucking it into my pocket with the picture from last night. "I'll go. But I'm serious. When I get back, that's it. You're telling me everything."

I head to the back door and slip my shoes on, feeling the lucky penny slide up against my big toe. The sky outside is a heavy gray. The clouds just sit there, pregnant, long overdue. It's as if the whole world is holding its breath.

"I mean it," I say, looking back at him. "As soon as I get back."

Benjamin Edson nods, and I start to close the door behind me.

"Michael," he says, stopping me. I turn. I'm guessing there is a quote coming. Gandhi or Schopenhauer or Oprah. Or maybe he's going to tell me he loves me. He does that sometimes.

"Be sure to look both ways," he says.

I guess I should have seen that one coming.

One more piece. I'm not even sure Aziz is open this early, but he sleeps in a loft above his shop, so if worse comes to worst, I'll just toss a rock at his window. I take my bike to get there faster, hoping to beat out the rain, but it's a lost cause. The smoke-gray clouds turn angry charcoal, and the sky growls once in warning. *Trust me,* it says, *you don't want to be out here much longer.*

Nor does anyone else, apparently. The streets are practically empty, save for the cops. That's all I see, perhaps because they appear in little swarms, like bees around a Dumpster. Probably they are out looking for the Dictator, trying to trace his signal, track him down. Or maybe they are just putting on a show. Either way, I have to take the long path, cutting down alleys and cross streets, doubling back, pausing to hide behind vans as patrol cars pass. I know they don't know me. I'm not wearing a silver mask or a blue one. But there are too many questions cops could ask that I don't have answers for. Questions about who I am, what my purpose is.

Even if I knew, I wouldn't tell them.

I pedal as fast as I can, but it's no use. The clouds unleash. It is pouring before I even get to Main Street. The kind of summer rain that teases you with a couple of big fat droplets before instantly unloading on you in sheets. I've got my hood up, but I still have to wipe off my face constantly as I skim across one growing puddle after another. The water splashes up and soaks through my new shoes into my socks. The shops are all closed. There is no traffic. Nobody is coming out today. Maybe they are camped out in front of their televisions already, waiting for six o'clock to roll around. Waiting for the revolution to start.

Or maybe they are all packing for Winnipeg.

I take two more detours to avoid the fuzz and circle around the back of Aziz's shop, parking my bike in the alley. I check the street to make sure it's clear, then run to his door. The sign says he's closed, but I knock anyway. It takes a minute, maybe more, before I see his face in the window. I'm soaked to the skin, staring up at the sky, looking for the sorry excuse for a sun.

Aziz opens and stands there, confused. He smells like licorice.

"Mr. Morn—what exactly are you doing standing out there in the rain like that?" He pulls me inside and I shake like a dog, wiping my eyes clear. "The store doesn't open for another hour," he continues. "Your father must be hard at work to send you out so early, especially on a day like this." I assume he means the rain. Or maybe Aziz, like all the others, is holing himself up as well. Nobody knows what to expect around here anymore. I reach into my back pocket and pull out the Post-it Dad gave me. It is sopping, like me, and it nearly tears in half as I try to unfold it. The rain has smeared the ink, but the numbers are still legible. *111000111.*

"It's the last part he needs to finish this big project of his," I say, handing it over, following the nodding Indian to the front of the store. I consider asking Aziz if he knows what it is my father is working on, but I doubt even he knows. It's all right. I can wait. I'll be home soon enough.

Aziz takes the paper, his brow creased in confusion. "One minute," he says, circling back around the counter. He types something into the computer. Then frowns. Types something. Frowns again.

"Where is your father now?" he asks sternly, his whole body rigid. I wonder what my dad could possibly have asked for that would cause Aziz to suddenly act this way, considering all the things he's helped us with in the past.

"He's at home. Why? Is there a problem?"

I wait for the head jiggle, *No sir, no problem at all,* but Aziz just continues to grimace at me, biting lip and V-shaped brow.

"Did he give you anything else? Say anything else?"

I shake my head. "Just that he's almost finished. Why? What's going on?" Now I'm worried. Cops on every street. A supervillain on the television. A masked hero who comes and goes as he pleases. But it takes Aziz's fallen face to push me over the edge.

The store owner doesn't say anything. Just walks to the front door and peers through the blanket of rain, making me even more nervous. Then he circles back around to his cash register, opening it and taking out all the money inside, tens, twenties, fifties. He doesn't even bother to count it. He puts on the jacket that was sitting on the stool behind him and zips it up, stuffing the huge wad of bills inside.

"Aziz," I say, "tell me what's going on!" But I can't catch his eyes to be any more persuasive, because he's ducked behind the counter. I hear him fiddling with something.

He pops back up with a gun in his hands.

A small black pistol that I've never seen before. It's not pointed at me. Not exactly. My hands shoot out in front of me, like I'm just going to swat the bullets away. As if.

"Jesus, Aziz! What the hell is *that* for?"

I consider diving behind one of the shelves, but before I can, Aziz just checks to make sure the gun is loaded, then stuffs it in the back of his pants *Lethal Weapon*–style: a five-foot-six, Hindi-speaking techno-geek with a Beretta in his belt.

"Come on," he says, motioning to me. "We are leaving. Now."

"What? Where?"

Aziz skirts around the corner and takes me by the hand, pulling me toward the storeroom, musty with dust and smelling of cardamom, past hundreds more metal shelves filled with cardboard boxes. Boxes and shelves. Kindred spirits, he and my father. Best of friends. The only other person Benjamin Edson really trusts, besides me. At least since my birth father died.

"One one one, zero zero zero, one one one," the storeowner mumbles, though he isn't looking at any of the boxes or heading down any of the aisles. He's not picking anything up. He seems flustered but determined.

"What is it?" I ask again. "What does my father want?"

"One one one, zero zero zero, one one one."

That's all he says. Over and over again. Shaking his head.

Then I realize that it's not a part number at all.

It's a code.

Aziz throws open the back door leading into the alley and looks around, keeping one hand behind him, resting on the butt of his pistol. The other hand still holds mine, a little too tightly. I've never been afraid of this man in my life. Of course I've never seen him with a gun before, either.

"Come on," he says.

But I stop him. Pull hard, wriggling my hand free.

Aziz knows about my power—the only person my father ever told. I guess we both got to tell somebody. He knows to look away, but he's distracted, nervous, and he doesn't do it in time. I manage to meet his eyes, only for a second, but it's just long enough to grab hold.

"Tell me what's going on," I say. It's a demand this time. I stay focused, mustering all my concentration, and I watch his pupils blow, black over brown. I've got him. I just need to hold on.

"The number," he says, just loud enough to be heard over the still-pounding rain that runs in ribbons along our cheeks. "It's a message. An SOS. It means I'm supposed to get you out of here."

"Out of here? You mean out of the city?"

Aziz nods. I can see he's trying to look away, but I don't let him. I am completely locked in.

"Because he's in trouble?"

Aziz nods.

"What kind of trouble, Aziz?"

"I don't know," he says finally, "but whatever it is, it's bad enough that he's afraid for your life."

Whatever my father is building, it's not for Tony. Tony would never threaten my father like that. I know exactly who it's for.

And this last favor was just another trick. My father's last-ditch effort to get me out of New Liberty before the ax came down.

"He loves you, Michael. He wants to keep you safe."

I keep my gaze fixed on Aziz, trying to stay focused, but it's difficult. It's happening again. The magic trick. He's trying to make me disappear. But I'm not a child anymore. I can make my own choices.

"Give me your gun," I say.

I can see the store owner's mouth twitch, his eyes straining, trying to look away. His whole body starts to shake.

"Aziz. Give me your gun . . . right . . . now."

His hand shakes as he reaches behind him, pulling the pistol free. I concentrate, my voice calm, measured. I know he doesn't want to, that he is resisting me with everything he's got, and that makes it all the more difficult. I can feel his mind wriggling, slipping free. In a moment I will lose him. Some minds are stronger than others, and I'm asking an awful lot of my father's friend.

I reach out and take the gun from his hands, prying his fingers loose and holding it in both of mine. I point it at his chest. My concentration finally breaks, and he shakes his head. I can't convince him of anything anymore. Not that way, at least.

"Go back in the store," I demand.

Aziz puts out both of his hands; it's just instinct, I guess. His glasses are streaked with rain. "Michael, please. I promised your father."

"Yeah, there's a lot of that going around," I say. "I'll tell him that you did your best, but that I wouldn't cooperate. Now get back in the store."

I wave the pistol around a little, the way I've always seen them do in movies. I've robbed banks before, but this is the first time I've ever held a gun. It's a lot heavier than I expected. But Aziz doesn't move. He doesn't look at my face either, just stares over my shoulder.

"You won't shoot me, Michael," he says, taking a step toward me. "I know you. I know your father. You would never kill anyone, either of you. You're not that type." He takes another step, close enough to reach out and grab the gun. I hope to god I know what I'm doing.

"You're right," I say.

I aim as carefully as I can and pull the trigger.

"Haramzada!"

I take a quick step back, startled by the sound of the gunshot and the sound of his cursing and the way the pistol kicked up out of my hands like a wild animal. The store owner stumbles backward, hopping on one foot, the other already up in both hands. He spins and falls through his own backdoor into his storeroom like a drunken ballerina, landing on his side, curling up and clutching his wounded foot. There is a hole in the front of his left shoe. I'm pretty sure I have shot one of his toes off.

"I am *so* sorry," I say over and over again as he continues to curse me in a language I don't know. I throw the gun in a nearby Dumpster and hop on my bike just as Aziz manages to struggle to one foot, the other one dangling limp behind him. As I pedal down the alley, I can hear him shouting at me to come back, whether to save me or choke me to death, I don't know. All I know is that I can't let him take me away. I can't leave my father behind.

I careen out into the street and nearly run into a parked police car, the door just starting to open, one black boot

209

stepping free. The cop undoubtedly heard the gunshot. Blowing a man's toe off is an arrestable offense. I veer sharp left, nearly colliding with a lamppost and a mailbox before righting myself, pedaling as fast as I can, brushing the wet hair from my eyes. I take two more quick turns, shooting down side streets with no sidewalks, brushing against parked cars, listening for sirens, looking behind me constantly for flashing lights or cussing, spitting, hopping-mad Indians.

But no one is following me. At least no one I can see. The rain is starting to let up, but it makes no difference. I am already soaked clear through. My jeans are so stiff, my legs can hardly pump. My lungs burn. But I don't care. I have to get home. Whatever it is, whatever he's into, he has to know that I'm in it with him. I'm not technically his son, I guess. But I'm still his minion.

I pull up a block away from the house, drop the bike, and pull my hood tighter. The house looks normal. Windows unbroken. Door shut. The Honda sitting in the driveway—he hasn't gone anywhere, at least not of his own accord. There are no strange cars on the street. No unmarked vans. No police anywhere that I can see. I head around to the back, peeking in the windows, past half-closed curtains, into empty rooms, walking on tiptoe as if it matters. I'm no ninja. I can't even beat the girl of my dreams at a kung fu video game. Part of me wishes I had kept Aziz's gun.

The back door is locked, but at least I have a key to this one. I open it slowly, waiting for a hand to come out of nowhere and grab me by the arm, drag me inside, throw a pillow-case over my head or stuff a gag in my mouth. Waiting for the smell of chloroform, which I've never smelled before but assume is something like Windex.

But there is no hand. No gag. No Windex. No anything. The place is deserted.

I close the door softly and look around. The lights are all on. The basement door is shut. There is no sign of scuffle or forced entry. No bullet holes. No smashed glass. I call out his name—Dad, not Benjamin. Once. Twice. Three times. Louder and louder. No answer. If there is someone here, they would have surely leaped out and clubbed me by now.

That's when I notice the note sitting on the table. A single sheet. Typed up in neat capital letters.

YOUR FATHER IS SAFE
HE NEEDS YOUR HELP
COME ALONE

That's it. I flip the paper over to find more on the back. An address: 17878 County Line Road. I have no idea where that is. Somewhere outside the city proper. On the outskirts of New Liberty.

I stand there with the paper trembling in my hand. He is safe, maybe. But for how long? Until six o'clock? I scour the room looking for something else, anything else. No over-turned chairs, no missing knives. Even the rolling pin is where it should be. I'm no detective, but it looks like Dad didn't even try to put up a fight. It's as if my father met whoever it was at the door and just walked away.

As if they had an agreement.

My eyes return to the basement door. I pull one of the long knives out of the wooden block by the sink for good measure. I have as much business wielding a knife as I do wielding a gun, but it makes me feel better to wrap my fingers around something.

Three slow steps. Turn the handle. The door is unlocked. I flip the switch to turn on the light and think back to the day Benjamin—my father—showed me his pictures, or most of them, anyway. A whole line of box makers. "You won't be able to turn back," he said. Can't say he didn't warn me.

I take the steps carefully, leaving soggy prints, too conscious of the squishing sound my feet make. The lair looks the same as always. The computers are still humming away. The kitten is still hanging on for dear life. The shelves are still full. The only thing different is that the usual piles of parts that litter the workbench are gone. In their place sits one of my father's little black boxes, all by itself.

The label has an arrow pointing to the green button. It says, simply, PRESS ME.

Alice in Wonderland, I think. Sucker for the classics.

It could be a trap, of course. Though the writing on the label looks like my father's, that is no guarantee. Somebody could have made him write it. I could press the button and instantly be blown to chunks or paralyzed with electric currents or struck blind . . . again. And yet I'm not sure what other choice I have. I suppose I could call the police. Normal people do that, I guess, in situations like this. I could report that my father—an illegal weapons and gadgets manufacturer with known ties to the city's most wanted criminals—has gone missing. That would go over well. Or I could go back to Aziz and beg him to help me, even though I obliterated his big toe and left him wallowing in pain.

Or I could just press the button.

I take a deep breath and follow my instincts. The box hums to life. Suddenly my father's face appears on the ceiling, projected from a tiny lens in the box's top. He's dressed in the same clothes as this morning, as yesterday. His voice falters as he talks into the camera.

"Michael, if you are watching this, then that means that things didn't go as planned. Either Aziz couldn't help you, or you wouldn't let him. It also means that you are still in danger, but this time you will have to save yourself. I want you to know I am sorry I dragged you into all this. Sorry that I couldn't look after you the way I intended. I thought I could handle it, thought it would be worth it, but I was wrong. I underestimated him. I realized too late. Which is why you need to go. As far and as fast as you can. Start a new life. A good life. The kind you deserve.

"But before you leave, be sure to empty the trash. And also, *right* before you leave, press the red button on this box. It's okay

213

this time. Just wait until you are ready to walk out the door."

The image of my father on the ceiling pauses, then looks me in the eyes.

"I love you, Son," it says.

The picture blinks out, and I let myself fall into the chair, his chair, the box in my lap. I press the green button again, though I know I didn't miss anything. I just want to see his face. But nothing happens. The white button doesn't do anything either. The message has been programmed to play only once.

I don't press the red button yet.

Instead I walk to the corner and push over the hollowed-out missile, letting the crumpled papers and empty chip bags spill out over the floor. I dig through wads of discarded notes and blueprints till I find what I'm looking for at the bottom.

Buried treasure. Ten bulging wads of hundred-dollar bills. A hundred thousand dollars at least, probably more. Down payment, I presume, for whatever it is he's been working on. It's a plane ticket to Canada and a new life once I'm there. With my power I'm sure I could make it. People will believe just about anything.

But I've got an even better use for the money.

I leave the cash on the floor and go back upstairs and pick up the phone. It takes six rings, but eventually he picks up. I can hear more shouting in the background, even more voices this time.

"Zach," I say, "it's Michael. Listen. Tell your boss I have a proposition for him."

Two minutes later I hang up and go back downstairs. I peel ten bills off one of the stacks, then wad the rest of it up as best I can and stuff it in a backpack I brought from the front closet. I think again about Aziz's pistol. I certainly won't need it now. There will be plenty of guns to go around.

Zach said to give him ten, buying me a little time. Changing into dry clothes slows my shivering but doesn't stop it entirely. I stuff the thousand bucks in my back pocket and slip into some dry socks. My new cross trainers are still wet, but they are the only decent running shoes I've got, and I want to be able to move quickly. I reach inside the one and pull out the penny.

Good luck, she said. I sure hope it starts working soon. I tuck it back in, then sling the backpack full of cash over my shoulder just as a car pulls into the driveway.

Zach is at the front door, dressed all in black, down to the leather jacket and steel-tipped boots, pure Hell's Angels with extra spikes. He frowns at me but doesn't say a word. I already gave him the recap. The SUV rumbles behind him, waiting. I hand him the bag.

"A hundred grand," I say. "Give or take."

"It's not about the money," he says, but he takes the backpack anyway. "Are you ready?"

"Almost," I tell him. "Keep the car running."

Back downstairs, I just stand by the workbench and take a deep breath, looking over the shelves of little black boxes. My father's life's work. I don't know what all of them do exactly—some of them were before my time—but several I had a hand in. I think about what the cops would say if they found them. The secret cache of a criminal mastermind. The arsenal of the insane. That's what an outsider would see. But I just see another in a long line of Edsons, looking for a way to make it in the world. I take the one with PRESS ME in my cold hands.

"Never press the red button." That's what he told me. The one time I did was by accident. It destroyed his workbench and took off two sets of eyebrows. Thankfully, my father shielded me with his body or I might have lost more than that. That was his way.

I look over at the poster. "Sorry, kitty," I say. Then I press it. The light glows like an ember, and the little box in my hand starts to hum, warming instantly, whatever chemical or electrical or nuclear reaction I've just triggered already under way.

And it's not the only one. Suddenly all the other boxes start to hum. A hundred singing, buzzing boxes, rattling around on their shelves. The whole room seems to fill with magnetic energy. Kinetic. Frenzied. I look around the room to see a hundred little red buttons glowing. Then my father's voice comes through the speaker of the box in my hand, telling me I have exactly two minutes to get out of the house.

I hurtle up the basement stairs as quickly as I can, through the door, and into the waiting SUV, to find myself sitting beside Blades again. He looks the same as last time, save for his left arm being in a sling. Mario still sits behind the wheel.

Zach is riding shotgun, the backpack in his lap. I want to ask about Indiana Jones but decide better of it, remembering what the Comet did to him, the hole he left in the warehouse wall. Instead I hand up the piece of paper with the address on the back and tell Mario that he should probably step on it. We've only got about a minute left.

We squeal out of the driveway and zoom down the street. Zach is watching the side mirror. I twist to look through the back window and wave good-bye to the house—my home—just as it explodes.

It's right out of a movie. One lone black SUV barreling down the country road out of town, kicking up dust, sun just starting to crawl its way from behind spent clouds. There is nobody around. Just miles of grain fields and wild grass. Then suddenly another black SUV zooms in from the right, cutting through the brush onto the road. Then another comes from the left. Lining up, one behind the other, falling into place.

Soon there is a convoy. A cavalcade of all black four by fours with silver rims and tinted glass, thundering down the highway. I look behind me and count at least ten. I knew we would be joined by the rest of the Romano clan, but the presence of all those trucks full of hired guns makes me even more nervous.

"I didn't know Tony had this many men," I say to Zach, who turns and smiles at me.

"He doesn't," Zach says back. Beside me, Blades expertly twirls one of his knives with his good hand.

YOUR FATHER IS SAFE
HE NEEDS YOUR HELP
COME ALONE

Alone. Or maybe with a squad of three dozen heavily armed criminals, some of them blessed with extraordinary abilities. I'm suddenly wondering if I haven't made a huge mistake, bringing Tony and whoever else he's got with him to the doorstep of the maniac who has kidnapped my father. Zach is bristling beside me, the tips of his thorns peeking through the back of his neck.

"Don't worry," he says. "You're family. The Romanos take care of their family."

The Romanos "take care" of a lot of things. I'm not sure this makes me feel any better. Still, it's not something I could do alone.

The herd rumbles along the dirt road. As we drive, Zach tells me the plan. It's not complicated. We break in, guns blazing. Find and rescue Dad. We hug. Then he and I have permission to leave while Tony and the rest have a talk with the Dictator.

"I might have questions for him, too," I say.

"It won't be that kind of talk," Zach tells me.

"Are you sure we are headed the right way?" Mario asks

from the driver's seat, tapping on his GPS. "This says we only got three more miles." I look out the window. The city of New Liberty lies behind us, its skyline obscured by haze. Only cornfields and farmhouses stretch ahead. I start to doubt myself. I always thought supervillains made their homes in dormant volcanoes or abandoned medieval castles. Not out in the boonies. Maybe there's a lake or something concealing an underwater fortress or a platform hovering up in the clouds, but all I see are hollow barns and abandoned tractors.

"Maybe it's a phony address," Blades says. "Or maybe it's a trap. Did you ever think of that?"

Of course I thought of that.

Mario taps his screen again. The nice lady on the GPS says we have arrived at our destination. He pulls to the side of the road. "There's nothing here," Mario says.

But there is something. A mailbox with the address on it in peeling black letters: 17878. "I guess this is it," I say, pointing to the farmhouse across the road, set back a ways. A rickety-looking wooden two-story with a wraparound porch and dark windows. A large tin-roofed barn sits off to one side.

"Screams supervillain hideout to me," Zach says.

We sit in the car for a couple of minutes, waiting for something, I don't know what. For a rocket to plunge into our side or a tank to explode out the front of the house or the noses of a dozen machine guns to nuzzle their way through the windows and open fire. But nothing happens. The place seems deserted. Finally Mario's cell rings, and he answers. He says a few *uh-huhs* and a *yes sir*, looking at me long enough to say the word *clueless*. Then hangs up. "Boss says we're going in."

Twelve SUVs pull up onto the farmhouse lawn, and at least thirty men step out. One of them is Tony Romano with Rudy the red-nosed giant by his side. I do my best to avoid eye contact with either of them. Tony's dressed for business as usual: black suit, blue tie. His gold wolf-head cane twirls beside him. He walks over and puts both beefy hands on my shoulders.

"Don't worry, kid. We'll get your dad back."

One of the other Romanos, who I recognize from the night at the warehouse, scans the farmhouse and shakes his head.

"I don't know, boss. I mean, how come we can't just let that big blue guy take care a this? You know, like, shine a light in the sky or somethin'? Show him where to go?"

"Because," Tony says, gazing over the house and the fields beyond, "this is our city. And we have to look out for our own." I hear Tony's name called and turn to see another familiar face emerging from a truck, looking even more scarecrow than before.

"What's he doing here?" I whisper.

"Tony invited him," Zach says. "They agreed to play nice, just for today. It's for a good cause."

Mickey Six Fingers saunters over to join us, flanked by a dozen men armed with everything from baseball bats to double-barreled shotguns. Mickey himself carries a machine gun that looks almost as big as he is, the kind with the ammunition that feeds into it like one of those ticket-munching machines. His belt of bullets is slung across his shoulder and clashes with his double-breasted white suit and bright red tie.

"That's a big gun," Zach whispers.

"Only takes one finger to pull the trigger," I reply. I think about the backpack full of cash still stashed in the car. I'm not sure I brought enough to go around.

Mickey and Tony nod to each other curtly. "You want to settle up now or at the end?" Tony says, scratching at his chin with the top of his cane. Mickey shrugs.

"Let's just get it over with."

Then Tony turns to the group of hit men, heavies, and goons circled around him. "Listen up, people," he booms. "Somewhere around here is a steel-eyed freak that calls himself the Dictator and probably a whole bunch of those goose-stepping, metal-faced rats at his heels. Lucky for us, today we are in the extermination business. This Dictator fellow, he plans to hijack the TV at six o'clock, which, as many of you know, is when *The Simpsons* comes on, so I'm afraid we are going to have to cancel his evening plans."

The Romanos laugh. The Maloneys don't. They have agreed to work together, but old habits die hard. Tony gives a signal, and three dozen guns are unholstered and pointed houseward. I look up at him, eyebrows raised, just a little nudge to say, *Don't forget why we're here.*

"And one more thing," Tony calls out. "Benjamin Edson is being held hostage somewhere here as well. Skinny. Orange beard. Probably dressed in a Hawaiian shirt." Tony looks at me for confirmation and I nod. "He's this kid's father and a close personal associate of mine, so he's not to be harmed, understood?" He looks across the divide at Mickey. "Got anything you want to add?"

Six Fingers scratches his head with his lonely digit, then turns to his men. "Let's do business," Mickey says, then motions for his men to move in. Tony does the same, and thirty armed henchmen suddenly swarm up the drive and around the house, SWAT-team style. Several of them bunch around the front door. I follow behind Tony and stand on the porch by the swing. There is a mat that looks to be at least thirty years old, imploring us to wipe our paws. A wind chime with only two tubes left clangs solemnly above us. I try to look through the windows, but they are crusted with filth on the outside and blocked by dark curtains from the inside. I guess there *could be* a supervillain in there somewhere. Tony stares at the door, takes a moment to adjust his tie, then raises his cane, as if he's going to knock.

Instead there is a flash of thunder and lightning, and Tony's cane kicks up in his hand as the front door explodes, shattering inward in splinters. The crime boss gives the top of his cane a twist, and I hear it reload with a click as his henchmen pour inside.

"It's *mostly* for show," he says, then squeezes himself through the hole he's made.

I wait out on the steps for a moment, holding my breath, listening. I expect to hear an instant eruption of gunfire.

Shouting and grunting and grappling and the *kabloom kerpow* of some epic confrontation. But there is only the sound of boots pounding on hardwood floors and doors being thrown open or kicked in as both Tony and Mickey's men inspect every room. After thirty seconds, I step inside.

The place looks like it hasn't been lived in for years. Sparsely furnished with moth-eaten chairs, a thick layer of dust on every surface. Cobwebs decorate every corner. It smells like a shoe closet. From the Dark Ages.

"Quaint," Zach says, running his finger along a grimy window ledge.

It doesn't take long for thirty armed men to search a five-bedroom house. Mickey finds a spot on the musty sofa and settles down, pillowing up a plume of dust, inspecting his nails, his machine gun straddling his lap. After only a matter of seconds, Rudy, whose nose is still a little purple, gives the all clear.

"Dere's nobody 'ere, boss," he says.

"You checked every room?" Tony says. "Maybe we should get a jackhammer and bust through the floors, just in case. Could be a secret passageway or something."

"Or maybe dis little rund led us on a wild goose chase," Rudy says, looking at me with a gap-toothed grin. He and I will never be best friends, I guess.

"He has to be here somewhere," I say, desperate now. "I was told to come here. We have to find him."

"There's still the barn," Mickey suggests from the couch.

Tony and Mickey each summon their gangs, and the whole

lot of us heads in that direction. The morning's rainstorm has left puddles scattered about like land mines, and I seem to be the only one interested in dodging them. The penny is nestled back under my heel now, and as I walk, I try to picture Viola sitting on the park bench beside me, asking me where it went, not quite believing in magic but seeming to want to. She would like it in Montana, I bet. The sky probably lights up like Independence Day every night out there. Tony puts up his hand, and we all stop outside the door.

The barn looks newer than the house. A large, boxy affair, windowless and sided with aluminum. A simple padlock holds the two giant doors shut, but another blast from Tony's cane makes short work of it. A man takes either side as everyone else raises whatever weapon they brought, ready to unleash a hailstorm at whoever's inside. I want to remind them all what my father looks like—but I keep my mouth shut. Beside me, Zach is already prickled, and I make it a point to take a few steps to the side.

Tony nods, and the doors creak open.

The barn is empty. No animals. No hay. No tools or equipment. Certainly no maniacal masked men in black jumpsuits. It even smells clean. Brand-new. We all step inside to look around, but there is absolutely nothing to see. There aren't even any windows. Just an empty barn with a giant metal floor. A giant, smooth metal floor and four smooth metal walls.

And a button.

"Barns don't usually have buttons, do they?" I ask Zach.

But before he can answer, the button lights up and everything starts to vibrate underneath us.

The floor starts to move. We are surrounded by the sound of metal grinding on metal. The sudden hum of electricity. The flip-flop in your stomach as your feet suddenly give out beneath you.

It's not a barn.

It's an elevator.

And we are going down.

The aluminum walls soon give way to reinforced steel, as the entire floor drops deeper into the earth. Everyone around me is suddenly tense, muscles jumping, eyes darting, wondering how far this thing goes and what we've stumbled into. At least it's not a volcano.

"Stay calm, fellas," Tony says, though his cane sits ready in his hands. The barn floor is big enough to hold three times our numbers, so everyone spreads out, forming a perimeter. I stay near the center, next to Zach, the rest of the Romano family in front of me, the Maloney posse behind. The elevator finally comes to a shuddering halt, and we find ourselves in the corner of a huge, cavernous room, at least ten times the size of the barn above us. A trio of white vans like the one from the jewelry store robbery sits silent behind us. Several open doorways veer off into branching tunnels leading to god knows where. Banks of computers and monitors are stationed throughout the room, and a giant screen sits on the far wall. It

225

shows a picture of the barn outside and the house surrounded by black SUVs. Smaller screens show other shots, from both inside and out, a huge surveillance system that I didn't even notice. Just like the little black boxes that were supposedly watching me at St. Mary's. The whole place reminds of my father's lair, except much more ambitious. And without the dangling kitty poster.

In front of the screens is a chair. And in the chair sits a man with his back to us, head gleaming from the glare of the overhead lights.

"You're here," the man says, his voice echoing off the steel walls. I recognize it instantly this time. They kept playing it over and over on the news, and his voice got stuck in my head, like a bouncy bad pop song. I look around, but there is no sign of my father.

We all step off the elevator and fan out, Tony's men still taking the lead, Tony himself standing directly in front of me. The man in the chair swivels around to face us, his face hidden behind his mask.

I know it's him. Only villains swivel around slow like that. Like they have all the time in the world.

The Dictator crosses one leg and leans back in his chair. "And you brought guests," he adds, in a voice both annoyed and amused. He is all alone. Not even armed. I guess the sword was just for show. I take a step past Tony and stand at the front of the army I've brought with me, bought with a wad of hundred-dollar bills, probably *this* man's hundred-dollar bills.

What goes around comes around. Circle of life and whatever. "Where's my father?"

It's not a question. I'm not near close enough to look the Dictator in the eyes, if I even could, but I don't need to be. There are at least a dozen of Tony's men behind me, armed with guns and knives and spikes and exploding canes. And another dozen of Mickey's men standing behind them.

From his chair, the Dictator snaps his wrist and checks his watch.

"If you mean the professor, he's just finishing up. It's not even noon yet. We still have hours."

I feel something huge step up beside me. "Give the kid back his dad," Tony Romano grunts. "Then you and I can talk about how quickly you can pack up your things and leave New Liberty forever. Or, if you don't like that," he adds, lifting his cane to his shoulder, "we can pack for you."

I hear one of Tony's men snort, but I don't even crack a smile. Something is definitely not right here. The Dictator is just sitting there. Where are all his men? He had the cameras. He knew we were here. Knew how many of us there were, that we were armed. And yet he just sits there, calm as a pond.

"And why would I do that?" the Dictator asks, still sounding amused.

"Because you've gone and got everything all out of whack, see? We were perfectly content till you came along," Tony says. "So I'm going to make you a deal. You shuffle all your tin-faced goons into those white vans of yours and drive off

227

into the sunset, and Mickey and I will forgo our plan to see how far we can cram that mask of yours down your throat."

The Dictator drums his fingers along the arm of his chair for a moment as if in thought. "I've got a better deal," he says.

He snaps his fingers, and there is a flurry of motion as suddenly all Mickey Maloney's goons turn their guns away from the man in the chair and onto Tony's men, a dozen barrels viciously stabbing the Romanos in the back, taking them completely by surprise.

I spin around, helpless as Mickey himself presses the tip of his oversized machine gun into the back of Tony's head. Another of Mickey's henchmen nudges Zach with the barrel of his shotgun and tells him to suck it up. Zach spits on the ground, but his spikes reluctantly retract. It takes only a matter of seconds. By the time I process what has happened, it has already happened.

We have us surrounded.

"Lose the magic wand, Tony," Mickey orders.

With a growl, Tony drops his cane, and the rest of his men follow suit, weapons clattering to the cold stone floor. Across the way, the Dictator covers the slit of his mouth with his gloved hand in mock surprise.

"You turd-faced little goon," Tony cusses over his shoulder through clenched teeth. "When I get out of here, I am going to take that special finger of yours and shove it so far up your—" But before he can finish the sentence, Mickey gives the head of the Romano family a sudden blow to the base of his skull. Tony flops to the floor like a three-hundred-pound sack of flour.

From his front-row seat, the Dictator applauds. "You see, Michael," he says, leaning in to address me, "it probably would have been better if you *had* come alone. But I couldn't count on it."

I hear Mickey and his men laughing behind me. My skin burns and I'm chewing a hole in my lower lip, but there is nothing I can do. I can't look a dozen men in the eyes all at once and convince them to do what I say. I don't have that kind of power. I glance over at Zach, hoping for some help, but he's on his knees with his hands on his head. The rest of Tony's men are quickly huddled together in a circle and forced to kneel as well. I'm the only one allowed to remain standing, though Mickey keeps his gun trained on me, pushing me forward so I am only twenty feet away from the man in the steel mask. He's wearing his uniform, just like in the broadcast. Dressed to impress.

"Sorry, kid," Mickey says. "It's just business. Nothing personal."

"So glad you see it that way," the Dictator replies, then brushes something under the arm of his chair. I know that gesture. I've robbed enough banks in my time to know where you keep a hidden alarm.

I spin around with all the rest to see the four doors leading into the underground chamber open and at least thirty armed men enter the room. They all wear the same black garb as the

Dictator. They all share his same taste in headgear, except, unlike their leader, they are armed with assault rifles. It happens so quickly that Mickey and his men are too stunned to respond. The faceless soldiers quickly surround the Maloney gang, now outnumbered almost three to one. Mickey's machine gun is wrested from the fingers he has left as all his other henchmen are quickly disarmed.

"What! What's going on?" he shouts. "We had a deal!"

"And now we don't," the Dictator replies coolly.

"But you said if I helped you, you would give me New Liberty. You said you would leave and it would be all mine!" Mickey "Six Fingers" is practically spitting.

"And I *will* leave," the Dictator purrs from his chair. "Probably go live in the White House. Or Versailles. But I'm afraid New Liberty will not be yours. It will belong to everyone."

Mickey lunges toward the Dictator, but a swift kick to the back of his legs brings him to his knees, shutting him up. The Dictator's men produce handcuffs, and soon they have both gangs shackled, the sound of metal teeth clicked tight together. Mickey shows the Dictator his reattached finger, but the villain laughs. "Take them to holding," he says, "And keep the two groups separate for now. If they don't cooperate, we will throw them in the same cell with a couple of wrenches and let them tear each other apart."

"You'll never get away with this," Tony says, his last word on the subject before the butt of a rifle bloodies his lip. It sounds strange, that turn of phrase, coming from him, but I guess he has as much right to use it as any. I throw Zach an imploring look as he and all the others are pushed, prodded, or dragged screaming and cursing away. One of the Dictator's guards comes and stands behind me, gun in hand, nestled into my ribs.

I could have been on a plane to Manitoba. Convinced the airport security that my frequent-shopper card from the Piggly Wiggly is sufficient ID. Instead I'm sixty feet underground in the middle of nowhere, the army I bought taken captive, my father still unseen. My house is a smoking cinder, my best friend is in handcuffs, and the girl I like seems like half a world away.

Which means I have almost nothing to lose.

"I want to see my father," I say, doing my best to sound defiant, though it's hard when you're surrounded by men with guns.

"And you will. Once he's finished. I'm certain he will work even harder now that you're here." The Dictator finally stands up and walks toward me. He's even taller than he looks on camera. He doesn't have the stooped-over expression of a mad scientist type. It's pretty clear he works out. He looks at me sideways, then reaches out and strokes my cheek with one gloved finger, and I jerk back. "What a waste, someone with your gift. Your father was an idiot."

"My father is a genius," I spit.

"Then we must not be thinking of the same man."

I pull away even farther. Having him suddenly so close to me, that mask and those eyes. The man just exudes creepiness. Guys like him, they're the reason kids can only play in their own backyards anymore. "So what now?" I say. "Are you going to kill me?"

The Dictator steps back and starts to laugh. A shrill, hollow screech that echoes in the cavernous room. "*Kill* you? Oh, heavens, no, Michael. I need you. *You're* the last piece."

Needs *me*? What is he talking about? He needs my father and whatever he's building. He needs his hollow-faced goons. He needs his huge underground lair and his cache of pirated weapons and his stash of stolen cash. He's got everything a supervillain could want. What does he need me for?

"But we have a few more hours still, so for now . . ." He snaps his fingers again, and I feel the henchman behind me move, but I'm not quick enough to do anything about it. The pain in the back of my skull is sharp and sudden. I feel every muscle give way as all the lights blink out.

I wake up to a herd of elephants stampeding behind my eyes, threatening to bust right through my corneas. My stomach rebounds off of my rib cage. There is throbbing in the back of my head, coursing down my neck, all the way down my spine to my very sore butt. I take a deep breath and try to focus.

I am sitting in a chair, steel, of course, in the same room as before—the huge one with the screens and the spiderweb of corridors, the getaway vans and the barn-turned-elevator. Most of the lights are off. Only the one directly above me shines down. Thick leather straps bind my wrists to the arm-rests, leaving just enough room to waggle my fingers. My feet are duct taped to the chair's legs. A rope is wound three times around my waist. I am anchored in place.

And all I can think is, They've got the wrong guy.

After all, this is the kind of mess superheroes always find themselves in. Except if I was a superhero, this would be nothing. I'd tear through these ropes like licorice. I strain once, just to be sure, but only succeed in hurting my wrists.

I close my eyes again and wait for the elephants to settle down.

It could be worse, I think. At least you are still alive. Just slow down and concentrate on getting free of these straps somehow. Then you can find your father and get the heck out of here.

I open my eyes again.

"Boo!"

Every muscle jerks. The whole chair nearly topples over. I'm sure my heart is about to burst. The metal face that was pressed right against my face retreats a bit.

"Sorry, did I scare you?" it says. "It's the mask, I know. Kind of the whole point, really. Fear breeds compliance. Plus it helps if you all look alike. Never know who's the real me. But you do, don't you?" The man reaches up with his gloved hand and removes his mask, revealing his face.

I've seen this face before.

"You," I whisper.

The Dictator smiles and bows. His gray eyes flash. I thought maybe I recognized the voice, too, that moment in Gulliver's when he came on TV. Now I realize why. I thought I had done enough that day at the zoo to make him forget about me, but I guess I was wrong.

"Not just me," the Dictator says, sweeping his arm to indicate the rest of the room. "All of us." The rest of the lights suddenly blink to life, and I see that we are far from alone. I count the guards first, a dozen of the Dictator's henchmen, buttoned to the collar and outfitted with rifles. A couple more are occupied at the banks of computers, clattering away at the keys, metal heads bobbing up and down.

And another man. Bound and gagged, strapped to a chair same as me. His frond-covered shirt is torn half open, and he's no longer wearing any shoes. He sits beside a workbench, much like the one back in his basement at home—before it blew up, at least. There is a bag sitting on top of the bench that I recognize. He doesn't appear to be hurt, though the guard standing beside him could change that in a heartbeat. I feel myself slump in relief, or as much as I can with all this rope twisted around me. When he sees me, my father tries to speak, but the bandanna around his mouth makes it impossible.

"Let him go!" I shout, bucking against the chair again, though all I manage to do is snap my head back and forth, sending sharper pains down my neck and goading the elephants on again.

The Dictator stands before me, mask in his hand, entertained by my gyrations, judging by his smile. I kind of expected him to be disfigured somehow. Scarred or burned or noseless. All

Phantom of the Opera melted flesh and whatnot, but the man is just as handsome and clean-cut as the first time I bumped into him.

"Of course . . . once our work is finished, I will let him go."

"Right," I fire back. "Why should I believe you?"

"Why shouldn't you? Am I really so different from him?" The Dictator points over at Dad. "Am I that much less trustworthy than the man who calls himself your father? Or the thug who calls himself your friend? Do you trust me less than Tony Romano? Is it because I wear a mask? At least *I've* never lied to you. You're still alive. So is your father. I haven't broken any promises."

"I still don't believe you."

"You're too young to know what to believe in, Michael. But don't worry. By the time we are finished, you will."

"Why don't you look me in the eye and tell me that?" I say. But the Dictator grins and continues to look over my shoulder, the way he has since the mask came off. He knows. Of course he knows.

"You'd like that, wouldn't you?" he says. "But you need to save your energy for what's coming."

"I'll never help you," I say, a little surprised at how easily the words come. I'm not sure I believe it—I'm strapped to a chair in the middle of an underground lair with a psychopath breathing down my neck and armed guards all around—it's not as if I've got a lot of leverage..

The Dictator sets his mask on the floor and slowly walks

around the chair so he's standing behind me. I can no longer see him, which totally freaks me out. I can see the look in my father's eyes, though, and that freaks me out even more.

Fingers suddenly weave into my hair, taking fistfuls and jerking my head backward. The pain sharpens as my head presses against the metal. I am staring at the Dictator's upside-down face, the man still looking past my chin, never in the eyes.

"Do you know what power is, Michael?"

I think about the crimes the Dictator has committed so far. Banks and jewelry stores. The hit on the police station to get more guns, probably to rob more banks and jewelry stores. Round and round it goes. It seems to all boil down to one thing in the end.

"Money?" I manage to choke out. I can feel my hair stretching at the roots, pain blazing across my scalp.

"*Pffffff,*" he says, rolling his eyes.

I didn't know supervillains said *pffffff*.

"Money is a fence," he scoffs, "nothing more. You of all people should know that. It keeps the rabble out. No, Michael. Real power is *control*. Of your life. Your surroundings. The people. The environment. Money is useful only to the extent that it can help you to establish that control." He releases me, and my head snaps forward again. I feel like my entire skull is on fire. The Dictator circles back around the chair, facing me again. "How much did you pay Tony to come along with you today? And all it took for Mickey to turn on him was the

236

promise of control. Money can build you a lair or buy you an army, but it doesn't guarantee dominance." The Dictator looks down on me again. His face is set in a snarl. The more he talks, the uglier he gets. I'm starting to prefer him with his mask on.

"Even with money, there is still so much that can't be dictated, Michael. So many *choices*, see? So much potential for rebellion."

I nod, even though I don't see. I just don't want him to jerk my head back again. I think my hair is throbbing.

"We aren't so different, you and I," he says. And somehow that hurts just as much as him jerking my head around. He gestures to the guards surrounding us. "I can be persuasive when I want to be. But my methods are much too complicated. Take Number Forty-Six here." The Dictator makes a motion, and one of those guards steps up next to him. He is massive—a slab of pure muscle barely captured in a black leather uniform. The cold steel machine gun hangs obediently by his side. The man's lips are pressed tight, snapped together like Legos.

"Do you know how hard it was to get him to obey the simplest of commands? First I had to kidnap him. Then I had to insert the microchip into his skull that connected him to my mind-control device, which cost millions of dollars, by the way, and requires constant maintenance. Then there's the hours upon hours of programming, brainwashing, memory restructuring—I could go on, but you get the idea.

It's exhausting. And I had to do it for each of them. One by one." He pushes a finger into the henchman's chest with each word—*one by one*. Number Forty-Six doesn't budge an inch. "But you . . . you make it so *simple*. Just a few magic words, and voilà, your wish is their command."

"It's not that easy," I croak. Though if I could ever get this maniac to look me in the eyes, I'd certainly give it a try. But he obviously knows more about me than I do about him.

"Don't try to fool me. I know what you are capable of."

I look over at Dad. Dad, who yelled at me for telling Zach about my power. Did he tell the Dictator about me before or after he was captured? Did they beat it out of him? Was that part of the payment? The Dictator follows my gaze and shakes his head. "Don't blame your father for everything," he says.

Dad lets his head drop. He's only bound to his chair by his wrists—but the man standing next to him is incentive enough to keep still. My father's not a fighter. At least I can say I've shot somebody. A real toe killer. Still, if he could somehow get free, wrestle the gun away from the guard . . .

The thought of my dad as an action hero almost makes me laugh.

"You see," the Dictator continues, "There is nothing extraordinary about me. Yes, I have a genius IQ, a burning passion, and a vision for a better world, but I don't have your gift. *My* father wasn't a telepath."

"How do you know about my father?" I say, snapping back to those gray eyes.

The Dictator kneels down and whispers in my ear. "She told me all about him. You too, son."

She. My mother. The woman I never knew. So she was the one. She had connections. She was ambitious. When she left us, there was no telling where she went.

Or who she would have run into.

"People like us," the Dictator explains, "our circles overlap. Your mother had a history. It didn't take much to get her to share."

"What did you do to her?" I ask, suddenly imagining the worst. The Dictator throws up his hands, pleading innocence.

"I didn't do anything. I let her follow me for a while and then set her loose, though at the rate she was going, I don't think she was bound to last much longer. Your mother was misguided, Michael. A lost and wandering soul. She didn't recognize the value of what she had in your father, what she had in you. But I do. In you I see a whole new world." The Dictator smiles, revealing a row of polished ivory too white to be real. Then he bends down to retrieve his mask, his loyal guard standing beside him.

This is my chance. I hiss to get Number Forty-Six's attention. He looks me in the eyes, just for a second, but that's all I need.

"Stop him!" I command, making the demand before I'm even sure I've got him fully under my control. "Shoot him! Free yourself!" It's a desperate move, I know, but I think . . . I can't be sure . . . but I think maybe I see something change in the henchman's face, a shift in the eyes or a twitch of the mouth. The hand that is holding the rifle trembles, fingers clench. He turns to the Dictator just as the man is standing up, his silver mask back in hand. The brainwashed soldier actually starts to raise his gun.

"Number Forty-Six!" the Dictator shouts.

The behemoth instantly lowers his rifle and snaps back to attention, eyes fixed back on the wall behind me. I feel all the air go out of the room.

"Number Forty-Six . . . shame on you," the Dictator chastises. "You were going to shoot me, weren't you?"

"No, sir," the guard barks.

The Dictator clicks his tongue. "Oh, I think you were. I'm not sure I can trust you, Number Forty-Six. I can't have people I don't trust in my organization. Trust is crucial. Isn't that right, Michael?"

A pocket of worms suddenly opens in my stomach. I can see where this is headed. I'm afraid to say anything that will make it worse. I'm afraid I already have.

"So how about you shoot yourself instead," the Dictator commands.

There is a pause—a glossy-eyed, unblinking pause. Then suddenly the guard raises his rifle and turns the barrel of it on himself, pressing the muzzle beneath his own chin. A man I don't even know, who may or may not have been a criminal when the Dictator found him and stuck a chip in his head, who might even have a family out there somewhere, wondering where he's been the past few weeks or months or years—this man is about to take his own life, just to prove a point.

The Dictator shakes his head. "No, no, no. Through the heart, please, Number Forty-Six. I don't want you to ruin the hardware implanted in your skull. It's terribly expensive and I can always reprogram it for another."

The barrel of the gun slips down until it is pointed at the man's chest. The Dictator nods appreciatively as Number Forty-Six reaches for the trigger.

"No, don't!" I shout.

The Dictator raises a hand, and the guard stops. I stare at them both in disbelief. "Tell him to put the gun down. Please."

Another motion from the Dictator, and Number Forty-Six shoulders his weapon, snapping back to attention. The Dictator turns back to me, smiling. Smug.

"You're a monster," I whisper. "You would have just shot one of your own guards. . . ."

"Of course not," the Dictator says. "I would have made one of my own guards shoot *himself*." He turns back to the henchman and points to one of the halls beside us. "Report to Number Seven for reprogramming," he orders.

The guard salutes briskly and then marches off toward one of the open doors without giving us so much as a second glance. The Dictator watches him go and then takes a step closer to me, bending over so I can smell his breath. Wintergreen.

"*That* is power," he whispers. He nods his head toward my father, still bound and gagged no more than thirty feet from me. The only one in the room who will look me in the eyes.

And I realize that he has me. That I'm completely trapped. If it was just me, I could resist. Maybe. I would try, at least. But he has me because he has both of us. And whatever he needs me to do, I will do it. For both of us.

The Dictator tucks his mask under his arm and checks his watch. His hair is a little mussed, and he smoothes it with one swipe. "Twenty minutes," he says. "Time to show you what your dad's been working so hard on."

I look down at my shoes. Looks like my luck's run out.

LIGHTS, CAMERA, AND
A WHOLE LOT OF ACTION

He tells me the plan. From start to finish.

That's what I never understood about people like him. Why they always have to let you in on all their dirty little secrets. I suppose in my case, it makes sense. Turns out I'm an integral part of the process. But it's not just that. I think he's actually looking for my approval. For me to tell him what a genius he is.

For brainwashing a small army of henchmen, using technology that my professor father invented years ago, before I was even an Edson by association.

For fashioning an elaborate underground lair in the middle of a cornfield.

For pirating a satellite so that he can broadcast his message to the living rooms of ordinary schmucks whenever he wants.

For hunting the two of us down and suckering Dad in with

the promise of millions for one little box—money that my father dreamed would take us far, far away.

For kidnapping Dad to make sure he got the job finished in time *and* to act as bait to lure me here once my father realized what was really going on. To use him as leverage against me. Because, as the Dictator makes abundantly clear, it is both of our lives at stake, and I will have to watch my father go first.

And now, finally, he has everything he needs, including the contraption on top of my head. He shows it to me before he straps it on. It doesn't look at all the same as it did the first time I tried it. Gone is the metal spaghetti strainer, replaced with a shimmering circlet that nestles perfectly on my head like a crown. Gone are the obnoxious wires and the suction cups, somehow now integrated into the thin metal strip itself. Of the original invention, only the box remains, polished to a gleaming obsidian, attached to the back of the apparatus, half hidden by my mop of hair. It's heavy; I have to strain to keep my chin up.

Turns out my father has been working on this particular box for a while. Long enough for someone like the Dictator to take notice. To germinate the seed of a master plan.

I don't think he's going to ask me to make him pee his pants.

"The neural amplifier," the Dictator coos as he secures it to my head. "It takes your natural mental ability and magnifies it, allowing it to project over miles and making you exponentially more convincing than you could ever be on your own. Your father thought he was building it for me, but as it turns out, *I* don't actually have any superpowers." The Dictator shrugs. "I'm not an extraordinary hiccup of nature. I'm just an ordinary guy with a zombie army, a hoard of cash, and a big dream. But *you* . . . you can convince just about anyone of anything—at least *now* you can."

As long as I look them in the eyes, I think, but that's what the camera is for. Two of the Dictator's goons are setting it up in front of us. Another is rigging spotlights. My five minutes of fame are being cued. The Dictator pulls up his chair and sits down next to me, and I suddenly feel like a guest on the most demented talk show in history.

"With the neural amplifier, your control will be instant, all consuming. It will harness your brainwaves, those magnificent mental manipulations of yours, and project them across the entire city. Of course, not everyone will be watching," the Dictator muses, "but if I can get even half of New Liberty pledging their allegiance, I can use them to . . . *persuade* the rest."

That's the plan. I do what I do. The box on the back of my head makes what I do a thousand times stronger, projecting it beyond the underground walls of this underground lair that is a lair and not just a converted basement. The camera ensures I have the city's attention, and before you know it, the Dictator gets an army.

I picture it: a mob half a million strong chanting his name, parading down the streets, breaking down doors and busting through windows, corralling the uninitiated. Banners and torches. Burned-out cars. His metal face flying on flags draped from rooftops. A revolution, he called it, though in my mind it looks more like an apocalypse.

"And this is only the beginning," he continues with eager eyes and smacking lips. "A test run, really. After this we can make modifications. Increase the amplification. Start broadcasting on a much wider scale. Which reminds me," he adds, leaning over to me, "how is your Chinese?" Before I can answer, he shakes his head. "We can worry about that later. Speaking of which . . ." The corners of his mouth twitch. "You still need your lines."

The Dictator snaps his fingers again, and another of his masked henchmen comes shambling up with oversize index cards in his hands. This is scripted television.

"Let's do a dry run, shall we?"

I look at the cards. It's a sizeable stack. A big speech. I can't give it, but I can't *not* give it. I can't hand this maniac sitting beside me a gigantic army of brainwashed bystanders. But if I don't, I don't know what the Dictator will do to me. Or to Dad.

All I know is that this completely psycho steel-faced freak is wrong. So wrong. Power is recognizing that you have a choice.

The trouble is making it.

"Don't worry about tone," the Dictator instructs. "Let's just make sure it flows."

I look at the first card. My throat is raw. My voice is all

246

croaks and squeaks. I think about Zach making rat faces at me. I hope he's all right.

The Dictator shakes his head. "Enunciate," he says.

"'The Dictator is your ruler,'" I say, trying again, reading off the card, hearing the tremor in my own voice. "'You will do whatever he commands.'" There is more. So much more. At least twenty cards' worth. Orders to gather cash and valuables. To arm themselves with whatever weapons they can find. To apprehend anyone who hasn't sworn allegiance to the Dictator, with extreme force if necessary—a line I stumble over twice. I look over at Dad again. I want to tell him I'm sorry, but I think he understands. "'All hail the Dictator,'" I finish.

The villain rolls his eyes. "Really? That's the best you can do? We are building an empire here. Let's have a *little* fervor."

He stands up and walks over to the video monitors, checking the outer perimeter of the barn and farmhouse one last time. SUVs sit idle in empty fields. The sky is clear, a washed-out uniform blue. Streakless. "Six minutes till showtime," he says, walking back to me and sitting down again. "Are you comfortable? Do you want some water or something? Number Seventeen could get you a straw—"

"Why are you doing this?" I say, interrupting. It's the one part of his plan he hasn't revealed. Not that I really care. Only that maybe if I knew why, I could come up with something, some reason to call it off, something I could say that would at least give him pause, buy me some more time. I've already tried convincing him it won't work, that I'm not powerful

247

enough, but he insists Dad's contraption will make up for that.

"Let me ask *you* a question, Michael. What do you believe in?"

I flash back to that first conversation at St. Mary's. My father asking me about God and me looking at him like he was insane. I stare now at the Dictator, who *is* insane. He takes my silence as an answer.

"Exactly." He sighs. "Nobody really *believes* in anything anymore. They say they do, but it's all for show. We are a nation of fence-sitters and teeter-totterers. Gone are the good old days when you could control men's hearts and minds through a fiery speech and some well-placed propaganda. Now we're too self-absorbed, caught up in our screens and pads, closed off from any real engagement with the world. I'm going to give everyone something to believe in again. Something to fight for. Something to *die* for. It's actually quite admirable, if you stop to think about it."

Admirable. Using a thirteen—hold up, *fourteen*-year-old boy to control the minds of hundreds of thousands of people, making them your slaves so that you can begin your takeover of the world. There are so many better words to describe that.

"You're not *giving* them anything," I snap back. "You're taking away the only thing that makes them human."

I get a flash of Dad standing at the top of the stairs, pictures in one hand, key in the other. You don't get to choose the box that's handed to you, but you at least choose whether you open it or not.

"It's not right," I add, though I realize how ridiculous that probably sounds coming from me.

"Who is to say that the world I create will not be better than the one we have now?" the Dictator says. "This isn't about good or evil. It's about winners and losers, and the winners get to be right."

"Except you haven't won yet," I say spitefully, glancing toward the ceiling.

He follows my upward glance, bemused.

"Oh," he says. "*Him*. I know. He's been on my mind as well. But it's too late even for him. He hasn't found me yet, and there's nothing to lead him here now."

I wonder if we are thinking about the same guy.

The Dictator continues. "In less than ten minutes, the city's savior will have his hands full trying to stop a mob marching under my control: ordinary citizens he can't hurt but will still have to find some way to stop. Or better yet," he adds, suddenly inspired, "maybe *he* will be watching too. Maybe you can convince the Comet to join the cause and I'll get my very own superhero to play with. Wouldn't *that* be something?"

Could that really happen? I have no idea how strong the device my father built will make me. Could I really convince the Comet to switch sides? He'd have to be watching, of course.

But if he *is* watching . . .

I start to improvise a plan.

"Two minutes," the guard standing by the camera says.

The Dictator dons his mask again, giving me a reprieve from his smug, irritating little grin, then presses another button on his chair. The giant screen in front of us is suddenly filled with his steely face. "Keep the camera on me until I give the signal," he says. "I don't want our comrade straying from his script.

"And you," he says, pointing at the guard standing next to my father. "If the boy so much as gets one word out of place, shoot the professor. Somewhere nonfatal but excruciatingly painful."

The masked henchman beside Dad nods. My father mumbles something behind his gag.

I need a better plan.

"I have to remember not to look at the screen while you're talking," the Dictator whispers in my ear. "I don't want to brainwash myself."

"One minute," the mindless henchman operating the camera says.

The spotlights come on, bathing us in a fluorescent pool. Beside me, the Dictator shifts uncomfortably in his seat, then reaches up and adjusts his mask.

"How do I look?" he asks.

"Terrifying," I mumble.

"Excellent," he says.

The henchman behind the camera counts down from five. The red light on the camera clicks on, and I realize that millions of people could be watching us right now. They won't be able to resist. It's human nature to gaze upon spectacle, be it triumph or tragedy, car wrecks, home runs, kidnappings, celebrity weddings, terrorist bombings, battles in the night sky. Besides, he promised them a better world. He has their undivided attention.

I have their undivided attention.

"Greetings, citizens of New Liberty. Thank you for joining me on this historic evening. Tonight we embark on a new journey: to throw off the shackles of apathy that enslave us, and to forge a new civilization. One uniformly joined in common cause. I promise that I will lead us all to a glory that past empires have never known. But I will require your unconditional allegiance. And so, to that end, I would like you to listen very carefully to the following message."

That's my cue.

On the giant screen before me, I see the Dictator reach behind me to the little black box at the back of my skull. Three buttons: green, white, and red, just like Christmas. And I think about what it would be like if he pressed the wrong one and my head simply exploded.

There is a moment, before you open it, when a box can hold almost anything. It's the best and worst moment, full of anticipation and possibility. The problem with me is I always open it. I can't resist.

I steal one last glance at the man who has raised me for the past four years, then look at the cue card beside the camera.

I've made my choice.

The Dictator presses the little green button.

I know exactly what I'm going to say.

I open my mouth to speak, but nothing comes out. Because I'm suddenly not there anymore. The camera is pointed right at me, but I have disappeared. There is nothing but darkness. The giant screen in front of us has instantly zapped to black.

In fact, all the video screens have gone dark. I look over at the video camera itself. The red light has vanished too. We are no longer live. The Dictator's would-be army isn't watching us anymore. They've probably gone back to their regularly scheduled programming.

The Dictator pounds his fist on the chair, furious.

"What's going on? What happened to the cameras? Was there a power surge? Number Seventeen?"

The henchman working the camera fidgets with the buttons. Another types frantically at a keyboard by the giant screen. "Everything else is up and running, sir. It's the camera systems," one of the henchmen says in his monotone. "They've all just stopped working."

The camera systems. All shut down.

My professor can fit just about anything into one of those little black boxes. I glance over at Dad. I think he is smiling, or at least is trying to, behind that gag of his. There is no neural amplifier. Or if there is, my father didn't hand it over. Or he tinkered with it to make it do this instead. On my head is another version of the Scrambler, scourge of bank security systems everywhere. It's the oldest magic trick in the book. The false bottom. The old switcheroo. Marvelo would be proud.

The Dictator turns on me, voice quivering, livid with rage. I can't see his face behind the mask, but for once I wish I could. "You," he hisses. "You . . . and him . . . What have you done?" I know he's not looking at me. Not in the eyes, anyway. I know it won't work, but I don't care. I'm going to say it regardless.

"Go piss yourself."

The Dictator reaches back with his one gloved fist, and I realize I'm about to have my nose broken. At least I can see it coming. Unlike Rudy. I close my eyes and then feel the whole world shake.

An explosion sends everyone not strapped to a chair stumbling. It comes from far away, but it's sizeable enough to resonate clear through the walls. A dozen guns are suddenly at the ready.

"What was that?" the Dictator yells, forgetting me for the moment and holding himself against his chair, spinning and checking all the doors. I can hear shouting coming from one of the hallways. The man who would create an empire is suddenly all finger points and orders. "You—get those cameras back up and running. You—take three men and go to the surface. Check all three entrances, put guards at the staircases. And get at least fifteen more men down in this room now! And you," he says, pointing to the guard standing beside my father. "Start removing fingers from that man until he tells you what he has done with my amplifier!"

The henchman guarding my father shoulders his rifle, rolls up his sleeves, and pulls out a wicked-looking knife, lined with jagged teeth. I can't help it—I think about Mickey Maloney. Leave the middle one, I think, so he can let everyone know just how he feels.

But the guard doesn't even get to the pinky.

It comes out of nowhere, just like the night outside the warehouse—a black ribbon, darting out of the shadows like a whip snake. The cord wraps around the goon's legs and drops him to the ground, chin first, hard enough to send his knife skittering from his grip and across the floor. I wince a little, watching. I know how much that hurts.

I catch a glimpse of gold stripes on a black body, the reflection off a pair of infrared goggles, those big red bug eyes, the shadow dancing along the wall. The sidekick nobody's heard of. The one who nobody else seems to know about. Except me.

I know.

The shadow moves quickly to my father and, in flash of steel that I just catch a glint of, frees his hands. He stands on wavering legs, leaning against the workbench for support. The five guards who are still in the main chamber immediately train their rifles on the two of them. My father's flaming caterpillar eyebrows crowd together in a look of defiance, but the Comet's partner steps in front of him, shielding him. I glance at the ceiling again, waiting, breathless. Totally figures. The one time I *want* him to show.

The guns stand ready. The Dictator growls beside me, looking back and forth from me to my father. "Oh, well," he says, throwing his hands up. "I have the boy. I can always find another inventor. Kill them."

I scream. In a blur my father's rescuer manages to kick over the workbench and push him behind it, collapsing on top of him as the masked men open fire. Bullets start to turn the bench to kindling. I strain at my restraints, pulling with every muscle. Then I see one of the Dictator's henchmen go down, struck by a shot to the leg. Then another. There is gunfire coming from somewhere else.

I twist my head as far as I can, with that stupid crown still wrapped around it, and see a dozen men charging through one set of big metal doors. Tony leads the pack, cane in hand, belching fire. Zach follows close behind, all thorns and holding a metal pipe for good measure. I twist all the way to the other side to see the men the Dictator had called for running through the opposite door. Fifteen metal faces and fifteen machine guns. Two waves cresting through the corridors, about to crash.

And me smack-dab in the middle. Again.

"Don't shoot the boy!" the Dictator screams as the room erupts. He reaches down to the injured guard on the floor beside him and pulls a knife from a boot, quickly slicing through the tape on my legs, muttering curses. I feel every muscle tense as my legs are freed. I clench my teeth and take a deep breath as he cuts the rope around my waist. I've been waiting for this.

When he saws through the leather band binding my left hand, I take my shot. I'm not a southpaw, and to be perfectly honest, I've never really been in a fight. Never had the need. But I am ticked. I just want to hit him. Hard.

"Geeeyyyaaaahhhh!"

It's a perfect punch. Nestled in that sweet pocket right beneath his eye. Unfortunately, the steel of his mask is much harder than my fist. My soft fingers smash into the unforgiving metal, and I can almost hear them break, knuckles aflame. I quickly stuff them in my mouth to try and suck away the pain.

The Dictator just cocks his head to the side as if to say "Really?" Then he ducks and maneuvers behind me, wrapping an arm around my neck, cutting off the air. I start to struggle but soon find the tip of the knife tickling my chin.

"Time to go," he says. I start to say something in protest, something that would get me into loads of trouble at St. Mary's, but the ten-inch blade pressed against my Adam's apple discourages any response. The whole room is quickly filled with smoke and bodies. Bodies flying, firing, tackling, punching, kicking, biting. I don't know where they all came from. More masked men pour into the room. Numbers Forty through Fifty. Or Sixty. An endless supply, cranked out by some henchman-making machine, I suppose. Another knife sails past us, and I look to see Blades crouched behind a bank of computers, emptying his jacket with his one good arm. Tony's giant frame looms large in one corner, like a bald-headed dragon, cane outstretched, wreathed in smoke. In the confusion I can't seem to find my father. Or his rescuer. I look toward the bench, no more than shards and splinters, but they aren't there anymore. I struggle as much as I can against the man who holds me, but every move causes the point of the knife to dig even deeper into my skin. The Dictator drags me backward, toward the only doorway that doesn't seem to be vomiting men with guns.

We make it all the way to the corridor before the whole room finally turns blue.

The sound of gunfire is nothing compared to the sonic boom of his arrival. I'm not sure how he got there. All I know is he is standing right in front of us, blocking the entry, so close I could touch him if I wanted to. I look into his eyes, wreathed by wrinkled spandex. I didn't think I would ever be so happy to see a superhero in all my life.

"Unggh," the Dictator groans, as if he's just stepped in something rank. I think I see the suggestion of a smile cross the Comet's face. The Super looks over at me.

"It's your lucky day," he says in that grizzly voice of his.

That's one way to look at it, I guess.

I feel the knife go slack, only for an instant, but it is just enough. I drive my elbow as hard as I can into the Dictator's gut, causing both of us to stumble backward; then I duck out of the way just as the Comet's fist flies.

I watch from the ground. It's a direct hit, a jackhammer, a pile driver, just like mine, right in the chin. Except this time the Dictator flies six feet, landing in a heap and skidding along the stone floor. When he raises his head, I can actually see the imprint of the Comet's fist emblazoned in the villain's steel mask, can actually count the knuckle marks pressed into the metal. Underneath, I'm certain the man's jaw is shattered.

"Of course, when *you* do it," I say.

Suddenly the entire room seems alerted to the Comet's presence. It's as if the whole melee is put on pause. The gunfire stops. All eyes turn to us. Then both the Dictator's zombies and Tony's men turn their weapons toward the superhero. The new threat, bigger than any of the rest of them.

Only the Dictator's men open fire, though. Tony's know better. They've been through this once already. I spot Zach in the chaos, fleeing through one of the tunnels, his boss huffing it right behind him.

The Comet stands in front of me, deflecting bullets from the henchmen's rifles with ease, shielding me from the attack. Then, in a flash, he is on the offensive, darting into the swarm of brainwashed thugs, bending steel and breaking bones, delivering punch after punch, sending the Dictator's numbered brutes airborne, piling them up behind him unconscious. I get the same feeling as before. At once terrified and mesmerized and impressed.

I feel a pair of hands under my shoulders, pulling me up. They are hands I recognize. Slightly hairy with nimble, blistered fingers. I look up at my father. Beside him is the Comet's sidekick.

"Come on," the husky voice says from behind the mask. "We have to get you two out of here." My father grabs my hand and drags me along as we follow the black-and-gold suit down the hall. Dad has the bag from the workbench slung over his shoulder, his shirt flapping open, his feet bare. He is grinning like an idiot.

As I look back into the central chamber, the last thing I see is the Comet standing in the middle of the room, lifting the Dictator up off the ground by his mashed metal face, the hero's free hand curled into a hammer, a five-fingered bomb, ready to explode.

A grunt startles me, and I turn to see a numbered henchman materializing out of one of the rooms along the tunnel, finger on the trigger of his gun. But a swift kick from the black-suited sidekick sends the weapon flying, and another planted square between the henchman's thighs drops him to his knees.

"Wow," I say, breathless. "You are totally awesome."

It's a stupid thing to say, I know, but it's the best I can come up with under the circumstances. The figure shrugs, then points down the hall. I can see a ladder at the end of it, only a dozen feet away.

"Climb!" the mask growls. My father doesn't wait, running to the end of the corridor, practically leaping up the rungs, bag slapping against his side. Down the hall the other way, you can still hear gunfire and shouting. I look up to see my father disappearing into the darkness above me, bare feet slipping on the slick steel, scrambling to the surface, not looking back.

I know I should hurry. Be right on his heels. There are still all of Tony's men, probably looking for their own way out. And Mickey's men, who must still be trapped in here somewhere. And no telling how many brainwashed soldiers the Dictator has left. Not to mention the Comet. I start to climb, but three rungs up, I freeze and look back.

I just have to know. After all, motive is everything.

"Why are you helping us?" I ask.

The Comet's sidekick glances over one shoulder, then back up at me. I can't see anything beyond the mask.

"Because," she growls, "I know which side you're on."

Then she turns and disappears down the hall, leaving me hanging.

My father reaches the hatch and pushes it open, and we crawl up and out into the middle of the cornfield next to the barn. The farmhouse sits empty behind us, the line of black SUVs surrounding it. I catch a large figure looming over me out of the corner of my eye and turn to karate chop it or something, but it's just a scarecrow, a real one, half of its stuffing spilling from a wound in its chest. Dad closes the hatch, sealing off the sound of the scuffle below. I wonder if the Dictator's men have all been subdued. If Tony's men have found a way out. If Zach is all right. Wonder who is winning.

I feel a pair of hairy arms squeeze around me and look up at the man who saved me once.

"I told you not to come," he says, clutching me so tight that

I can count his heartbeats against my cheek.

"You told me to do something. So I did."

"Listen, Michael," he starts to say, but I interrupt. If this is about my other father or my mother or his lies or Winnipeg or anything *but* getting the heck out of here, it will have to wait.

"This *really* isn't the time," I tell him.

I pull him by his torn Hawaiian shirt, and we smash our way through cornstalks toward the house. I just hope one of those SUVs still has the keys in it and that my father is in good enough shape to drive. We've made it to the back porch when my father points to the road. We are too late.

The cavalry has arrived.

At least twenty of them, hornets burst from their hive. Flashing blues and reds coming from both directions. I think I can even hear a helicopter in the distance. I scan the clouds, then look back at the barn. Any moment those doors will open, and out will come Tony's men. Or Mickey's men. Or the Comet himself. A superhero rock and a whole mess of hard-place cops. We will be cuffed and taken in for sure.

Dad turns to me, a determined look on his face. "Do you have any of that money left?"

"A few hundred dollars."

"Do you know how to drive?"

"What?"

"You know," he says. "Put the car in gear. Press on the gas. Try not to hit anything." He starts running for one of the SUVs. I follow behind, yelling at him.

"What are you talking about?"

"Head back to the city," he shouts. "Cut through the fields. Ditch the car in the first parking lot you find. Stay in the shadows. Don't draw attention to yourself. Then, first chance you get, take a train."

"Take a train? Take a train where? What are you saying?"

He opens the door to one of the cars and fumbles around on the floor, finding the keys. He pushes me inside. I push back, but he's still stronger than I am. Even after everything that has happened. This was the summer I was going to start working out.

"Somewhere safe," he says. He actually reaches over and buckles my seat belt for me.

"You're insane. Get in the freakin' car, Dad. I'm not driving this thing. And I'm not going to leave without you! Haven't you figured that out by now?"

He reaches over again and turns the key. The SUV purrs to life. The sirens are getting louder.

"It's all right," he says. "I'll be all right now. You came back for me. And I'm glad. But now you have to go. Here. Take this." He fishes in the bag still slung on his shoulder and pulls out a box. This one is smaller than most of the others, about two inches square. Small enough to cup in the palm of his hand. There are only two buttons on it. Green and yellow. The label says FOR MICHAEL.

"We still have so much to talk about, I know," he says. Then he looks me in the eye. And I want to tell him to stop being such an idiot and get in the stupid car. Not ask him. Just tell

262

him. But I don't. Because I promised I wouldn't. Just like he promised he would look after me. You have to draw the line somewhere.

Then, before I can even say good-bye, he slams the door, turns, and runs toward the approaching police cars, pulling out another box from his bag and pressing the red button before pitching it overhead toward the convoy. It hits the ground, rolls several feet, and then explodes with a force much bigger than its size could ever suggest, creating a crater that the first patrol car unwittingly rolls into. He reaches into his bag and pulls out three more boxes, activating their self-destruct and rolling them toward the oncoming cruisers. He isn't trying to hurt anyone. If anything, it's just the opposite. He is only trying to buy me time.

I gun the engine and throw the SUV into drive, squealing and kicking clods of mud before catapulting forward, plowing through the field. Out my side window I see the doors to the barn open and at least a dozen men pour out, Tony's and Mickey's both, punching and kicking each other, not even realizing whose hands they are tumbling into.

And in the rearview mirror I see my father. One of several and yet the only one I've ever really had. All out of boxes. Standing there with his hands up in surrender as a swarm of cops surrounds him.

UNDER THE STARS

New Liberty welcomes me quietly.

I make it to a part of the city that I am at least familiar with before ditching the car. I'm surprised I made it this far. Surprised that I didn't crash into anything, or at least anything that didn't give easily, mailboxes notwithstanding. Surprised the police helicopter didn't track me down. Surprised I wasn't followed by sirens. Then again, they probably had their hands full. A mastermind and his army. A vigilante hero and his sidekick. Two criminal organizations at each other's necks. I was the least of their worries.

I find a parking lot and leave the keys in the ignition—first come, first served. Let someone else steal it and create another trail. I tuck the box—my father's last box—into my pocket and do my best to clean my face. The knuckles on my left hand are skinned raw from my unfortunate attempt at boxing.

I have chafe marks around my wrists and ankles. There's a scratch beneath my chin where the knife got too close, but otherwise I look normal. For me, anyway. I look up to see that I've parked right across the street from a White Castle. Not *the* White Castle, just *a* White Castle, but I still can't help but feel like I'm back at the beginning.

I start walking, away from the sun that has nearly finished setting behind me. Heroes always ride into the sunset, I tell myself, and sure enough, there it is in the sky—the big blue smudge set against the bright orange-and-pink backdrop. The Comet. His work is finished. Which means the worst of it is over. I half expect him to just land right in front of me. Materializing from out of nowhere like a magic trick. But he doesn't. Maybe I'm the least of his worries too.

I rub my raw wrists and shuffle down the sidewalk, keeping my head low. I don't want to draw attention. I need to find a television. Just to see. Just to make sure he wasn't hurt. The last time the cops surrounded a father of mine, I ended up an orphan.

I pass a group of people coming out of a restaurant called the Fighting Irishman. One of them holds the door open for me. I say thanks, then stop him just as he is about to leave. "Hey, did you watch that big announcement?" I fish. "I'm afraid I didn't get home in time."

"Total bust," the guy says, snorting and shaking his head. "Some big spiel about pledging our allegiance or some crap, then all of a sudden the camera cuts out. Apparently the Comet showed up, took down the Dictator and a whole mess of other guys. It's all over the news."

No doubt. I thank him and slink through the door. Restaurants like these always have bars and the bars always have televisions. The hostess looks at me strangely. Probably they don't get a lot of teenage boys with swollen fingers and torn clothes smelling like sweat and gun smoke on a Monday night. I force an innocent smile. "Just one," I say.

She lets me seat myself, and I find a booth right across from one of the four television sets, all of them tuned to the news. Most of the faces are tuned to it as well, soaking it in eagerly. Tragedy and triumph. Hard to resist. When the waitress comes, I order a diet soda just so she will leave me alone for a minute.

There's live coverage from the news chopper hovering over the scene. It's a mess. There is smoke coming out of one of the windows of the farmhouse. One police car sits in a ditch, riddled with bullets. Another sits belly up. There is a giant chasm in the side of the barn, with an SUV wedged into it—a getaway attempt gone awry, I guess. There are cops of every kind swarming the field, probably looking for clues. And that's just what is happening on the surface. Imagine what they found underneath.

Between the cops and the reporters and the mob of eager onlookers, it's hard to make out any one face in the crowd. I see a few of the men who Mickey brought being cuffed and stuffed into the backs of cruisers. I see one gloved officer carrying a stack of steel masks, carefully tucking them into plastic bags. At one point I think I even catch a glimpse of Zach glancing out the back of an armored van. If these are Tony's cops, they aren't doing their job. Everyone is being rounded up, taken in, no matter what group they belong to. Tony will have to rely on his paid judges to get him out of trouble now.

Nowhere do I see the Dictator. Nor do I see my father. My only hope is that he was one of the first ones taken. The camera cuts to the on-scene reporter, the same blonde I've been watching off and on all week, the one with the overly dramatic pauses and too-large teeth. I ask the passing waitress if she minds turning the volume up a little.

"Yes, John, I am here . . . live . . . on the scene of what is, undoubtedly, the biggest bust in New Liberty's history. Turns out this simple farm right behind me sits on top of the huge underground lair of the villain known only as . . . the Dictator. The same man who vowed to change the world has been brought to justice by the city's latest . . . and perhaps greatest hero . . . who has once again left his calling card for all to see." She points, and the camera pans up to show the streak of blue starting to blend into the darkening sky.

I look toward the windows of the pub instinctively, but all the blinds have been closed. It's all right. I've had my fill of that big blue stain.

The reporter continues. "It has been confirmed that the Dictator is in police custody, along with thirty of his personal henchmen and at least twenty other known criminals, including Tony Romano and Mickey 'Six Fingers' Maloney. In fact, the first to be arrested was this man . . ."

The camera cuts to footage of a man with bushy orange hair being loaded into a patrol car. As they shut the door on him, my father turns and smiles at the camera. Smiles at me.

I take a deep breath and let my whole body go limp. I reach for my glass to take a drink.

". . . a self-proclaimed inventor who is currently believed to have been working for the Dictator and may even be the mastermind behind the whole operation. . . ."

And snarf it, the bubbles burning their way up my sinuses, the soda squirting out of both nostrils, splattering the table in a fizzy mess.

My father. The mastermind.

The waitress comes back to the table, towel in hand. Her name is Darlene. She looks glumly at the puddle I've waterfalled through my nose but wipes it up anyway. "You okay?" she asks.

I'm not about to answer that question for real, so I just nod.

"Crazy, ain't it?" she says, following my gaze. "I tell you, I've lived here for fifteen years and I've never seen *anything* like this. That Comet is somethin' else. Can you believe he did that all by himself?"

I shake my head.

"I guess we were lucky to have him. Though between you and me," she says, leaning down and whispering, "I kinda wish I knew what else that fella in the silver mask was going to say."

"You really don't," I tell her.

She gives me a dirty look and then asks me if I'm going to order something to eat. I shake my head and she pulls out her pad, writing up the bill for the soda that's still burning my nostrils. On TV they've cut back to the news desk for more updates. It's all stuff I already know, of course, but to them it is late breaking. The weapons found in the lair, along with all the equipment the Dictator used to create his little army. Details about the nature of the shootout itself. Then they say something that gives me pause.

"Authorities say that at least one suspect, a young Caucasian male in his early teens, managed to flee the scene in a black SUV. They are currently looking for any clues regarding his identity or whereabouts."

I swallow hard. I'm a wanted man.

It feels strange being wanted. Sort of sickening and awesome at the same time. I look up at the waitress, but she is oblivious. She slaps my bill on the table.

"He's a hero, I guess," she says. I can only assume she is referring to the Comet. I wait for her to go, then take a look. I owe a dollar seventy, but I don't have any small bills. I guess tonight Darlene will have two heroes.

I leave the hundred on the table and head back outside, making it a point not to look anyone in the eye. Who knows what Tony's or Mickey's men are telling the police right now.

And the Dictator. There's no way he's going to let me off the hook. The authorities may have him now, but guys like him, they find a way to get free. To start over. I need to find someplace to go, at least for the night. At least until I figure out what to do next.

Someplace safe.

I run my fingers along the box in my pocket, hoping that it is what I think it is. Hoping that I still know the way.

It takes almost two hours on foot. I don't want to risk taking a bus or a taxi. After what they said on the news, I'm thinking the fewer people I meet tonight, the better. I keep to the shadows and alleys, feeling every bit like I'm up to no good. I only pass one police car, headlights shining but its driver looking the other way. All the rest are probably either at the barn, back at the station, or somewhere in between. Still, I give a wide berth to every stranger I pass. Every dog bark, honked horn, and slammed car door makes me jump. Only when I get to the neighborhood just past the baseball diamonds do I calm down a little.

Everything here is still just as it should be, untouched. I keep to the rows of manicured bushes and evergreens, dodging the pools of gold cast by the streetlamps. The houses are all quiet, and I marvel for a moment at how peaceful it is, how the driveway lights automatically bloom when you pass them, how there are no cars parked anywhere along the street. I retrace my steps till I am standing right outside her house. I circle around the back, sneaking through the fence left open, remembering which room she said was hers. The master bedroom. Her light is on. It takes some scrounging to find a rock the right size. I don't want to break the glass.

For once my aim is spot-on.

I wait for a few seconds, holding my breath, until finally a hand pulls back the curtains and opens the window. Arise, fair sun, I think, and please, for the love of god, let me come in. Her face appears in the window.

Viola.

The instrument, not the cross-dresser. This isn't Shakespeare. I look up at her and smile, but she just stands there for a moment, as if she doesn't recognize me, as if we've never even met, and I suddenly feel like I've made a horrible mistake.

Then she leans out the window, propped up on her elbows, chin in hands.

"What are you doing here?" she whispers.

"I brought you something," I say. I already told myself I wouldn't use my powers. I won't force my way in. She'll either have me or she won't. I reach in my jacket and pull out the box.

She bites her lip, then glances behind her, and for a moment I think I've lost everything. My house in ashes. My father in police custody. And now she's going to turn me away. But then she points to the giant recycling bin by the corner of the house.

"Climb," she says.

So I do. It's a bit of a struggle—the bin buys me only an extra five feet—but Viola reaches over the ledge and takes both of my hands in hers, hoisting me up without much apparent effort, though she seems to wince a little just as she pulls me inside. She puts a finger to my lips as I get to my feet.

"*Shhh.* My mother will kill you if she finds you here."

I look around. It looks like a typical teenage girl's room. Pastel-flowered bedspread. Purple walls spattered with peel-off butterflies. I notice the telescope in the corner and one shelf lined with softball trophies. There are posters of a few pop bands and a vampire heartthrob from the latest trilogy. A stuffed animal—Mikey the Chickopotamus—watches me from the bed.

"You kept it," I whisper, pointing to the prize.

"Of course," she says.

Viola comes up and stands beside me. She is wearing pink flannel pajamas with satin cuffs, decorated with peace signs. Her hair is damp. She smells like soap, and perhaps the faintest hint of smoke. Or maybe that's just me. I can't even imagine what I must smell like, what I must look like, what she must think of me.

"Where's your dad?" I ask.

"Working late," she whispers. She sits on the edge of the bed and pats the comforter, and I take a seat next to her. I listen for sirens. For helicopter blades. For her mother's footsteps or the sound of her father opening the door. A few hours ago I was strapped in a chair, surrounded by men with guns, about to be forced to brainwash an entire city; yet sitting here, next to her, I am just as nervous. Maybe more.

But I had to come. I didn't know where else to go.

"I won't stay," I say. "I just wanted to give you this."

I dig in my pocket and hand her the black box. She takes it gingerly, hesitantly, running her fingers over the smooth metal and the two sleek buttons, stopping at the label with my name on it. She looks at me. "Are you sure it's for me?"

"Only one way to find out," I say. I take the box from her and tell her to just watch. Then I tiptoe over to her door and turn out the light.

"Michael?" she says, her voice clipped, suddenly not quite hers.

"Don't worry," I say, sitting on the bed next to her. I press the green button.

Suddenly her ceiling explodes as it transforms into the dome of the sky. It's as if the whole universe is unzipped and laid bare. Planets and moons and meteors, shimmering and streaking. And stars. Thousands of stars. Millions of them. I hear Viola catch her breath as she falls backward on the bed, enveloped in starlight. No walls. No boundaries. Just nebulous infinity.

"It's beautiful," she says.

I set the box on the floor, the galaxy still spinning above us. "It's genius," I say.

I sit there, watching her as she traces the patterns with her eyes.

"It's just like I remember," she says. Then she reaches up and takes me by the arm, pulling me down next to her. The two of us, lying in her bed, side by side. I can feel her heartbeat racing even through her pajamas. She begins naming the planets and the constellations, pointing with one hand even as the other reaches out and takes mine.

"It's amazing, isn't it?"

I don't say anything. It is amazing, it's all amazing, but it only reminds me of my father. I imagine him, lying on a cot in some cell, staring up at his gray ceiling, stuck in another box, while I lie here beneath this perfect system that he created without my even having to ask.

"There could be anything out there," she says.

I turn to look at her, eyes twinkling in the glow of a thousand brilliant suns, so bright I can't even stand it and have to look away. I'm not an idiot. I know what she means. There is an offer here. An opportunity. There could be anything, but you still have to choose. You can't have it both ways.

And it feels so good here beside her.

But this isn't me.

I've made my choice. I can't stay, but I'm not going to run either. I've been thinking about it the whole walk over, weighing my options. I'm going to bust Dad out of prison. I figure it won't be that hard. I just have to talk to the right people. Get their undivided attention. I can be very persuasive when I want to be. Then maybe, together, he and I can track down my mother. Ask her what her damage is. Why she told the Dictator about me. Why she left in the first place. If she ever really loved my father. I'm not looking for a weepy reunion. I know better. I'd just like some answers.

I twist my head and see that Viola isn't looking up at the artificial sky anymore. She's looking straight into my eyes.

"I should go," I tell her, though it takes every ounce of will I have to say it. She rolls over onto her side, grimacing slightly at the shift. She still has my hand in hers, fingers entwined, pulling me in. And I'm certain, so suddenly certain of all the things I've suspected. About fathers and heroes and promises. And girls you just happen to run into at the mall. Who laugh like pianos and give you pennies for more than just good luck. Who know your magic trick already but still act impressed when you do it.

Viola squeezes tighter. "It's all right," she whispers.

"Stay here," she says.

"I know which side you're on."

Acknowledgments

Getting a novel to print is a task requiring almost super-human effort, on the part of not just the author (who gets to mostly play pretend), but the entire league of extraordinary editors, agents, proofreaders, publicists, booksellers, family, and friends who combine their powers to create something worth reading. This book certainly wouldn't be possible without the enduring faith of my agent, Quinlan Lee, and the rest of the Adams Literary crew. Then of course there is the noble, keen-eyed cadre of copy editors, proofreaders, designers, and directors at HarperCollins, including Renée Cafiero, Erin Fitzsimmons, Amy Ryan, Viana Siniscalchi, and Ray Colón, who work in the background to make the book look good, as well as marketing geniuses such as Jenna Lisanti and Caroline Sun, who give it a big flashy cape before sending it to do battle on the shelves. Thanks also, of course, to Shannon Tindle for making Michael look so suspiciously cool on the cover, and to Debbie Kovacs for championing *Minion* from start to finish. A special commendation goes to wonder-girl Kellie Celia, who works tirelessly to give the book some legs. Finally, thanks to the leader of the super crew—the professor to our literary X-men—Jordan Brown, whose insights inform every page of this book and who always makes me feel like I know what I'm doing.

Special thanks to my parents, Wes and Shiela, who still hold out hope that I'll grow up someday and who love me anyways, and to all of my family and friends who encourage me with every page. And finally, to Alithea, the Alfred to my Bruce, the Arthur to my Tick, the Invisible Woman to my Mr. Fantastic, the better half that I can't do without, thanks for everything.